Celia Fremlin (1914–2009) was born in Kent. Her first published novel of suspense was *The Hours Before Dawn* (1958), which went on to win the Mystery Writers of America's Edgar Award for Best Novel in 1960. Over the next thirty-five years Fremlin published a further eighteen titles.

'Britain's equivalent to Patricia Highsmith, Celia Fremlin wrote psychological thrillers that changed the landscape of crime fiction for ever: her novels are domestic, subtle, penetrating – and quite horribly chilling.' Andrew Taylor

also by Celia Fremlin

fiction

UNCLE PAUL

SEVEN LEAN YEARS

THE TROUBLE-MAKERS

THE JEALOUS ONE

PRISONER'S BASE

POSSESSION

APPOINTMENT WITH YESTERDAY

THE LONG SHADOW

THE SPIDER-ORCHID

WITH NO CRYING

THE PARASITE PERSON

LISTENING IN THE DUSK

DANGEROUS THOUGHTS

ECHOING STONES

KING OF THE WORLD

short stories

DON'T GO TO SLEEP IN THE DARK

BY HORROR HAUNTED

A LOVELY DAY TO DIE

The Hours Before Dawn

CELIA FREMLIN

FABER & FABER

This edition first published in 2017
by Faber & Faber Ltd
Bloomsbury House, 74–77 Great Russell Street
London WC1B 3DA

Typeset by by Faber & Faber Ltd
Printed and bound by CPI Group (UK) Ltd, Croydon, CR0 4YY

A CIP record for this book is available from the British Library

ISBN 978–0–571–33812–2

2 4 6 8 10 9 7 5 3 1

Foreword

The Hours Before Dawn (1958) was the first of Celia Fremlin's sixteen novels and the one for which she is best known, although – given her contribution to the crime-fiction genre – she has been, to date, woefully underrated and not remembered nearly so often, nor so vociferously, as she deserves. Fremlin's métier was psychological suspense in a domestic setting; no Grand Guignol or melodrama, but something a thousand times creepier and more insidious in its small-scale, suburban gentility.

In the preface to the 1988 edition of the novel Fremlin wrote that it had been inspired by her experience, with her second baby, of sleepless nights and subsequent exhaustion. The simple plea in the first sentence – 'I'd give any-thing – *anything* – for a night's sleep,' – takes us straight to the heart of the sleep deprivation bordering on torture that is often the lot of mothers with young babies. Louise Henderson, harassed parent of two primary-school-age girls as well as screaming infant Michael, struggles to ser-vice the needs of her family, keep things on an even keel with husband Mark, keep the noise down for the neigh-bours and keep up appearances in middle-class London. Written at a time when gender-demarcation was well-nigh absolute and motherhood fetishised as woman's highest calling, Louise, ears ringing with well-meant advice and other mothers' war stories, struggles on, uncomplaining, despite her growing depression, anxiety and fatigue.

Michael's arrival has necessitated taking in a lodger, the respectable spinster schoolmistress Vera Brandon. Soon after her arrival, Louise begins to wonder if she's imagining things: is Miss Brandon creeping about the house and spying on them? Is she making a play for Mark? Has she met her somewhere before? With a series of incidents for which there might – or might not – be an innocent explanation, Fremlin expertly ratchets up the tension, notch by notch, as Louise's imagination becomes ever more febrile . . . or does it?

Tightly plotted and admirably concise, Fremlin's fiction is characterised by precise observation and the inclusion of small, telling details – skills surely honed by her time working for the Mass Observation movement during the Second World War – which ensures that all of her characters, including the children, are fully formed and pitch-perfect. More surprising, perhaps, as well as wholly delightful, is the wit – effortless, acerbic and just enough of it – that gives her work its distinctive and memorable pungency.

Laura Wilson

I

'I'd give anything – *anything* – for a night's sleep.'

For one awful moment Louise thought she had spoken aloud. She jerked up her head and blinked round at the swinging streaks of colour that were rapidly resolving themselves into Mrs Hooper and her baby, Mrs Tomlinson and her baby, and that Mrs What's-her-name in the smart blue suit whose baby did exactly what the books said, for all the world as if he and his mother studied the Behaviour Charts and Average Weight Tables together.

Louise fought back her drowsiness and hoisted Michael into a safer position on her lap. It was all right. No one was staring at her; no one was looking shocked, not even Nurse Fordham. Indeed, she could not have been dozing for more than a second or two altogether, for Mrs Hooper still hadn't finished the sentence she had begun while Louise was properly awake.

'. . . And so I thought I'd bring Christine to be weighed today after all. Just out of interest, of course – I shan't worry if she hasn't gained. In fact, I shan't worry if she's *lost*—' Here Mrs Hooper leaned further across the placid bulk of Mrs Tomlinson to peer expectantly into Louise's face. Louise knew that Mrs Hooper wanted to be reproved for this casual attitude – no theory of child-management can thrive if no one disagrees with it – but this afternoon she felt too tired to disagree with anyone.

1

'Yes, I think you're quite right,' she said uncooperatively. Mrs Hooper was only momentarily disconcerted; soon she began again, in the hushed yet piercing tones used habitually by the mothers, who felt that they should not disturb the solemnity of the Infant Welfare Clinic by anything above a whisper, and yet wished to converse continually with neighbours several chairs and several crying babies away.

'I don't believe in all this worrying,' continued Mrs Hooper truculently. 'I think it's absurd the way most mothers worry about a few ounces this way or that. After all, *Nature* doesn't worry. She doesn't provide baby-scales for rabbits, does she? Or for cats? *They* bring up their babies all right without all this fuss.'

Mrs Hooper paused, anxious as a child, and watched Louise hopefully for some sign of disapproval. She had an uneasy feeling that people were less shocked at this sort of remark now than they had been nine years ago, when her elder child was a baby.

'Don't they?' she prompted, with an oddly touching sort of aggressiveness.

'Don't who? – Oh – I'm sorry! Yes. Cats and rabbits.' Louise hastily collected her wits. 'Yes. Of course. But the trouble is that *we* expect our babies to survive. Cats and rabbits are content to bring up about two out of seven, and so—'

'You're next, ain't you, duck?' enquired Mrs Tomlinson, across whose amiable bulk this conversation was taking place. 'You come in after her with the pink coat, I saw you, and she was two in front of Mrs Rogers, but Mrs Rogers ain't waiting, see, and so that only leaves her what's up there now, and then—'

Louise could not quite follow the intricacies of this calculation, but like most laymen she did not query the methods of the expert. She thankfully accepted the conclusion, and was about to get to her feet when Mrs Hooper intervened.

'No – excuse me – I'm sorry – but *I* was here first,' she protested. 'I've been here since half past one. I think it's scandalous the way they keep us waiting. I came here early on purpose so as to get away early. I've got to be at my pottery class by five.'

'Never mind,' said Louise soothingly – and she would have liked to have added that mother rabbits get on all right without pottery classes; instead, she went on: 'Don't worry, you go in front of me if you like – but *please* don't ask her a lot of complicated questions. I've got to get away early, too, to fetch the girls from school.'

'Of course I shan't ask her any questions!' retorted Mrs Hooper, scandalised. 'I *never* ask advice about my children. I feel that my own mother-instincts . . .'

Her sentence remained unfinished, for Nurse Fordham had already called out 'Next, please' a second time, and Mrs Hooper's mother-instincts were proving somewhat inadequate when it came to the task of disentangling her baby's outdoor garments from the feet and chair legs of her neighbours with one hand, while with the other she clutched a handbag and a weight-card as well as her almost upside-down and loudly protesting daughter.

But Nurse Fordham was patient. You could tell that she had schooled herself to be patient with the mothers; and when Louise, a few minutes later, settled herself in the chair facing Nurse Fordham, she felt the patience in that bright smile like the sting of an April wind. Michael, seeming heavier and damper than ever, was wriggling discontentedly in her lap. He was already beginning those uneasy, rasping grunts which meant that soon he would be yelling beyond all hope of control. Louise jigged him gently from side to side in a delaying action, praying that the interview with Nurse Fordham would be over before he really let himself go. When a baby cried, Nurse Fordham's patience with the mother became so intense that one could no longer meet her eyes nor remember what one was trying to say.

'So you see,' Louise hastened on, 'the trouble is that he wakes up and cries *every* night. Whether I give him a feed or not, I mean.' As she spoke, she jigged Michael with mounting violence, feeling through her palms, through her thighs, the tide of boredom rising within him. Harder – harder – it was like baling out a boat when you know without any doubt that the water will win in the end . . . And the patience in Nurse Fordham's voice was like the swell of the sea, in which a thousand boats can sink unnoticed.

'You see, Mrs Henderson,' she was explaining, choosing her words carefully, as if Louise could understand human speech little better than the writhing baby in her arms – 'you see, as I'm always telling you mothers, you mustn't *worry*. He's gaining splendidly – he's very strong and active for seven months old. There's nothing to worry about.'

'No – I know——' said Louise, senselessly apologetic by now. 'But you see he keeps us awake half the night. My husband can't stand it either, he——'

'You mustn't *worry*, Mrs Henderson,' repeated Nurse

Fordham, the patience crackling from her starched sleeve like machine-gun fire as she reached for the case-sheets. 'That's the mistake all you young mothers make. You worry too much. Your worry communicates itself to the baby, and there you are!'

Such was the self-confident triumph in Nurse Fordham's voice that for a moment Louise felt as if Nurse Fordham really *did* know where she, Louise, was. Knew what it felt like when you dragged yourself out of bed at two in the morning . . . and again at quarter past three . . . and again at five. Knew what you could say to a husband when he shouted at you in the light of the crazy, dying moon: 'For God's sake make him shut up! I can't stand it any longer! Make him SHUT UP!' Knew, too, how to make yourself cope with the next day – how to remain bright and good-tempered and attractive – to get the children off to school in time – to answer their questions, plan the meals, never letting tiredness get the better of you . . .

'Just stop *worrying*, you see,' repeated Nurse Fordham (you had to repeat things over and over again to these mothers, they never seemed to take anything in the first time, and really, this woman was still looking quite blank). 'Just stop worrying, and then your baby will stop worrying, too. Create a calm tranquil atmosphere . . .'

Michael's first real yell filled the clinic from wall to wall, and Louise hastily gathered him up and rose from her chair. Under the scorching beam of Nurse Fordham's patience she got him to the back of the room, bundled him pell-mell into leggings, coat and bonnet, and fled from the room like an escaping burglar.

Once outside in the cold spring sunlight, with the

cold spring wind flicking across the rows of empty prams, Michael's yells subsided; and he maintained a guarded silence as Louise settled him in his pram, his breath indrawn ready to scream again at once if she should attempt to lie him down instead of propping him up in a sitting position. Like any general of a defeated army, Louise gladly accepted such moderate terms, and was about to embark on the familiar task of disentangling her pram from the four adjoining ones, when she noticed with surprise that one of these contained a baby. At first she did not recognise the child, as half its face was hidden by the grubby pink bonnet which had slipped down over its eyes, and the other half by a cauliflower, at which it gnawed with absent-minded greed. The pram she could not immediately recognise either, though it undoubtedly must belong to one of the higher-income-group mothers, for it was scratched and muddy, the hood was lurching sideways where a screw was missing, and the end away from the baby was filled with potatoes. The prams from the poorer parts of the neighbourhood were invariably brand-new and shining, with satin eiderdowns and embroidered pillows. A moment later Louise was able to identify the bonnet and the cauliflower as Christine Hooper; for Mrs Hooper herself could now be seen picking her way among the prams towards them, her sturdy legs blue above their unseasonable sandals, and her sparse red hair held back as always by an Alice-in-Wonderland ribbon – a style which was growing yearly more unbecoming as she floundered further and further into the thirties.

'Hullo – I thought you were in such a hurry to get to

your pottery class,' remarked Louise. 'Look – can you get your pram out first? No – turn it a bit sideways – that's right.'

A violent jolt from her mother's rather heavy-handed manoeuvres sent Christine's cauliflower bouncing on to the gravel, and her shrill, peevish wail silenced further conversation until the cauliflower, rather battered by now, had been restored.

'I always think that's such a *natural* way for them to get their vitamins,' beamed Mrs Hooper, as a muddy, mangled bit of stalk dribbled from Christine's mouth on to her knitted jacket. 'She got it all by herself, you know, out of the end of the pram. When Tony was a baby, I always used to let him help himself to the shopping on the way home. I remember once he got hold of a mutton chop. Raw. People were terribly shocked,' she added wistfully, with the faraway look of one recalling past triumphs.

'I'm sure they were,' said Louise kindly, 'But listen; why are you coming this way? Surely you have to take Christine home before the class?'

'Oh – yes – well, the thing is, I was going to ask you, actually, if you'd be an absolute angel and have Christine with you for an hour or two? Then I won't need to go home at all, you see, I can just walk along with you now and leave her at your house and go straight on from there.'

'Oh.' Louise thought quickly. 'But what about Tony?' she suggested hopefully. 'Don't you have to go back and give him his tea? Won't he wonder where you are when he gets in from school?'

'Oh *no*!' Mrs Hooper looked horrified. 'He's *quite* used to it. When he finds I'm not there, he'll just go in to one of the neighbours for tea. I believe in children learning to be independent, you know.'

'Oh.' Louise looked gloomily at the dribbling Christine and wished, not for the first time, that Mrs Hooper's children could be independent in some way that didn't involve the neighbours' having to feed them so often. She tried again: 'I'm not going straight home, you know; I'm going round by the school. I've got to meet Margery and Harriet.'

'*Meet* them!' Mrs Hooper's expression was that of a scandalised Victorian grandparent, '*Meet* them? But my dear, how ridiculous! Margery's eight now, isn't she, and Harriet's nearly seven? Why, Tony was coming home alone *long* before that. It never worried him a bit. I remember once when he was barely five he was knocked down by a bicycle crossing the main road. Some kind lady took him home with her and bandaged him up and brought him back in her car as cheerful as a cricket. He didn't mind in the least. I'd always trained him to be independent, you see.'

'If all children were as independent as that, there mightn't be enough kind ladies to go round,' remarked Louise sourly. 'Anyway, since I am meeting the girls, I'm afraid it means I can't have Christine. You don't want to come dragging up to the school with me, I'm sure. Besides,' she added, with sudden inspiration, 'I couldn't have her in any case, not this evening. I've got a prospective tenant coming to look at the room.'

'My dear! You're *not* letting that room, are you?' cried Mrs Hooper, stopping dead with an access of interest which nearly flung Christine through the hood of the pram. 'But how dreadful! I mean, I should have thought you needed *more* space now you've got Michael, not less. And then, everyone knows that two women can't share a kitchen, and—'

'We've thought of all that,' Louise interrupted. 'But unfortunately another child means you want more money as well as more space. Besides, it isn't really sharing, you know. She'll have her own gas ring up there, and that little basin on the landing ought to be enough for washing-up. She can't have much washing-up, just one person by herself.'

'Don't you believe it!' said Mrs Hooper, resuming her rapid stride along the pavement, the pram clearing the way before her with the efficiency of a battering-ram. 'We were sharing with a girl once, and she had parties every night. *Every* night; and never less than fifteen people. She always used our crockery for them, too. At least,' admitted Mrs Hooper reflectively, 'she did after we'd *got* some crockery of our own.'

Louise could not help feeling that Mrs Hooper and her fellow tenant must have been well matched. She also noticed that Mrs Hooper was still marching relentlessly at her side in the direction of the school, and had managed deftly to turn the conversation right away from Louise's objections to looking after Christine for the evening. She hastily interposed:

'Well, I don't think this woman will be like that. She's a schoolteacher, and she sounded very respectable on the phone. In fact, I expect the trouble will be that she'll think *we* aren't quiet enough for *her*. I told her we've got children – but, well, you do see, don't you, that I don't want an extra baby around just when she's coming to look at the

9

room? I mean, *two* prams in the hall – it'll make the place look like a day-nursery.'

'Let her put up with it,' advised Mrs Hooper airily. 'Let her see you as you really are. Why should you be always putting yourself out for other people?'

Before Louise had thought of a suitable reply to this a screech of 'Mummy!' put an end to the discussion. Two little girls had detached themselves from the squealing crowd round the school gates and were running towards her. Margery, the elder, ran clumsily, heavily, a bulging satchel with a broken strap banging her ankle at every step; and even as Louise watched, one of the gym shoes clutched in her other hand skidded to the ground, followed by a crumpled paper bag of crayons, spilling this way and that among the hurrying feet. Harriet, smaller, darker, carrying nothing, free as air, flew past her woebegone sister, skimming like a dryad across the crowded pavement and into Louise's arms.

2

It would, of course, happen that the new tenant should arrive at exactly the moment when Mark got back from work, tired and irritable. And it was equally inevitable that this moment should be the very one when Louise had at last decided to bring the howling Christine indoors, and both prams were now wedged across the narrow hall, locked by their mudguards in a dismal and indissoluble embrace. This was the moment, too, chosen by Margery to sit on the bottom step of the stairs and pick bread and jam off her socks – the result of Harriet's Teddy bear's tea having been laid out in its usual place – on the floor just inside the kitchen door. What with one thing and another, Louise could hardly wonder that Mark should give her one hunted glance, and disappear headlong into the kitchen. She had only time for a fleeting, desperate hope that he had not landed, as Margery had done, in the middle of Teddy's bread and jam, before she had to turn and greet the tall figure silhouetted in the doorway.

'Mrs Henderson?' the figure was saying, in the clear, decisive tones of one used to commanding attention. 'I'm Vera Brandon. I telephoned yesterday—'

'Yes. How nice. I mean, do come up. Come and see the room—' Exerting what felt like a degree of physical strength equal to throwing a sack of coal across the hall, Louise radiated silent will-power in four directions at once:

to Margery to get herself and her jammy socks off the stairs without any of that laboured discussion with which Margery always liked to surround herself and her doings: to Harriet to keep her shrill argument with her father well behind the closed kitchen door: to Michael to slobber over his sodden rusk for a few minutes longer before dropping it through the bars of the playpen and screaming: and to Christine to remain in the state of stunned silence to which the appearance of so many strangers at once had fortunately reduced her.

The will-power worked – as it always does, thought Louise, when you put every ounce of strength you've got into it, and leave yourself weak and empty – and she conducted the visitor upstairs to the vacant room – the Rubbish Room as the children still persisted in calling it, in spite of the fact that it had been cleared out some days since and furnished in readiness for its new occupant. And, as it happened, this title turned out to be a good deal more appropriate than Louise could have wished, and she began to apologise to her rather disconcertingly silent visitor:

'I'm sorry we haven't quite got the shelves cleared yet,' she explained nervously. 'Those are my mother-in-law's books, she's fetching them at the week-end. And of course the dolls' pram will be gone, too, and that – that—' Louise sought for the right word to indicate the swaying structure of cardboard grocery boxes in which Harriet had spent a happy afternoon last week being a Tiger in its Den. Mark had been quite right, of course. He had always said that she shouldn't let the children come up here and play while there was no tenant. They'd only get into the habit of it, he'd said, and there'd be an awful job keeping them out after the room *was* let. But it was such a temptation, especially at week-ends, when Mark himself wanted some peace and quiet in the sitting-room. And she'd been so sure that she would remember to clear everything away before anyone came to look at the room. She *would* have remembered, too, if only it hadn't been for Mark dashing home unexpectedly for lunch, today of all days, just when she had to be at the clinic by half past one. And then Christine this evening . . . Oh, well, it couldn't be helped now; and if this woman didn't like it, there were plenty of other people looking for rooms nowadays.

But Miss Brandon didn't seem to care at all; nor did she show any dismay at learning that there was only a gas ring to cook on, and that she would have to do all her washing-up at the minute hand-basin on the landing. Louise was a little surprised. Miss Brandon, in both voice and appearance, gave the impression of being a successful woman of the world, both critical and self-assured; not at all the sort of person whom one would expect to choose for her home an inconvenient, ill-equipped attic in someone else's house. Louise felt suddenly ill at ease. She had expected a different kind of applicant altogether – a young art student, perhaps, who would giggle happily about her hardships, and boast to her friends that she was starving in a garret. Or one of those silent young men whom you never see on the stairs, who never have any washing, and who have all their meals out. Or maybe someone elderly – this was what Louise had visualised when this woman had spoken to her on the phone, and told her that she was a schoolteacher. Someone past middle-age, Louise had thought, perhaps on the verge of retiring. Someone who had learned slowly and painfully – or maybe proudly, and with undefeated courage – to accept without complaint all the numerous small discomforts that life brought her way.

But Miss Brandon did not fit this picture at all. As to her age, it was difficult to tell. She could hardly be much past forty, Louise thought, watching her visitor glancing round the room with an odd sort of impatience; not so much as if she thought the room was inadequate, but rather as if she was completely indifferent to it, and was irritated only by the necessity for making a decision.

'I'll take it,' she said brusquely, without either prodding the bed for broken springs or peering under it for spider-webs – actions which Louise had always understood tenants to perform before they rented rooms. 'When can I come in?'

'Well – that is – of course—' Louise stammered a little under Miss Brandon's clear, commanding gaze – 'just as soon as you like. Except that my mother-in-law won't be fetching her books till the week-end, and so—'

'Never mind about that,' said Miss Brandon, still with this air of restrained impatience. 'I shan't need those shelves. I haven't a lot of books of my own just now. Tell your mother-in-law she can fetch them whenever it suits her. I shall have no objection.'

The remark, still more the manner of it, struck Louise as a trifle arrogant – rather like the mistress of the house giving instructions to her housekeeper. Then she remembered that Miss Brandon was, after all, a schoolteacher, and the giving of instructions probably occupied the greater part of her waking life, and this manner had no doubt become habitual. All the same, it was odd that a woman so self-assured should display so little interest in the amenities (or lack of them) in the place she proposed to make her home. With almost perverse honesty, Louise began pointing out the disadvantages of the room: the low, sloping ceiling; the lack of storage space – the only built-in cupboard being shallow and inconvenient, with a jagged hole in the plaster at the top which the men still hadn't come to mend.

But Miss Brandon seemed quite unperturbed – or, rather, uninterested. Indeed, she seemed to find Louise's frankness merely irritating, and she brushed it aside impatiently, simply repeating that she wished to take the room. Her only concern seemed to be that she should come in *soon* – say tomorrow evening?

This being agreed, the two set off down the stairs again, Louise making rapid calculations about how to fit in the cleaning and preparing of the room tomorrow. Mark would definitely be home for lunch, which meant extra cooking; and the scullery and passage simply *must* be scrubbed – they couldn't go another day . . .

At the foot of the stairs, Miss Brandon seemed suddenly to lose her air of restive indifference. 'Good God!' she exclaimed.

Louise really couldn't feel surprised at the exclamation. Anyone other than a mother must surely be horrified at the sight of a baby in the position in which Christine Hooper had managed to get herself. There she lay, sound asleep, her head hanging over the edge of the pram, and her spine bent backwards at an angle which must surely have resulted in instant death to anyone much over seven months old. Louise, of course, recognised these symptoms as indicating merely that Christine was all set to sleep peacefully for hours; but she appreciated that to a less experienced eye the situation might look alarming.

'It's all right,' she began hastily; but Miss Brandon was already bending over the pram, rearranging the outraged Christine into the comfortable position which babies so detest. 'She's all right, really,' repeated Louise, as Miss Brandon, her strong features flushed with stooping, straightened herself, and looked accusingly at Louise.

'This isn't *your* baby, is it?' she said.

'Why – no,' answered Louise, rather taken aback. 'I'm just looking after her for a friend of mine—' She stopped rather awkwardly, realising that 'looking after' must seem to her listener something of an exaggeration. It was true that she had abandoned Christine and her pram rather unceremoniously in the middle of the hall when the visitor arrived; but what else could she do, with the doorbell ringing, and Mark arriving home, and such pandemonium everywhere? And anyway, hadn't Mrs Hooper assured her that Christine could be left in her pram indefinitely, anywhere, anyhow?

'Don't worry about her, my dear,' Mrs Hooper had said. '*I* never do. Just leave her anywhere – out in the front, if you like. I'll be back in time for her feed.' And then, as if conferring a great favour, she called over her shoulder: 'If you like, you can give her a bottle when you give Michael his. Any milk mixture will do.'

But, of course, Miss Brandon didn't know Mrs Hooper and her methods. And anyway, it occurred now to Louise that the accusing stare which was fastened on her so uncomfortably probably had no reference to her neglect or otherwise of the superfluous Christine, but simply to the fact of her owning a baby at all. After all, she had only said three *children* on the phone, and who would choose to come and live in a house with a baby in it if they could possibly live elsewhere? Apologetically, she plunged into explanations:

'Actually, I *have* got a baby about that age. And two older girls. I thought I told you when you rang up. But I don't think they'll bother you at all, your room is right up at the top, on a floor by itself—'

Miss Brandon seemed in some indefinable way to have relaxed, and her voice was noticeably less hostile as she spoke again:

'Yes, yes,' she reassured Louise. 'I remember now, you did tell me. Dear little things, I'm sure, I'd love to meet them. And your husband, too, of course,' she added, as if in afterthought. She hesitated a moment, almost, thought Louise wonderingly, as if she really *did* want to meet them all, here and now. Not that Louise had any intention of ushering a stranger in to her family without warning at this hour of the evening. Not one of them would have their shoes on, not even Mark. Harriet would giggle, and bury her head ostentatiously in a cushion, displaying a large expanse of torn knicker which Louise still hadn't found time to mend. Michael would go red in the face and roar – not, as everyone would fondly suppose, because he was shy of strangers, but because the sight of his mother coming into the room would remind him that she hadn't been there all this time. Margery would stare in ill-concealed and speechless horror, and so, in all probability, would Mark. Louise firmly escorted her visitor to the front door.

Mark was still scowling when Louise rejoined her

family, and she could guess at the withering comments hovering on the tip of his tongue. It was something of a relief to know that he would have to postpone them while she fed and changed Michael and put him in his cot; while she dished up supper; while she wrestled with the children's table manners, tooth-brushing, and finally got them to bed; while she washed up supper, finished the ironing, and ran upstairs to see how it could be that Margery's eiderdown should have slipped off her bed and vanished without trace in the space of half an hour.

It was nearly half past nine by the time all this had been lived through and Louise could throw herself wearily into the armchair opposite to Mark. For a minute she watched the unresponsive back of the evening paper in silence, wondering dejectedly whether quarrels were improved or worsened by being left to simmer like this for three and a half hours? Did a husband's anger fritter itself away as one interruption succeeded another and prevented its expression? Or did it gather itself together into one bitter spurt of rage? Or did the delay merely leave him defeated, bewildered, as weary as oneself . . . ?

Louise woke with a start, and opened her eyes to find that the evening paper had been flung aside, and that Mark was already half way through a sentence:

'. . . Why, on top of everything, you had to have that wretched Hooper brat here just when you knew someone was coming to look at the room? *Why?*'

Louise fought back the drowsiness which always, now, lay in wait for her, ready to pounce; she tried to gather together her rather scattered defences.

'Well, you see,' she began, 'I couldn't really avoid it. I

mean, Mrs Hooper simply dumped her on me – you know what she is.'

'Of course I know what she is!' exploded Mark. 'And that's just exactly why I can't understand why you're eternally putting yourself out to oblige her. And putting *me* out, too – that's the point. Do you know that damn kid was yelling without a break the whole time you were upstairs?'

'No, she wasn't,' contradicted Louise, conscious even as she spoke of the childish folly of such an appeal to accuracy in an argument of this nature. 'She couldn't have been. She was sound asleep when I came down.' Fortunately Mark paid no attention to this ill-judged appeal to facts, and went on as if she had not spoken:

'As if it wasn't bad enough to have to come home to my own kids' yelling! God, what a shambles! I'm surprised that woman didn't turn straight round and walk out again!'

'Well, she didn't,' retorted Louise; and then, in an attempt to change the subject, she continued: 'She really seemed to like the room, you know. She wants to come in tomorrow. She doesn't mind about your mother's books, or anything.'

'The woman must be mad,' muttered Mark; but his voice was perceptibly mellowed as he asked: 'And what did you think of *her*, Louise? Do you think she'll do?'

'Yes – oh, yes!' said Louise, with a misleading enthusiasm which stemmed more from her relief at having successfully changed the subject than from any liking for the new tenant. 'Yes, I think she's just what we want. And I think she must be quite fond of children – she simply rushed to pick up Christine when she thought something was wrong. Or' – Louise's brief enthusiasm waned – 'do you think it just means that she's interfering?'

'More likely it means she was trying to strangle the brat,' said Mark with gloomy relish. 'For two pins I'd have done it myself. But listen, Louise, seriously, we *must* see that there is less uproar in the house now that someone else is living here. Particularly at night. You've *got* to see that Michael stops crying at night. You can't expect anyone else to put up with it. I've had just about all I can stand myself.'

Louise was conscious of an aching, helpless weariness; and as she glanced at her husband's face, the tired lines more deeply drawn in the lamplight, she felt a tiny stab of fear. For the first time, she wondered: Does it sometimes happen like this? Do men sometimes stand up in the divorce court, tired and bewildered, and say simply 'Yes, I still love my wife; yes, I still love my children; no, there isn't another woman; it's just that I can't go on any longer without any sleep.' Do they? And why does it never get into the papers . . . ?

Scream upon scream from upstairs. Louise was at Margery's bedside and with her arms round the little girl before her conscious mind had even registered which child it was that called her. And, after all, it was only one of Margery's dreams.

'The Rubbish Room!' sobbed Margery, as soon as she could speak. 'I dreamed I went to the Rubbish Room, and there was a horrid brown lady in it, and she was looking for something, and when she turned round I saw she had enormous hands. Oh, Mummy, they were *enormous*! Like –

like great flapping cardigans. And I couldn't move, and she came at me—'

It was half an hour before Margery was soothed and sleepy again; and by that time Michael was demanding his ten o'clock feed. Another night was beginning.

3

'Oi!'

The syllable used by Mrs Morgan was not exactly 'Oi.' It was something so discreet, and at the same time so peremptory, that it defies transcription. But it was sufficient to make Louise set down the basin of steaming nappies on to the grass, and go to the wall over which Mrs Morgan's small brown eyes glinted excitedly. It was barely eleven o'clock, and so Mrs Morgan had not yet made herself up ready for her daily shopping expedition, and the wisps of untidy grey hair protruding from her hairnet added to the air of illicit conspiracy with which she beckoned Louise to the wall.

'She's come, then?' Mrs Morgan spoke in a penetrating undertone, at the same time glancing cautiously to right and left.

'Who's come?' asked Louise, who was always rather slow at switching her mind off the problem of what to cook for lunch that would be ready if Mark was early; wouldn't spoil if he was late; and wouldn't matter if he didn't come at all. Besides, conversations with Mrs Morgan nearly always started off at cross-purposes because of Mrs Morgan's habit of referring to everyone as '*She*' – with a nervous backward glance as if the subject of her remarks might be lurking unseen among the wisps of London Pride by her back door.

'*She. Her,*' explained Mrs Morgan obligingly. 'Her that's took your top room. I saw her come up last night. In a taxi. Not wanting to be nosey, it's not my business of course, but she didn't bring much with her, did she? Isn't she stopping long?'

'Why – yes, I think so,' said Louise. 'At least, I suppose she will, if she likes the place. She didn't say anything about it being temporary.'

'Ah!' Mrs Morgan allowed the significance of this observation to sink in. Then: 'Well, it's none of my business, but you're only young, dear, and I wouldn't like to see you took advantage of. Where did you say she come from?'

'Why, I – well, to tell you the truth, Mrs Morgan, I never thought of asking her. I suppose from some other lodgings somewhere.'

'Ah.' You could tell that the conversation was taking the turn that Mrs Morgan was hoping for. 'You didn't have no references, then?' she proceeded, moving in for the kill.

'No. Why, should I have?' asked Louise, settling her elbows less painfully on the roughness of the brick wall, ready for the drama that was to follow. By rights, she supposed, she should have felt bored and restive at being thus cornered by such an old gossip. Other intelligent women did. They sighed and fidgeted, and bemoaned the impossibility of getting away without giving offence. But Louise felt as if she was waiting for the curtain to go up at the theatre. All sense of hurry and overwork left her; the wet piles of washing seemed to dwindle, and the bitter spring wind felt suddenly warm on her bare, damp arms as Mrs Morgan began, in hoarse, conspiratorial tones: 'Well, I don't want to upset you, dear, but . . .'

This time it was even more absorbing than usual. It appeared that Mrs Morgan had a friend, and a very good friend she'd always been, too, who had once let a room without asking for a reference, two very nice ladies they had seemed, respectable you know, nicely dressed. They had paid a week's rent right away, and had said they would come back that evening. And back that evening they came, this time carrying between them a very long, heavy-looking parcel, which they had hurried upstairs and into their room without so much as a word. Well, Mrs Morgan's very good friend hadn't wanted to be nosey, just like Mrs Morgan herself never wanted to be nosey, but all the same she felt it was her duty to know if anything was going on. So the next morning, when the two ladies had gone out to business – Mrs Morgan's friend never took in ladies that weren't business ladies, it was just asking for trouble – well, after they'd gone, she felt it her duty to slip into their room, seeing she happened to have an extra key. Just slip in for a moment, see, just to make sure that everything was as it should be. And when Mrs Morgan's friend went in the door, what did Louise think she found?

'A corpse,' said Louise promptly, though a little sorry for thus robbing Mrs Morgan of her climax. But apparently she had robbed Mrs Morgan of nothing of the kind, for the grey head only shook triumphantly.

'No – that's just where you're wrong, dear. Of course, that was what my friend – though she was never one for throwing no aspersions at anybody, you understand – that was just what my friend had it in mind that she might see. But she didn't. She saw worse than that. She saw an imbecile. Lying there on the bed, gibbering and rolling its eyes something horrible, and not even the wits to move hand or foot! That was the parcel what they brought in, their sister, see. They couldn't get no one to take her in, poor thing, not like she was, so they'd schemed it up like I told you, to bring her into my friend's house done up like a parcel, and leave her there. It was a great shock to my friend, of course, and after that she always asked for references from her ladies. Because as she said, you never know.'

This seemed to Louise a rather tame sort of moral to be drawn from such a horrific experience; however, she admitted that perhaps she should have asked Miss Brandon for references, adding: 'But I'm sure she's all right. She teaches at the grammar school, you know, so I could always find out about her from them if I wanted to, she knows that. Besides, you saw yourself that she didn't bring much luggage. Not enough to include a corpse, *or* an imbecile sister!'

But Mrs Morgan would not smile. 'You never know,' she said, shaking her head. 'There might be other things what you haven't thought of. And she's a funny age, too,' she added darkly, as was her habit when the victim of her discourse happened to be a female anywhere between the ages of thirty and sixty-five. 'You can't never be certain, not when a woman gets to a funny age.'

'What *does* worry me,' Louise went on, 'is Michael. He still cries every night, you know. He didn't stop till five o'clock this morning, and I know it disturbed her. I heard her door opening and shutting softly two or three times – you know, as if she was thinking of coming down to complain, and then thought better of it. I don't know what to do about it. I *can't* get him to settle.'

'Don't you worry,' said Mrs Morgan, just as Nurse Fordham had said, and Mrs Hooper had said – as everyone, in fact, said, who didn't actually have to live through those weary hours before the dawn. 'Don't you worry, duck, he's cutting his teeth on the cross, see? My Herbert, he cut his teeth on the cross, and he was a proper terror. I never got a wink of sleep for three years. Not a wink.'

For a moment Louise seemed to glimpse, beyond the young, pinched leaves of the lilac, beyond the grey, scudding clouds, a far-off time in which she, too, would be able to lean at peace on someone else's wall, and talk with comfortable reminiscence of the long-ago days when she never got a wink of sleep. How trivial the phrase sounded, even a little farcical. How little it described the gnawing, relentless weariness that could suck every joy out of body and mind . . . could batter to pulp all the contentment in a marriage . . .

'Did your husband mind?' she asked suddenly. 'Did he complain?'

'Oh. *Him!*' Into Mrs Morgan's voice was gathered forty rewarding years of putting the male sex in its place. '*Him!* I should worry! The men get it easy all the way, dear, don't you worry about them! Let me tell you—'

But already the church clock was chiming the half hour. Louise eased her elbows, deeply patterned by the brickwork, off the top of the wall.

'I must go,' she said. 'They'll all be back for lunch in an hour, and I haven't even finished the washing yet!' She hurried back to her basin of clammy garments, and began pegging them out in hasty, uneven loops, while Mrs Morgan shook her head in pitying tolerance.

'There, dear, don't fluster yourself,' she admonished, radiating the philosophical calm which is born of not having anyone expected back for lunch. 'Don't worry. What I always say is, the work'll still be there when you're gone.'

Like other, more eminent philosophers, Mrs Morgan managed to deliver her pet aphorism with such conviction that it was some moments before her hearer realised that it had no meaning. And yet, somehow, the senseless, irrational optimism of it was like the spring itself; it was a part of this gay, sharp wind which was already billowing out the nappies into lovely, glittering curves; filling Louise's soul with that unrehearsed, unsolicited joy which comes so strangely and so unfailingly as the wind first catches a line of washing.

It was nearly six before Louise had occasion to think about her new tenant again. The gusty, chilly morning had worsened, and now a steady, hopeless rain was falling. Louise shifted Michael to her other breast, and stared out at the almost colourless garden, where the nappies she had forgotten to bring in hung still and sodden on the line. The dull, relentless daylight of a wet spring evening was still undiminished; it seemed to go on – and on – and on. Would it never be time to switch on the lights, draw the curtains, and let it slip back into firelit winter again?

'Never mind, my precious – only two hundred more scrubbing days till autumn!' said Louise, addressing Michael with unguarded idiocy. 'And then we can both—' She stopped, embarrassed, realising that she and Michael were no longer alone. Miss Brandon was standing in the doorway, her brown costume dark with damp, her neat school case dripping.

'Oh – good evening. Won't you come in by the fire for a bit?' exclaimed Louise, with awkward hospitality, conscious of the extreme social disadvantage of the noisily sucking Michael still clamped to her. 'You must excuse me – the baby – he's nearly finished—' She waved her free hand in an ambiguous gesture of apology, explanation and invitation.

Miss Brandon approached, with a reassuringly bright smile.

'But of course – I understand – thank you so much. Perhaps I *will* dry off a bit before I go upstairs, since you are so kind. That little electric fire in my room – it's more for the summer, isn't it?'

Now it's coming, thought Louise. She wished she had had more experience as a landlady. Was it usually at the end of only twenty-four hours that tenants came to lodge their first complaints? And was one expected to take a firm, take-it-or-leave-it sort of attitude? (Well really, Miss Brandon, I'm sorry you're not satisfied, but you must realise that at the rent you're paying . . .') Or did one meekly, ineffectively, promise to put everything right . . . ?

But, to Louise's surprise, Miss Brandon did not pursue the subject of the one-bar electric fire which, according to Mark, was all that the wiring in that part of the house would stand. Nor did she embark on the other dangerous topic – that of the baby's crying in the night. She merely moved closer to the fire, and, standing with her back to the warmth, she gazed with interest at Louise and Michael. Louise felt a little embarrassed under this scrutiny.

28

She drew the shawl more closely around Michael, and said, to break the silence:

'A dreadful evening, isn't it?'

Her visitor started a little, as if her mind was elsewhere. Then she answered:

'Why – yes. Most unpleasant. More like winter again.'

Clearly the conversation was not going to prosper. Michael drew away with one final, smacking suck, and his head, heavy with the sudden sleep of satiation, flopped against Louise's shoulder. If only he would sleep like this at night! thought Louise, shifting him higher on to her shoulder, so that the dead weight of his head lay warm and with lovely trustfulness against her neck. From now until half past nine or ten he would sleep as if drugged; as if stunned; no power on earth would wake him. But after that . . .

'He's a lovely baby. Very big and forward for his age, is he not?'

Louise looked up to meet Miss Brandon's civil, enquiring gaze.

'Why, yes,' she answered, pleased both at the compliment and at the breaking of the uneasy silence. 'I suppose he is. He's quite different from my other two. They were both quite small babies: Harriet was barely six pounds when she was born.'

'Indeed?' Miss Brandon was clearly making an effort to keep the conversation going. 'But then, you're not so very big yourself are you? I suppose this one takes after your husband?'

'Well – no – I don't know that he does, really,' said Louise, squinting round towards the pouting, unconscious little face so close to her own. 'He's so much darker, for one thing. Now Margery, when she was a baby, she was the image of her father. Some people say she still is—'

Louise stopped, uneasily conscious that she was beginning to run on about her children in just the kind of way that up-to-date mothers must be so careful to avoid. To talk shop if you are a mother is not socially permissible as it is if you are a typist or a bus conductress.

But to her relief, Miss Brandon did not look bored at all. On the contrary, she pursued the subject of her own accord:

'Margery? That's the older one, isn't it? Yes, I suppose she *is* like her father – she has his colouring, anyway. That shade of red hair – most unusual.'

Louise was a little surprised that Miss Brandon should already have noticed so exactly the colour of Mark's hair. Last night Mark had been working late, and had not encountered Miss Brandon at all; and the evening before – the evening when Miss Brandon had come to look at the room – she and Mark had only met for that few moments on the doorstep, in the deepening dusk, before Mark had bolted so unceremoniously into the kitchen.

It's nice of her, though, thought Louise, to try to take an interest in my family like this. Or perhaps, she reflected more cynically, this is just a rather cultured way of making me put a two-bar fire in her room. I expect she believes that the way to a woman's heart is through her children. Of course, she doesn't know that it isn't a matter of my heart at all; it's a matter of the wiring on the top floor.

The conversation seemed in this last minute to have petered out. Miss Brandon leaned closer to the fire, though her usually pale face already looked scarlet with the heat. Before the silence had had time to become painful, the slam of the front door and a cheery shout announced that Mark had returned from work; and had returned in high good humour, too, in spite of everything. He swung into the room, his coppery curls glistening with raindrops, and had given both Louise and the baby a resounding kiss before he noticed the visitor by the fire.

'Why – hullo – good evening,' he said, glancing at Louise enquiringly.

'I asked Miss Brandon to come in and warm herself, and meet some more of the family,' said Louise hastily, trying to remember what, if anything, she and Mark had decided about 'keeping themselves to themselves' or otherwise. Was he going to be annoyed that she had so readily invited this new tenant into the family sitting-room? Was he going to—?

'Mum-mee! I can't find my other garter, they were on my grey ones, and the ones in the drawer you said look in are Margery's, and the other—'

By this time Louise had reached the upstairs landing, and was able to stem the flow of this ear-splitting narrative.

'Hush, dear, hush! Why can't you come downstairs and tell me instead of standing there yelling like that? Look – aren't those yours? Under the chair?'

By the time Harriet and her garters were re-united, and Michael was settled in his cot, it was time to turn the potatoes down and put the fish in the oven. Louise was surprised, when she returned to the sitting-room, to find that Miss Brandon was still there, and deep in conversation with Mark, who was looking both pleased and interested.

'I should have thought the *Medea* was a bit advanced for your fifth-form girls,' he was saying. 'The theme of it, I mean. – Her feelings about Jason. I should have thought the point would be rather lost on teenagers who've seen nothing of life.'

'It isn't life I'm supposed to be teaching them,' retorted Miss Brandon. 'It's Greek. And as far as language goes, the *Medea* is a great deal simpler than many plays with possibly more suitable themes. Particularly the choruses—'

'Yes, yes!' interposed Mark eagerly. 'I agree entirely. But surely the theme is important too? How can those girls understand the play if they don't understand the complexity of Medea's character? They don't know anything about the feelings of a real grown woman.'

'Hardly anyone nowadays does know anything about the feelings of a real grown woman,' said Miss Brandon quietly. 'Most women simply feel what novels and magazines tell them they feel. And as for most men – why, if they ever came across a real grown woman, you wouldn't see their heels for the dust! She'd be too strong for them, you see. True femininity isn't weak at all; it's the strongest, fiercest thing on earth. Euripides sees that clearly enough. What he *doesn't* see – what he gets quite upside down – is the mainspring – the motive – of that strength and fierceness.'

'But, good Lord, I should have thought that's just exactly what he *does* see!' exclaimed Mark, obviously enjoying himself. 'It's a wonderful piece of character-drawing! What stronger motive could she have? What worse injury can a man possibly do to a woman than to desert her, with two little children, after she had given up everything for him? Her home – her reputation – years of her life – and has even done murder for him?'

'I don't agree,' insisted Miss Brandon quietly and obstinately. 'Men *can* do women a worse injury than that. And they do. Often feeling themselves very virtuous in the process. However,' she continued, with a sudden change of tone, 'there are some very fine speeches in the *Medea*. Particularly where her jealousy and hatred are laid bare. Her hatred . . .' As she repeated the word, Miss Brandon's glance fell, somehow, on Louise. Only for a moment; a second later she was looking once again into Mark's eager face as he defended his best-known classical author:

'A splendid piece of writing,' he was saying. 'Even you can't deny that. You remember the speech after Aegeus has gone out—?' He broke off: 'Look, have you got a copy of it handy? Let's thrash this thing out properly, while we're about it.'

'I've got eighteen copies of it, to be exact,' said Miss Brandon with a little smile. 'I've to distribute them in class tomorrow. Would you care to come up—?'

'Oh – jolly good! Rather!' and a moment later Louise watched the two of them going up the stairs together, still arguing enthusiastically.

When Mark came down to supper, after having to be called three times, he was still bubbling over with eagerness.

'Damned interesting woman, that,' he announced, as he drew up his chair. 'Did you know she'd written a book on Homeric civilisation? Apparently it was very well reviewed. I told her she was wasted, teaching those lumps of grammar-school girls, but, as she says, there's very little else you can do with a classics degree. Unless you get a University lectureship, of course. Apparently she came very near that a few months ago, but it fell through. Still, she'll get other chances – *Margery!* Louise, *can't* you get that child to look what she's doing occasionally?'

'Margery! Oh dear—! Well, you'd better get the cloth, dear, and wipe it up. But Mark, isn't it rather puzzling? I mean, if she's written books and all that sort of thing, why should she be pigging it in our attic? – No, Margery, not the *floor* cloth – the one hanging by the sink – I mean, you'd think she must be quite well off.'

'Don't you believe it! A scholarly work like that doesn't bring in anything. Anyone'll tell you. But there's an odd thing, Louise – all the while I was talking to her, I had the feeling that I'd met her before somewhere, but I couldn't for the life of me think where. As if she'd looked very different before – or in very different surroundings – something like that—'

'Perhaps you met her when you were up at Cambridge,' suggested Louise. 'Naturally she'd have looked very different then.'

'Maybe,' said Mark thoughtfully. 'I must ask her some time what year she was up.'

'If you want her to go on contradicting you about Euripides, I wouldn't ask anything so tactless,' said Louise, smiling. 'She was probably up years before your time, and she won't thank you for forcing her to admit it! – Margery! – For goodness sake don't flap it all over the food like that! – Here, I'd better do it. – But I still think it's funny –

34

her taking a room like that, I mean. Harriet, that's far too much butter! No no – it's no use putting it back now it's all jammy—' And for the time being the subject of Vera Brandon had to be shelved.

4

It was Saturday, the first Saturday in April, and it seemed to Louise that with one dizzying lurch of the thermometer summer had struck. The radiance of the afternoon sun seemed to be soaking gloriously into her tired limbs just as if, she reflected ruefully, her tired limbs really *were* out in the sunshine like everyone else's, instead of grovelling about in this tool-cupboard in search of Mark's canvas shoes. But then, she remembered, as a tin half full of dried-up paint fell viciously on her elbow, the first sudden sunshine of the year was always like that once you had become a housewife. It drove you not outdoors, but in. Fishing in long-shut drawers for the children's summer frocks. Ironing them. Restoring missing buttons. Rootling about in dark cupboards for the garden cushions; for the deckchairs; for the ropes of the swing. And now Mark's shoes, for which she could only search half-heartedly because of a growing conviction that they must have been left behind at Westcliff last summer – a mishap which would undoubtedly prove to have been all her, Louise's, fault. By the time all this grubbing about was finished, the sunshine would probably be over, and she would have missed it all. And yet, somehow, mysteriously, she wouldn't have missed it at all; not while Harriet's voice sounded out there, piercing as a blackbird's through the sun-warmed air; not while the sturdy thudding of the two pairs of sandalled feet sounded so purposefully on the stone path and then on the linoleum. In and out . . . In and out. Into the kitchen . . . Into the garden . . . Back into the kitchen again . . . What *were* they doing?

Oh, the Tent, of course. Louise felt suddenly very tired when she thought about the Tent – that fearsome erection of kitchen chairs, table, clothes horse, ironing board . . . all of which would have to be brought in again at nightfall, by Louise . . . And they'd want the ground-sheet too, of course . . . it was probably somewhere in here . . .

At this point in her meditations, Louise was interrupted by Mark's voice – already edged with that grim patience which a week-end so often calls forth in fathers.

'I say, Louise!' he yelled from somewhere upstairs. 'Can't you make those kids keep the back door shut? There's a howling draught up here – my papers are blowing all over the place.'

'Harriet – Margery!' yelled Louise obediently. 'Shut the door!'

A vigorous slam was followed barely five seconds later by a renewed bursting open of the offending door, and a fresh hurtling of breathless small bodies along the passage.

'Shut the door!' called Louise, this time mechanically. Another slam. Another scurrying of feet. Again the door was open. Again Mark yelled down in protest. 'Shut the *door*!' called Louise; and again: '*Shut* the *door*!'

Well, here was the ground-sheet, anyway – this stiff, sticky, unyielding block of obstinacy. She yanked it out, accompanied by a clatter of miscellaneous metalware, and dragged it into the garden.

'Here you are, children—' she was beginning, when a voice from over the fence interrupted her – a precise, over-ladylike voice, trembling with something more than ladylike emotion:

'Mrs Henderson,' it said, 'I don't want to seem to complain. I can put up with a lot, anyone will tell you that. But that blessed door of yours' (the ladylike diction began to slip as justifiable indignation came into its own). 'That blessed door has been going slam, slam, slam the whole blessed afternoon till I can't put up with it any more. It's more than anybody's nerves can stand, Mrs Henderson, and I don't mind telling you. It's just about driving me crazy . . .

'I'm sorry, Mrs Philips,' said Louise helplessly. 'I'll see it doesn't happen again.' She turned back towards the house. 'Don't shut the door!' she nearly called; and then, remembering Mark still within, she substituted, 'Shut the door *quietly*!' Even as she spoke, she was overwhelmed by the futility of such a command. As if the children *could* shut doors quietly! Better, perhaps, to prop it open a few inches . . .

'*Louise!*' came Mark's voice for the third time, as the draught whistled through the house all over again. '*Can't* you get those damn kids to—'

For a moment Louise stood quite still. What would they all do, she wondered, if she were to lie down on the floor, then and there, and have hysterics? If she screamed, and sobbed and gibbered, and yelled out: 'I can't – I *can't* do any more about any of you! I CAN'T.' Would Mark rush downstairs, all concern and tenderness? Would Mrs Philips wipe that expression of watchful disapproval off her face and hurry round with offers of neighbourly assistance? Would the children stand round, awed and bewildered, shocked at last into silence . . . ?

'Mummy!'

For one mad second, Louise wondered if it had happened; if she had in fact fallen into hysterics. For Margery's eyes were round, and a little awed; her voice rather prim and unnatural: 'Mummy,' she repeated. 'There's a lady out in the front, and she says do you know baby's crying? She says he was crying when she started out to do her shopping, and he was still crying when she came back, and so she said she thought she'd better enquire if he was being looked after, and she said—'

Louise knew that this recital would continue without intermission for as long as she cared to stand there listening to it. Hastily pulling herself together, she managed to say brightly: 'All right – thank you, darling. I'll go and see to it. Oh – and Margery. I *wish* you and Harriet would try to shut the back door quietly. You heard Mrs Philips complaining, didn't you? Or, better still, don't keep on coming indoors. Can't you stay in the garden and play with the things you've taken out already? What do you keep coming in *for*?'

'What?' said Margery, bringing her gaze back from the vacancy she had been so comfortably contemplating since her mother began speaking. 'What, Mummy?'

But Michael's yells from the front garden had now reached a pitch that could leave no doubt as to which was the most urgent task. Louise hurried through the house, leaving Margery, Mrs Philips and the back door to unravel their destiny as best they could.

It was nearly teatime before Louise remembered that her mother-in-law was expected that evening.

'I wish I'd thought of it this morning,' she said, as she set a plate of bread-and-jam on the rickety garden table. 'Then I could have asked Miss Brandon about it before she went out. We can't very well barge into her room and take the books without asking her.'

'Why not? Does she lock her door?' asked Mark obtusely, heaving himself up in his deckchair. 'I say – it's getting damn cold. D'you think it's such a good idea having tea out here after all?'

'Well—' Louise looked across the lilacs to the sinking sun. Half an hour ago it had been so brilliant, tea indoors had seemed out of the question. Now the sun hung red and dimmed, surrounded by a thickening mist that augured rain for tomorrow. And thank goodness, too! thought Louise. I couldn't have stood another day of Mrs Philips and the back door . . .

Aloud she said: 'I think we might as well have it here now it's ready. And with Michael just settled on his rug, too – he'll only scream if we go in. Children! Tea! – Listen, Mark, about your mother coming this afternoon—'

'Is Granny coming?' interrupted Harriet, shrill and inquisitive through her bread-and-jam.

'Yes, dear, she's coming after tea, and so—'

'Who is?' enquired Margery, waking up as usual in time to hear the tail-end of every conversation.

'Granny, dear,' repeated Louise patiently. 'So do you think, Mark—?'

But it was no use. It never was any use trying to discuss anything at mealtimes. And it isn't as if I've deliberately *tried* to bring them up on progressive lines, thought Louise dismally, as she scooped an imaginary beetle out of Harriet's milk. I haven't had any theories about letting them express themselves – why do they behave so exactly as if I had? Is it something in the air of the present century? And was there something different in the air of previous centuries – something which children breathed in – and lo and behold found themselves quiet and docile and in awe of their elders? Or is it that the disciplining of children is a lost art, like the making of frumenty, or the medieval staining of glass? In that case, then the only difference between progressive parents and others is that the progressive ones are making the best of a bad job by parading the universal incompetence as a special virtue of their own . . .

'*Granny!*'

With a screech like a parakeet Harriet was across the lawn and clinging to her grandmother with arms sticky to the elbow. Children are just like cats, thought Louise. They have an unerring instinct for the person who most wants to avoid them, and they cling and clamber on that person with relentless and unsnubbable devotion. If only Mark's mother had been the kind of grandmother who revels in just the sort of affection with which Harriet was now belabouring her! Only, of course, if she had been, Harriet wouldn't be doing it . . .

Mrs Henderson senior meanwhile had picked Harriet off her skirt as if she was a burr, and was continuing on her way across the lawn, her smart black suit, her sheer nylons and her flawless nail-varnish putting Louise and her crumpled overall utterly to shame.

'Oh – hullo, Mother – come and have some tea,' said

Louise, getting herself clumsily out of her deckchair. 'Do sit down.'

'No – no, thank you, dear, I can only stay a moment. I've got to go straight on to that wretched cocktail party. Besides, you know, now my children are grown up I like to make the most of never having to have meals in the garden at all, ever. My present flat hasn't even *got* a garden,' she added, with undisguised satisfaction. 'But finish your own tea, dear, and then perhaps we can collect those books of mine and be done with it. Half of them want getting rid of, really, but I don't know when I'll get a minute to go through them.' She glanced at her watch; and Louise, hastily gulping down the last of her tea, led the way into the house.

'There's just one thing,' she said, as they mounted the top flight of stairs – 'it's a bit awkward – Miss Brandon's been out since this morning, she won't be back till quite late, and I forgot to tell her you were coming. Mightn't she think it's rather a cheek if we just walk into her room while she's out . . . ?'

'If she's out she can't think anything, can she?' said Mrs Henderson practically. 'And if by any chance she comes in while we're at it— Oh, don't you worry, dear! I've been caught red-handed at worse than this in my time!' She laughed merrily, pushed the door open with a flourish, and stepped briskly into the room.

But a second later even her assurance faltered. She stopped dead, and Louise, following on behind, nearly tripped over the enviable high heels. For there by the window sat Miss Brandon, quite motionless, staring out into the garden.

'Oh – I'm so sorry! I really do apologise. I understood you were out.'

It was Mrs Henderson senior who spoke. Louise herself was too much taken aback to say a word. Miss Brandon had *said* she was going to be out all day – had, in fact, sought out Louise in the kitchen especially to tell her so. And quite unnecessarily, too – she had her own key, and her comings and goings were no business of Louise's. When had she come back then? How long had she been sitting up here, silent, and apparently unoccupied? For there were no books or papers laid out, no sewing – nothing to suggest that she had spent the afternoon either working or amusing herself. Of course, it might be that she had only just come in, while they were all out in the garden and wouldn't have noticed; but something in that hunched, motionless pose seemed to preclude this possibility. It was not the pose of a woman who is simply resting for a few minutes between one activity and the next . . . Louise felt suddenly ill at ease. There was something unnerving in the thought that this woman had been sitting there motionless, perhaps for hours, simply staring out into the garden – a silent witness of Louise's ignominious encounter with Mrs Philips; of the untidy, ill-managed picnic tea; of all the ineffective, half-hearted tussles with the children which had mingled with the golden afternoon. And above all, why, if she had planned to spend the afternoon thus, had Miss Brandon announced so positively that she would be out . . . ?

Louise checked herself. This was absurd! She was allowing herself to become the very caricature of an inquisitive landlady! Miss Brandon surely had a perfect right to change

43

her plans without coming and announcing it to Louise; had a right, too, to spend Saturday afternoon doing nothing in her own room if she wished. Even had a right to amuse herself by watching the goings-on in the gardens within her view. Goodness knows Mrs Morgan next door spent enough time doing just that; no doubt she too had been enjoying her ringside view of the row with Mrs Philips, and was even now watching hopefully for the second round – which could not be long delayed, reflected Louise gloomily, unless someone quickly stopped Harriet dragging that watering-can across the flagstones by a piece of string. Perhaps Mark would stop her. Or perhaps Mrs Philips had set off already for her evening stroll. Or perhaps . . .

'Louise, dear,' Mrs Henderson was saying crisply, 'don't stand there dreaming – really, I sometimes think you're worse than Margery! – Miss Brandon is asking you, haven't you got some kind of a box we could borrow? A packing-case? Grocery box? Anything to put the books in—?'

'Well—' began Louise doubtfully, her mind hastily but without much hope ransacking the untidier recesses of her home. 'There might be. But our grocer always sends such big floppy boxes, and then the children get hold of them to be dog-kennels or something—'

'My dear, you needn't say any more!' interrupted Mrs Henderson. 'The word "Children" is enough. It goes without saying, that if there are children in the house, there won't be a single container of any sort in less than eight mangled pieces! Don't you think,' she went on, turning to Miss Brandon, 'that the most wonderful moment in a woman's life is when her last child clears off and leaves her free – *free?*'

Miss Brandon did not reply; unabashed, Mrs Henderson continued: 'Look; isn't that a suitcase you've got up there on the wardrobe? Could you possibly lend it to me? I think it'll just about hold all this lot.'

For a moment Miss Brandon still did not speak. Then, as if rousing herself with an effort, she said:

'Of course. Let me get it down—'

With a powerful and oddly graceful movement she hoisted the case off the top of the wardrobe and laid it before her visitor. Quite a big case it was, reflected Louise, in spite of Mrs Morgan's neighbourly disparagement. She hadn't particularly noticed it herself in the darkness and bustle of that evening of arrival; but now she looked at it with interest. Such a distinguished-looking case, with its rich dark blue leather, and its array of foreign labels. Greece Miss Brandon seemed to have been to – that would be in connection with the book on Homer, no doubt. Turkey too, and Sardinia; Helsinki; Portugal . . . How absurdly out of place such a case seemed in a suburban street like this . . .

Louise was aware of a queer, lurching giddiness. When – where – had she thought exactly these thoughts before? Where had she seen that suitcase – or one the very double of it – and had found herself thinking, exactly as she was thinking now: How out of place that is! Fancy seeing a suitcase like that *here*, of all places!

But what place? Louise passed her hand across her forehead. What *would* be the most unlikely place to find a suitcase covered with foreign labels? A Church jumble sale? A Westcliff boarding house? Louise shook her head. Was she, after all, merely experiencing that well-known sensation of 'having-done-all-this-before'? Didn't they say that this sensation was very commonly caused by lack of sleep?

She became aware that Miss Brandon was watching her. Watching her interest in the suitcase, her puzzlement. With an awkward, hasty movement the older woman pushed the suitcase nearer to the wall, planted herself in front of it and began packing the books with hasty, nervous movements.

The task was soon finished, though with shockingly little help from Louise, and the party set off down the stairs; Miss Brandon, at her own insistence, carrying the case, while Louise followed with the remainder of the books piled in her arms, and Mrs Henderson went in search of Mark.

When she saw Mrs Henderson's miniature three-wheeler drawn up in front of the house, Miss Brandon dumped the case down on the pavement in surprise.

'Don't make me laugh!' she exclaimed, with the schoolgirlish brusqueness which occasionally marred her poise. 'Don't tell me that your mother-in-law's proposing to get all this lot in there! And the seat's all covered with dinner-plates already,' she added, peering in through the toylike window.

'I expect she'll manage,' began Louise uncertainly; and at that moment Mrs Henderson reappeared, followed by the reluctant Mark, who, hidden in the bedroom, had begun to hope that he was escaping the whole of this book business.

'Manage? Of course I'll manage!' she exclaimed, always alert to defend her little car against any hint of criticism.

'And thank you *so* much, Miss Brandon – you've been most kind . . . What's that, Mark?' she added, as Miss Brandon turned back towards the house – 'but of course it'll go in, dear. You just have to get it up a little farther – slantways – no – the *other* corner, dear. You'll soon get the knack—'

'For God's sake – it weighs about a ton!' protested the panting Mark as a corner of the blue suitcase caught him savagely on the ear. 'How on earth did you manage to get the thing downstairs?'

'Miss Brandon carried it,' explained Louise anxiously. 'She insisted. I did ask her if it was too heavy, but—'

'She must be Strong Sam of the Fair in disguise!' gasped Mark giving the suitcase a final shove. 'Mother, I do wish you'd get a bigger car if you want to cart all this junk about. It wouldn't be any more expensive in the long run – in fact, it would work out cheaper, because—'

'You know very well that a small car suits me better for business,' interrupted his mother. 'The smaller the better for parking in town. You'd know that if you were a motorist. And in any case,' she added, plunging into the recesses of the queer little vehicle to rearrange a soup tureen under the steering wheel, 'in any case, I absolutely refuse to own a car that could possibly be big enough for Family Outings. The very first Family Outing I ever took you for, Mark, when you were only five months old, I remember resolving then and there that the greatest pleasure of my old age would be the knowledge that I'd never, never, *never* have to go on a Family Outing again. And it has been, too,' she added complacently, settling herself into the driving seat. 'At least, *one* of the greatest pleasures.' As she spoke, she glanced with genuine pity

47

towards Louise, who was sagging untidily against the garden gate.

'Cheer up, child!' she admonished gaily. 'Only another twenty years, and then you'll be able to have some fun, too!'

Louise started.

'I *do* have some fun!' she began indignantly. 'I'm very happy—' She stopped, wondering if the words sounded insincere. For she wasn't happy exactly, not just now; she was too sleepy most of the time. It was more that she *possessed* happiness, as one might possess an evening dress tucked away in the back of a wardrobe. Even though one might find no time to wear it, it was still there; it wasn't like not having an evening dress at all . . .

Her thoughts were interrupted by an agonised snort from the overworked little car; and with a wave of her elegantly gloved hand, Mrs Henderson was gone.

5

'Hullo – Hullo! Is that you, my dear? This is Jean Hooper speaking. Listen. Can you be an absolute angel? Can you do something for me?'

Louise sighed. Would it be Christine? Or Tony? Or both? And would it be for the whole day, or only for tea? She asked herself the question that Mark had asked her, in masculine bewilderment, only a few days before: 'Why on earth do you put yourself out for the woman?'

Well, why did she? Not for friendship's sake, certainly – why, she and Mrs Hooper didn't even call each other by their Christian names yet. Though, of course, that was largely because their acquaintance had begun in adjacent beds at the maternity hospital where Michael was born; and there everyone was so firmly '*Mrs*' So-and-So that you got into the way of it, even with someone who became an intimate friend. Not that Mrs Hooper *had* become an intimate friend – far from it. And yet, reflected Louise, there was undoubtedly something likeable about her, in spite of everything. Her very selfishness had such a childlike, confiding quality that one scarcely knew how to resent it. But all the same, decided Louise grimly, I don't like her all *that* much! Not enough to have Christine dribbling and screaming in the sitting-room all the evening – especially on a Monday with Mark home early, and Margery to be got off to her music lesson. No, most decidedly not.

'Very well,' she heard herself saying: 'about five, then—' and flung the receiver back into its cradle as if *it* was the one to blame. How *did* Mrs Hooper do it? How did she always manage to twist things so that it was impossible to say 'No'? And could she do it to everybody, or was it just Louise who was the simpleton?

It was, in fact, barely half past three when the damp and lowering Christine was dumped into Michael's playpen; and when Mrs Hooper returned, long after the promised hour of seven, she brought with her an angular and somewhat haggard youngish woman whom she introduced as Magda. Late as it was, neither of them seemed to be in any hurry to collect the baby and go; and before long they were settled in armchairs, one on each side of the fire, without Louise having any clear idea of how this had come about. Which was a pity, because later on Mark was undoubtedly going to want an explanation of how it had come about, and in no uncertain terms; that much had been clear from every line of his body as he beat his precipitate retreat.

The young woman Magda, it appeared, had read just *everything* about psychology, and Mrs Hooper proceeded to put her through her paces in front of Louise, rather as one might display a performing seal. Unfortunately, the performance resolved itself at a very early stage into a recital of Magda's own life, beginning with the lack of understanding of her parents, and working through to the lack of understanding of her second husband, who had left her four years ago.

'Of course,' explained Magda tolerantly, 'I understood what his trouble was. He was neurotic. He lacked inner security. Subconsciously, he felt that he wasn't indispensable to me, and he resented it. Nothing I could do would convince him that he *was* indispensable. Nothing. I see now, of course, that it was hopeless from the start. Nothing would have convinced him, because, subconsciously, he didn't want to be convinced. It was his lack of inner security, you see.'

'I should have thought that the only thing that would convince a husband that he was indispensable would be if he *was* indispensable,' remarked Louise. 'Was he?'

The two friends stared at her reproachfully. It was as if she had dashed into the ring and rearranged the hoops.

'Of course he wasn't!' snapped Magda. 'I told you I was earning my own living at the time – I earned more than he did, actually. Besides, my own inner integrity—'

A ring at the front door released Louise from the rest of this sentence; and a minute later she returned with her mother-in-law, a bunch of syringa and Miss Brandon's blue suitcase. Louise noticed that among the numerous labels on the case there was now a raw patch of ragged white, as if a label had been torn off recently, and in haste; but there was no time to reflect on this now, as her visitors were waiting to be introduced.

'I'm on my way to Hugh's party, really,' explained Mrs Henderson. 'I have to fly; I only dropped in to get that suitcase off my conscience. Oh, and those flowers – you'd better keep them, dear. They're from a grateful client, you know, an absolute pet, but all the same I can't drag them around with me all evening, now can I?' She settled herself, legs elegantly crossed, on the arm of the sofa. 'I'll just smoke a cigarette, and then I must dash,' she explained. 'Don't let me interrupt whatever it is you're talking about.'

Magda, who had had no intention of letting anything or anybody interrupt what she was talking about, continued her recital. The husband was finished now – at least, this particular one was – and she had reached her son, now sixteen, who also didn't really understand her. Nor, it appeared, did she understand him; but then he was so impossible to understand. In spite of never having been repressed, in spite of having been educated at no less than eight progressive schools, all he seemed to want to do now was to pass the GCE and go in for the Civil Service. And worse still; although he had had the facts of life dinned into his ears ever since he could speak, he had so far showed no inclination to make any use of them whatever.

'Of course,' allowed Magda tolerantly, 'it may not be really his fault. In fact, I'm sure in my own mind that it's the girls who are to blame. They're repressed, you know. Most of them have a fearfully conventional upbringing, even nowadays. Of course, it's only thirty or forty years since they were all accepting meekly the notion that no nice girl ever thinks about sex at all.'

'And nowadays they're accepting equally meekly the notion that no nice girl ever thinks anything else,' retorted Mrs Henderson. 'If she does, then she's repressed, inhibited, full of complexes – in fact, not a nice girl at all. Yes, it's true: girls are very suggestible.'

It was some minutes now since Louise had heard Michael's first tentative squawks from upstairs. It wasn't really time for his ten o'clock feed yet, but she might as well fetch him before he worked himself into a rage over it. It was a wonder, really, that he hadn't done so already. Having once woken up he didn't usually stay quiet so long.

'It's time for Michael's ten o'clock feed,' she announced firmly, standing up; hoping as she did so that this would call the attention of her guests to the lateness of the hour.

But the results were disappointing. Her mother-in-law was the only one who leaped to her feet in proper dismay.

'Gracious heavens! I'd no idea! Hugh will be furious! Poor darling, I promised I'd be there early and give him moral support — he's an absolute baby when it comes to entertaining.'

A moment later she was gone, in a whirl of apologies for her short visit — though Louise suspected that her sudden departure was due less to concern for the incapable Hugh than to the imminent prospect of encountering one of her grandchildren while in her best clothes.

But the two remaining guests seemed to suffer from no such qualms. They sat on, evidently expecting Louise to bring the baby down and go on with the conversation while she fed him. Louise made one more half-hearted attempt:

'Isn't it time for Christine's feed, too?' she asked hope-fully. 'Oughtn't you to be getting her home?'

'Oh *no*!' Mrs Hooper was shocked. 'I believe in Demand Feeding. That's the natural way — feed a baby when it's hungry, not to a timetable.'

'Of course,' agreed Magda. 'I think any other method must be terribly frustrating to a child, it could affect him for the rest of his life. When Peter was small, I made *everything* give way to his demands. If I was in the middle of cooking the supper I'd leave it to burn rather than risk frustrating him.'

Louise could not help feeling that this method of

housekeeping might have contributed something to the lack of inner security suffered by the departed second husband; but before she had time to say anything there was a yell, sudden and terrifying, from upstairs. Not an ordinary yell of hunger; of boredom; of loneliness. Fear was it then? Or pain? Or sudden rage? Louise raced upstairs; and as she ran she was aware of the pattering of bare feet on the landing above.

'Margery!' she called; 'Harriet – whoever it is – get into bed! Whatever are you doing?'

There was no answer. But she had no time to spare for whichever tiresome little daughter it might be; she hurried past their room and into Michael's. He was still screaming, with the quick, breathless screams of real distress; his face was scarlet and beaded with sweat; and his arms and legs were flailing wildly. Louise snatched him up and tried to soothe him, and at the same time to find out what had happened. A pin? No, they were both secure. A sharp-cornered toy? Something left accidentally in the cot? But there was nothing; and as Michael's screams were now subsiding, Louise began to think about the footsteps she had heard. One of the girls must have been in and upset him somehow. She dismissed at once the possibility that either of them had hurt him on purpose. In spite of all the warnings one received nowadays about jealousy of a new baby, they had both seemed entirely delighted with him right from the start, and they handled him with an instinctive gentleness that seemed proof against any amount of provocation. But all the same, Margery was often clumsy; Harriet often heedless; there could easily have been some accident – a toy dropped on him – his finger pinched in the fittings of the cot – anything. It was Harriet, probably, scuttling away like that. If Margery had had any kind of mishap she would still have been standing there, tearful and inept, waiting for someone to come and scold her and put matters right. Settling Michael, now pacified, into the crook of her arm, Louise tiptoed into the girls' bedroom.

'Harriet – Margery!' she called softly. 'Which of you has been playing out of bed?'

There was no answer. Both little girls were breathing deeply, regularly. She switched on the light, and peered in turn into each of the apparently sleeping faces.

No, there was no shamming about it – nothing easier to recognise than a child pretending to be asleep. Odd that whichever child it was should have fallen asleep so quickly after her mischievous adventure. Louise wondered uneasily if either of them was developing the habit of sleep-walking? Wasn't it said to be fairly common in children of – well – some age or other? On her way downstairs, she thought of asking if Tony had ever done anything of the sort, but quickly dismissed the idea. With Magda there as well, she would certainly be told that sleep-walking was a symptom of repression, frustration, and, above all, of regular feeding in babyhood. Particularly since she had already told them that this was Michael's ten o'clock feed, and the clock was tactlessly striking ten at this very moment.

She was surprised when she returned to the sitting-room to find that the blue suitcase was gone. Apparently Miss Brandon had come in to collect it while Louise was upstairs, and must have gone on up to her room without Louise hearing her.

'And do you know – such a funny thing,' added Mrs

Hooper, 'I know her. That is, she didn't seem to recognise me, but I remember her very well – she came to our Sex and Society Group two or three times last winter. Such a pity – I thought she was going to become a regular member, but she quite suddenly dropped out. I don't know why.'

'Too repressed and frustrated,' chipped in Magda, eager as a child who has come to the bit of the lesson that it knows. 'That sort never go on coming long. They can't take it. Didn't you notice she went out early every time, as soon as the discussion began to get really intimate? And your Tony says—'

'Talking of Tony,' Louise interrupted, with sudden hope, 'won't he be wondering what's happened to you? Surely you should go back?'

But this only evoked a fresh assurance that it was *perfectly* all right; that Tony was with a neighbour, and didn't mind a bit how long he stayed there; he never worried a bit, even when left so late that the neighbour had to make up a bed for him on the sofa.

By this time Christine was complaining, in her thin, peevish fashion, and her pram in the corner of the room was jerking irritably. But it appeared that the Natural Method of feeding allowed a margin of time sufficient for her mother to hear an account of three further neurotic characters who didn't understand Magda; and it was nearly eleven before Mrs Hooper finally bumped her pram away into the darkness, while Magda set off at a loping stride in the opposite direction, to who knew what haunt of further misunderstanding.

Louise had to lock up herself that night, for Mark had

gone to bed without a word – in a fit of sulks, no doubt, about the unwelcome visitors. Louise, indeed, felt very much like having a fit of sulks herself, if only it would have done any good. All that ironing would have to wait till tomorrow now; tonight, she could hardly stand up for sleepiness. But what *could* you do with people who wouldn't take a hint? Even if you told Mrs Hooper point blank that you wanted her to go because you were tired, she would only beam at you and explain that it had been proved that tiredness was all psychological; and Magda would back her up, and tell you it was because you lacked inner security . . . Louise bolted the back door with a violence which nearly took the skin off her knuckles; and quite suddenly, as she stood there nursing them, her tiredness seemed to push her over some invisible frontier, and everything took on the quality of a dream. And in that dream it seemed very, very important that the house should be locked up thoroughly tonight. Half sleeping, half waking, she stumbled from room to room, fastening windows, trying latches. Downstairs, upstairs – even to the top floor of all, where there were only Miss Brandon's room and the lumber room. There was no bulb in the lumber room, but there was plenty of light from the landing to show her the way past Mark's fishing tackle, past the broken scooter, past the roll of underfelt. Plenty of light to cast wild, huge shadows on the white walls. Among the shadows her own head swayed and dipped, oval and distorted where the ceiling sloped nearly to the floor. For a moment the shadow seemed to quiver . . . to divide into two heads, vast and impossible; and then it was one again, swooping insanely across the ceiling, and vanishing as Louise stepped into the darkness at the far end of the room. Clumsily she made her way among the old chairs and lino; senselessly she latched the window which could scarcely have admitted a skilful cat; and then she hastened, trembling, down the stairs to the bedroom.

The dreamlike feeling was gone now, and she was awake; but Oh! so wearily awake! She was so tired that her whole body seemed to be swaying, rocking, and when she lay down it was as if she was being sucked into heaving, bottomless water. 'All-conquering sleep.' The phrase drifted into her mind – was it some quotation from the classics? And had the author of it been inspired by a weariness as deep as hers? Across the span of the centuries Louise reached out for the solace of a fellow-sufferer. But uselessly; for that long-ago poet had managed to put his torturing sleepiness into immortal verse; not, like Louise, into muddling the laundry list and snapping at the children.

6

What's more, that poet was wrong. This was Louise's first dazed thought as the relentless, intermittent crying from Michael's room forced her to battle her way back to consciousness a couple of hours later. For weeks now she had fought this nightly battle, and each night it grew a little harder. Each night, too, she would pause for a little in the midst of the struggle, allowing herself to think: Perhaps he'll stop: perhaps if I lie here and do nothing about it, he'll get tired and drop off again. He wouldn't: she knew with absolute certainty that he wouldn't, and yet the thought still gave her a sort of respite; gave her time to collect the strength needed to open her eyes and to move her limbs again.

Two o'clock. It was always two o'clock. There was no need, really, to peer into the little phosphorescent dial; no use, either, to cherish that flickering hope that possibly, this time, it would be three, giving a hope that his habits might be slowly changing.

The cries, which had been irregular, were continuous now, and growing louder. She must go to him, at once. If she delayed any longer Mark would wake up too, exhausted past endurance, and she would have a row on her hands as well as the crying baby.

The linoleum was icy on her bare feet as she felt about in the darkness for her slippers; her heavy dressing-gown gave, as always, its odd assurance of support, as if its enveloping warmth was a sort of relic of the blessed sleep which was gone. Clutching round her its delusive comfort, Louise padded through into the next room, and set herself to the nightly routine as one might set a machine in motion.

The routine had changed since Miss Brandon's arrival. As Mark had pointed out, one couldn't expect a stranger to put up with this nightly disturbance; and after that first night of hearing doors reproachfully opening and closing, Louise had evolved a new method. Instead of feeding Michael in his own room, and then rocking him, patting him, senselessly pleading with him, and at intervals trying to settle him back in his cot, she now took him straight down to the kitchen and sat with him there. Sounds seemed to carry upstairs less from here than from the sitting-room, and if his screams became really impossible, she could always carry him through into the scullery, thus putting two doors between him and the rest of the household. There she could sit, her feet propped on the mangle, her head drooping against the draining-board, and jig her baby up and down – up and down; while behind her the taps dripped in the darkness. There she would stay; and presently she would be neither sleeping nor waking; neither thinking nor at peace; scarcely aware of the cold striking up from the stone floor. And her head would sink further and further over the throbbing little body . . . the screams would become part of an uneasy dream . . . People, crowds of people, shouting, calling, demanding . . . rushing for a train in a station full of screams and whistles and roars . . . And then, quite suddenly, she would start awake, cold and deadly stiff, to find the baby relaxed and quiet in her lap, and the dawn breaking in the queer shapes and shadows of a downstairs room at this uninhabited hour.

Tonight Louise took Michael straight to the scullery. The comfort of the warm kitchen was out of the question with him screaming as loud as this. This time, even feeding him did not bring the usual temporary peace. He seemed restless, aggressive, pulling away from her breast, and would not settle to sucking steadily. Of course, it probably wasn't a feed that he needed at all – everybody said he was far too old to be needing a night feed. Except, of course, the people who said he was far too young to be denied one. Oh, there was so much advice to be had; and it was all so kind, and sound, and sensible. All the problems of child management seem to be solved, mused Louise, except the one problem which confronts *me*. Is that why I always feel so guilty when I'm talking to Nurse Fordham? She knows the answers to so many questions – it seems dreadful to bring just the question that doesn't fit any of her answers. As if I'd done it deliberately. Like going into a smart dress shop when you weigh about fifteen stone. Of course they can't fit you – and it's *your* fault, not theirs . . . 'No, Moddom, nothing like that at all, I'm afraid.' . . . It was Nurse Fordham's voice that rang so genteel and scornful in Louise's ears . . . Nurse Fordham who was advancing across the deep pile carpet, a slinky model gown draped over her arm . . .

Louise started awake, and clutched Michael more tightly. Somehow, one never actually *did* drop a baby, however much one drowsed and dreamed, but all the same there must be a risk. And this hard stone floor, too. She should have brought down a blanket to spread at her feet, just in case. Or an eiderdown. Yes, an eiderdown would be better. Only the floor was so dirty; you couldn't put an eiderdown on a floor like that. Thursday was supposed to be her scrubbing day; had she missed scrubbing it last Thursday? No, of course she hadn't, she remembered it very clearly, particularly the slimy scantiness of that old worn cloth. She would need a new cloth. Oh, most certainly she would . . .

Louise found that she could think about the new floor cloth better with her eyes shut . . . She could think really hard . . . But wait: this *was* a new cloth, wasn't it? New and white – but why so big? And so stiff? What is it that is stiff and white? A shroud? No, of course it couldn't be a shroud; no one would use a shroud for scrubbing floors. It must be a sail. A canvas sail for a ship . . .

Oh, but it was so heavy to work with! It needed all her strength to pull it out of the pail, heavy and dripping. Her arms ached. She had been scrubbing for hours, surely, and still the unwashed floor stretched ahead . . . yards of it . . . acres of it . . . all thick with grease and old sodden rubbish.

She must clear it all, though. They would make her. They were watching her even now, their eyes fastened on her, murderous, and without pity. Such eyes! All the hatred of the whole earth must be mirrored in those eyes . . . those bared teeth coming closer, closer . . . she could feel the hot breath on her face, and it smelt of hatred . . .

Panting, gulping with fear, Louise awoke. For a second she thought the baby had slipped off her lap while she slept. But no; if anything, he seemed even more securely pressed against her than before. She clung to him in relief, sat up straighter; but even now that she was fully awake

62

shreds of the nightmare still clung about her. The smell of hatred still seemed to hang like steam in the chill of the scullery; she seemed still to feel the damp threat of it on her cheek.

But at least Michael was quiet now. She staggered to her feet and cautiously, painfully, she carried him upstairs again, the giddiness of sleep compelling her to feel with her toes for every step.

But it was no use. The moment she bent towards the cot, Michael began to yell again. If she had been alone in the house it would have been worth putting him firmly in the cot and leaving him to it; something in the quality of the yells now told her that they would exhaust themselves in ten minutes or so. But ten minutes would be quite enough to rouse the household; there was nothing for it but to set off down the stairs once more.

She reached her uninviting destination, and sat down again on the chair by the sink. As she settled her feet against the mangle and leaned her head against the draining-board in the now familiar position, she felt for a moment that she was settling right back into the nightmare; as if it was waiting there, to go on for her exactly where it had left off.

But Louise knew the cure for this. She had only to shift her position a little, and the nightmare would shift too. As if it could only catch the people who were in one particular attitude; and now it must depart frustrated, and hover over the towns and cities of the world – waiting – watching – peering – until at last it found another woman with her feet propped against another mangle, her head resting on another draining-board. And perhaps that woman, too, would not have washed up the supper last night; she too would have the smell of stale tea-leaves in her nostrils, would see the stacks of dirty saucepans looming at her in the darkness, huge, like towers, like lumpish, shapeless bodies, with little gleaming eyes where the street lamp caught the curve of the enamel. Brown eyes of course, the saucepans were brown; it was only common sense that their eyes would be brown, too. Green saucepans would have had green eyes. Brown eyes, so brilliant and so hard. Enamel eyes, with all the hatred of all the earth mirrored in them . . .

But this time, as the face approached, Louise knew it was only a dream. She tried to cry out, to wake herself. She even knew that Michael was in her arms, and she clutched him more tightly to protect him from the nightmare. Closer came the face, and closer; and Louise saw now that the malignant eyes were filled with tears; the face was stupid with grief, sobbing, crying; and the tears poured down in great swollen streams. Suddenly the twisted mouth opened. 'Don't make me laugh!' it shrieked; and again, in rising agony, *'Don't make me laugh!'* And a moment later it *was* laughing, showing great teeth, pointed as nails – teeth set wide apart, like bars . . . And louder came the senseless laughter – louder – louder – until it seemed to fill the room . . .

'For God's sake, Louise, what the devil are you doing down here? What's happened?'

Mark's voice was loud and anxious, raised above the crying of his son, as he stood at the scullery door in his pyjamas. Louise blinked in bewilderment. For a moment she could only stare at the scullery window, barred by some careful previous tenant against burglars. The bars stood silhouetted against the dawn sky, and Louise said stupidly: 'They're just like the teeth. That's what must have made me dream about the teeth.'

Mark stepped forward and shook her roughly by the shoulder. 'Wake up!' he cried, his voice sharp with anxiety. 'Wake up! Come back to bed! What *is* all this?'

Louise fumbled hastily for her returning senses.

'Baby was crying,' she explained. 'I had to bring him down or he'd wake everyone up. I've been bringing him here for several nights now. Not to wake everyone up.'

Mark pulled her to her feet, anxiety, as often happens, making him lose his temper.

'You're killing yourself over that damn brat!' he exploded, steering her across the kitchen and out into the hall. 'We never ought to have had him! I told you from the start that two was enough—'

Louise didn't answer. She was too dazed to listen properly; too dazed even to talk sense herself, for she heard herself saying, mechanically: 'Harriet, get back into bed!' Why had she said that? Had she heard a movement from upstairs? – Footsteps? Too tired to explain it, too tired even to think about it, she crept into bed, leaving Mark to put Michael back into his cot. He wouldn't cry any more now that the dawn had broken. With the first shrill stirrings of the birds Michael always fell into a deep and tranquil sleep.

7

It was thoughtful of Mark to switch off the alarm so that Louise should have an extra hour's sleep after such a night. It was thoughtful of him, too, to get his own breakfast and to bring her a cup of tea when he left for work at half past eight. The only trouble was that by half past eight the girls also should have had their breakfast; should, indeed, have been almost ready for school instead of lying peacefully in their beds reading comics. Thus it happened that Louise was able to produce only the thinnest pretence of gratitude for all these attentions; and as she leapt out of bed and dashed into the girls' room, leaving her tea half slopped into its saucer, she knew very well that Mark's feelings must have been hurt. If only there was more time! Hurting someone's feelings was so often the quickest thing to do – the shortest route from one task to the next.

She knew, too, as she hustled the girls from their beds, that she was defeating her own purpose by all this hurrying. Harriet, perhaps, would stand up to it – would get herself sketchily dressed and then stuff herself with bread-and-butter in time to set off at ten to nine and run all the way to school. But Margery! Heaven help those who tried to hurry Margery. Even as she scolded, Louise knew exactly how it was going to be. With every exhortation from her, Margery would grow more exasperatingly slow and clumsy. Bit by bit she would become incapable of buttoning her dress – of finding her socks – even of putting on her shoes . . . and finally she would be sitting on the floor in floods of hopeless tears. Precious minutes, and even more precious self-control, would then have to be expended on comforting her, and then everything would have to be started again from the beginning. And, of course, there hadn't been time to give Michael his orange juice, or change him, or anything; his yells mingled with Margery's tears and with Louise's more and more strident instructions. And just at this point Miss Brandon had to appear on the stairs, neatly dressed and ready for school. She stood for a moment hesitating, as if about to intervene – whether with criticism or an offer of help Louise could not tell. Nor could she tell which of the two would have infuriated her most, and so it was well that Miss Brandon thought better of it and went on her way down the stairs.

It ended, of course, in Louise dressing Margery herself, as if she was a baby, and then running with her all the way to the school gates, pulling her by the hand and scolding. All the time she knew exactly what she looked like. No lipstick; hair scarcely combed; the shapeless old coat failing to hide her overall as she ran. She knew how she sounded, too, her voice shrill and ugly as she hustled along the dragging, tearful child. So many mothers just like this had she watched and despised; so many children just like this had she pitied as they took the brunt of their mothers' late-rising and mismanagement. And the more clearly she saw the picture, the more infuriating became Margery's sniffs and stumbles. By the time they reached the school gates she could joyfully have driven the child inside with a resounding slap.

And after all this, here was Margery kissing her good-bye. Kissing her wetly, passionately; hugging her as if in boundless gratitude. Had the little girl really not noticed that all the scolding and misery she had suffered that morning had been entirely her mother's fault? Or, noticing, had she so quickly forgiven? Or was the whole question of no importance to her – a mere ripple on the surface of that deep pool of self-absorption in which all lives begin?

Louise returned the little girl's kisses, and no longer felt ashamed of herself. Bent double like this, with Margery's arms locked tight about her neck she too was in that underwater world; she too could scarcely feel the ripples.

And perhaps I'm there all the time, really, she thought confusedly as she hurried home through the rain-spattered streets. 'At least,' she amended, 'three quarters of me is – all the part that needs to deal with the children – *really* deal with them. It's just my head that's above the surface, worrying at it intellectually—'

'Mrs Henderson, excuse me, I don't want to make trouble. Anyone will tell you that I'm not one to make trouble, but really, there are some things that no one could be expected to stand.'

Louise looked up. If only she hadn't been staring at the pavement all the way up the road she would have seen Mrs Philips coming out, and would certainly have managed not to be turning in at her own gate at exactly the moment when Mrs Philips was coming out of hers. Unless, of course, Mrs Philips had engineered it deliberately; in that case, no amount of dawdling, hurrying or plunging into the tobacconist's at the corner would have been any help. Louise knew when she was out-manoeuvred; and she stopped, looking as puzzled as she could at such short notice, and with Michael's yells already resounding in her ears through the open bedroom window.

'It's that baby of yours,' continued Mrs Philips. 'I don't know what's the matter with him, I'm sure, and of course it's not my business. Though, of course, if a complaint was to be made in some official quarter, and if they were to ask me the circumstances, me being the nearest neighbour, you understand, well, I wouldn't feel it was right to hold anything back. I'm telling you frankly, Mrs Henderson, I wouldn't feel it was right.'

'I'm so sorry, Mrs Philips—' began Louise, and then stopped helplessly. How could Mrs Philips, in her leisurely, well-ordered solitude, be made to understand the kind of rush and scramble that had made it necessary to leave Michael at home alone?

'And it isn't just this morning,' continued Mrs Philips inexorably. 'Though, of course, he's been screaming ever since breakfast time. Hasn't stopped for a moment. It's given me a bad head, Mrs Henderson, a real bad head.'

'I'm so sorry, Mrs Philips—' Louise wished she could ever think of any other answer. So far as she could remember, ever since she had lived here, these five words were the only ones she had ever managed to contribute to a conversation with Mrs Philips. Even their very first introduction of all, on the day when the Hendersons had moved in, had been over the question of the children's footsteps on the uncarpeted stairs.

She hurried indoors and up to Michael's room. Through the window she could see Mrs Philips still standing attentively by the gate. And though she couldn't see them, Louise was aware that the lace curtains at her other neighbour's window were stirring a little as Mrs Morgan peeped out, all agog. Praying, no doubt, that the Henderson baby would go on crying louder than ever, and that Mrs Philips really would make a Complaint. Mrs Morgan knew all about the possibilities opened up by a Complaint. Shouted insults – the police – furniture on the street – even the throwing of bricks. Why, some of the happiest days of Mrs Morgan's life had been ushered in by nothing more than a Complaint.

Understanding all this, Louise was not surprised that Mrs Morgan should seem a little down-hearted as she greeted her over the garden wall a couple of hours later. For Michael had been as good as gold for those whole two hours, and was still sleeping peacefully; and Mrs Philips had been heard actually humming as she weeded her rockery in the front. The morning that had begun with such belligerent promise looked as if it was going to peter out quite amicably, and so Mrs Morgan beckoned to Louise with something less than her usual gusto.

'Hullo,' said Louise, so dispiritedly that Mrs Morgan perked up at once. Perhaps it *hadn't* all blown over, after all? Perhaps it only needed a little stirring up?

'Don't you mind *her*,' she admonished with heart-warming partisanship. 'Don't let her upset you, dear. *She* don't know nothing about it. She's never had no kids of her own.'

'Hasn't she?' said Louise. 'I didn't know. I don't really know anything about her. I've never really talked to her, you see, apart from these rows—'

'Talk to her? Nobody can't talk to *her*!' declared Mrs Morgan encouragingly. 'None of us is good enough for her, that's what it is, duck. She don't even pass the time with you if you happen to meet down the shops. Keeps herself to herself, that's what *she* does.'

Louise had lived in this road long enough to know that while Keeping Oneself to Oneself could be a virtue of the highest order in Mrs Morgan herself, or in her Very Good Friend, in Mrs Philips it was a vice deserving the uttermost of neighbourly criticism. Mrs Philips' other shortcomings as a neighbour were then enlarged upon in a manner very soothing to Louise's wounded pride; though as these shortcomings turned out to have extended over a period of nearly thirty years, the balm to her pride was purchased at the price of her second largest saucepan, whose charred bottom she only smelt through the back door after it was too late.

Luckily it was Tuesday, and only the children would be home for lunch. As she transferred the un-burnt parts of the potatoes to her third largest saucepan, Louise felt oddly unperturbed. It really had been worth it. It had been such a comfort to bask in Mrs Morgan's eager partisanship; to allow herself to believe, for the space of half an hour, in all the very worst about Mrs Philips. Even though she knew very well that any minute now Mrs Morgan would be embarking on an exactly similar conversation with Mrs Philips herself, only this time with Louise as the victim. Undisciplined children, they would say: Hopeless fool of a mother: No consideration. And they would compare notes about their nerves and their headaches. Mark always said that Mrs Morgan was a back-biting old hypocrite, but then a man couldn't be expected to understand. It wasn't hypocrisy. Mrs Morgan really *did* feel warm and protective towards you, and hostile to your enemies, all the while it was you she was talking to. It was completely genuine. The only trouble was that as soon as she began talking to your enemy, she at once felt warm and protective towards her instead; and that was genuine, too.

The third largest saucepan came to the boil, and as Louise turned it down, Mrs Morgan's cracked, excited voice came to her once more through the window. No doubt she and Mrs Philips were at it already. Reluctantly drawn to try and hear the worst about herself, Louise peeped round the scullery door. But no: it wasn't Mrs Philips out there. Mrs Morgan was leaning over her further wall, with her back to Louise, deep in resounding conversation with an invisible Miss Larkins – or maybe it was Miss Larkins' niece, Edna? – somewhere indoors. I'm sure it's about me, thought Louise, as listeners usually do. Me and Mrs Philips – I suppose it makes a good story . . .

A shrill cackle of laughter from Mrs Morgan seemed to confirm this view – but it wasn't resentment that made Louise grow suddenly tense and let the saucepan lid go clattering to the floor. It was fear: sudden, unreasoning fear. That laugh reminded her of something – something horrible, and unpleasantly near.

In a second she remembered. It was that stupid dream, of course, that nightmare which had haunted her restless, exhausted vigil last night, right here in the scullery. That senseless, tormented laughter came back to her with horrid clearness, and the agonised words, too: 'Don't make me laugh! Don't make me laugh!' The words seemed familiar, as if she had just recently heard them – not merely in the dream, but in real life, too.

Well, and why not, indeed? It was a commonplace enough phrase nowadays, with its cynical, couldn't-careless sort of undertones. Anybody might have said it.

And then, quite suddenly, she remembered who *had* said it. Standing outside on the pavement, suitcase in hand, looking at Mark's mother's ridiculous little car.

It had been Miss Brandon.

8

It seemed that Mark had suddenly become worried about Louise's broken nights. He had known about them theoretically for weeks, of course – had, indeed, often complained bitterly about his own unavoidable share in them – but it was only after discovering her in the scullery last night that he began to display real concern on her behalf.

And if only this concern hadn't taken the form of coming home unexpectedly to lunch just as Louise had got everything cleared away, she might have been deeply touched by it. As it was, she enjoyed his solicitous embrace with only a quarter of her mind; the other three quarters were already busily ransacking in imagination the refrigerator and the depleted store of tins, racing to have an answer ready for the inevitable next stage of his greetings:

'I'm starving, I can tell you! I missed lunch at the canteen to dash back here. What is there? Something good?'

Louise hadn't the heart to tell him that there were four teaspoonfuls of sieved spinach warming through in a teacup – Michael's first course. The girls had finished their sausages and fried potatoes and gone back to school half an hour ago. There wasn't even any potato left.

'I'll make an omelette,' she hazarded, trying to remember how many eggs there were left, and at the same time to smile brightly and welcomingly. For after all, it *had* been terribly sweet of Mark to worry about her and dash home like this.

But the bright smile did not quite come off; and neither did the calculations about the eggs. Mark already seemed deflated even before he realised that his lunch was to consist of a tin of baked beans and a warmed-up sausage. And by this time Michael's spinach was far too hot, and would have to be left to cool again. So Louise had to placate Michael by picking him up and carrying him on her left arm wherever she went. She heated and dished up the beans clumsily, with one hand, watching whatever gay hopes Mark had come home with fading one by one. He spoke only once:

'Do you remember, before we were married, I used to come to your flat for lunch on Saturdays? You used to knock up the most marvellous little snacks then, when you got in from work. With mushrooms and things.'

And though he didn't pursue the subject, Louise felt the tears coming into her eyes. It *had* been fun, once. Even the three strenuous hours needed on Friday evenings to get the said snacks into a state in which they could be so nonchalantly 'knocked up' at one o'clock on Saturday – they had been fun, too. And in those days, with the April sun shining like this, she would have been wearing a new summer skirt and a white sweater, not this eternal overall.

Yet what could one do? What could *any* woman do? Not even the most brilliant fashion-designer had so far devised an outfit suitable both for fascinating a jaded husband and for having sieved spinach spat on to it. And yet, Louise knew, it wasn't only gaiety and glamour that Mark was looking for. He had come home really anxious about her; ready to be protective and tender. If he had found her utterly helpless and defeated, appealing to him for help, that would have done just as well as glamour – perhaps even better. But somehow she hadn't been able to do that, either. I just haven't the *energy* to be helpless, thought Louise dismally, as she watched the last of the spinach trickling from the corners of Michael's mouth.

'Well, what do you say? Shall we go?'

Louise blinked. Even sitting on a hard kitchen chair for five minutes was enough to make her drowsy now; apparently she could even doze over the shovelling of spinach into that obstinate pink mouth . . .

'Go where?' was the best she could do, and she watched Mark stifle a sigh of impatience.

'That film. The one I've been telling you about. And I must say, I thought you'd have been keen, too. It's just your kind of film. At least, it would have been once. Honestly, I don't know what you *do* like doing nowadays.'

It was on the tip of Louise's tongue to answer truthfully: 'I just like sleeping. Nothing else. There's nowhere you could take me – no entertainment on the face of this earth – that would mean a row of pins to me compared with a few hours' unbroken sleep.'

But, of course, she couldn't say it. Not with Mark's blue eyes already looking so hurt, so baffled.

'I planned it specially,' he was saying, 'because it seems to me you're overdoing things. I thought you needed a night out. I thought you'd enjoy it.'

'Of *course* I'd enjoy it!' Louise assured him hastily. 'I'd love it – it would be marvellous . . .' Her tongue gabbled on glibly, expertly, striving by itself to smooth the disappointment from his face, while her mind busied itself with rearranging the afternoon and evening. The ironing would have to wait then, yet another day. The stew would have to go on at once if they were to have supper so early – in fact, it should have gone on an hour ago. Perhaps it would be better to save it for tomorrow and just have bacon and eggs tonight. No – that wouldn't do – it must be something that could be got ready well beforehand, because Michael's meal would have to be squeezed in, too, just before their own supper – as late as possible or he would be wanting another feed long before they got home. And what about fetching Harriet from her dancing class? Perhaps Mrs Hammond would do it – or was Vicky Hammond still at home with chicken-pox? But even if not, Harriet still wouldn't be home till nearly seven, too late for this early supper. Perhaps she had better miss the class altogether this week? Oh, but that would never do: she was to be the Third Rabbit in the Easter show, and tonight's class was practically a dress-rehearsal; and besides, Miss Walters would be giving out the pattern for the rabbits' ears. Could Harriet be trusted to bring the pattern home safely if Louise didn't fetch her herself? And if not, would Louise be able to design a pair of ears that would do well enough? If only Miss Walters wasn't so exacting about the children's costumes – really, it was ridiculous – anyone would think it was a Royal Command performance at Covent Garden, not just a bunch of six- and seven-year-olds prancing about in a church hall. And yet, on the other hand, they really *did* look rather sweet all dressed exactly alike, with their plump little legs and grave faces . . .

Her tongue must have been doing its work well all this

time, for when Louise turned her attention to him, Mark seemed quite cheerful again; the hurt look was gone.

'Who are you going to get to baby-sit?' he was asking, tilting his chair back and running his fingers through the crisp, red-gold curls, of which Margery had so ineptly inherited the redness without either the curls or the golden lights.

'Oh – well – that's the trouble,' said Louise unhappily. 'It'll have to be one of the Short List, I'm afraid, as we're starting so early.'

At this, Mark looked doubtful, too. The Short List was very short indeed, consisting as it did of people who were willing not merely to sit, in the literal sense, but to supervise the going to bed and settling down which was involved if the parents left much before seven.

'Listen – why shouldn't we ask Vera – Miss Brandon?' Mark sounded eager and confident. 'I'm sure she'd do it.'

Louise wondered why she hesitated before answering. It was a good idea – of course it was. It couldn't put Miss Brandon out very much since she was living in the house; and since the children were still slightly in awe of her, they would probably behave well. She would be suitable in every way. Why then should Louise feel so uneasy – yes, so frightened – at the very idea? Mark was watching her face, puzzled.

'What's the matter?' he asked. 'You're looking quite scared. Don't you like the idea?'

Since Louise had been asking herself the very same questions, she found it almost a relief to be forced now to find some reasonable answer.

'It's just that it seems a bit awkward,' she explained

uncertainly. 'I mean, whether to ask her to do it as a favour or – or pay her, like a professional baby-sitter, I mean. That is, with her living in the house with us like this. It makes it awkward, don't you see?'

'No, I don't,' said Mark cheerfully. 'You're always looking for such complicated difficulties, Louise, just as if there weren't enough simple ones in the world. Well, never mind. Get someone else. Who is there?'

'I could try Mrs Hooper,' said Louise, not very hopefully. Mrs Hooper's skill in asking favours for herself was second only to her skill in evading the favours asked of her; and her talents were never more in evidence than in a telephone conversation with Louise.

'You'll never get her,' predicted Mark with gloomy confidence. 'It'll end up with you promising to go round and look after *her* brats tonight. I've heard you telephoning that woman before! Look, why not get What's-her-name? The fat girl with the trail of magenta knitting?'

'Edna Larkins, you mean? But she doesn't go to her shorthand classes any more,' said Louise elliptically. 'I mean, she only ever did come so that she could study without her aunt having the wireless on all the time.'

'*I* never saw her studying,' said Mark obstinately. 'She was always pawing mounds of wool about, like a dispirited kitten. Or do you mean she's stopped wearing home-made twin-sets, too?' he added, a little more hopefully.

'No – I mean I don't know. I could try her. Now I come to think of it, Miss Larkins *did* say something about Edna's starting German classes this spring. I'll go round and ask her about it as soon I've finished Michael . . .'

Miss Larkins was full of sympathy, as always, and very

much regretted that her niece wouldn't be able to go out tonight as she was going to wash her hair. Of course, Miss Larkins herself would have been only too delighted to help out if only *she* hadn't been going to wash her hair, too; and if only her rheumatism hadn't been playing her up lately, and if she hadn't been having too many late nights recently, and if she hadn't felt it was wrong to leave Edna by herself too much, a young girl was such a responsibility . . .

Louise was touched. It had not occurred to her that Edna could be regarded by anyone as a responsibility – not now that the shorthand classes had rendered her capable of keeping herself in knitting wool and suet pudding. But apparently her aunt could see through Edna's doughy exterior to all sorts of hidden complexities; and if only Louise had had nothing to do between now and supper-time, she could have heard about them all. As it was, she had to back down the road making those understanding noises which become so inadequate at a range of more than two yards; and she finally fled into her own house hoping that she hadn't hurt Miss Larkins' feelings. Or shut the door loud enough to rouse Mrs Philips? Or taken so long over the whole business that Mrs Hooper would have gone out before she could phone her?

For Mrs Hooper was the only remaining hope. Not a very bright one, to be sure, but after all, she had her sister staying with her this week, and hadn't she always said that when this sister was staying with her she was free as air, and could go out all the time? The sister who *worshipped* Tony and Christine, and *loved* to be left with them, all day and every day.

Except, apparently, today. Particularly this evening it would be difficult. Yes, the sister *was* here, and, yes, she still *adored* being with Tony and Christine, but, just this evening . . . At this crucial point in the explanation, Mrs Hooper gave one of those headlong twists to the conversation which are always so effective on the telephone, where your victim cannot register protest by look or gesture:

'My dear!' she cried exuberantly. 'What about your mother-in-law? You don't mean to tell me *she* won't help you out?' – and without waiting for a reply, she went on, with indignant sympathy: 'Old people make me sick, they really do! They'll never do a hand's turn to help. They simply batten on the young ones . . . interfering . . . possessive . . . working out their own frustrations . . .' So indignant had she become on Louise's behalf that Louise had to move the receiver a few inches away from her ear to let the technical terms shrill against her eardrums less painfully. As she listened to the stereotyped diatribe against mothers-in-law – this overworked blend of old music-hall jokes and half-digested modern psychology – Louise found herself wondering how much longer this legend would survive in the face of the real life mothers-in-law that one actually meets nowadays. Energetic, preoccupied women, often smart and attractive, never with a minute to spare. All of them as robustly determined not to interfere, intervene or assist as three generations of cruel jokes could make them . . .

'It's not like that at all. It's just that she's always busy—' began Louise; but before her defence of her mother-in-law could be developed further, she realised that Mrs Hooper was no longer listening – that is, if the degree of attention

Mrs Hooper accorded to other people's remarks ever could be described as listening. Pressing her ear close to the telephone, Louise could hear a muffled conversation going on between Mrs Hooper and someone else in the room; and when Mrs Hooper spoke again down the telephone she sounded surprisingly meek and unsure of herself:

'It's all right,' she said to Louise, uneasily. 'My sister says – that is – I *can* come this evening, as early as you like.'

This was so unexpected that Louise could hardly find a reply.

'It's terribly nice of you. Could you possibly manage half past six?' she got out at last; and when Mrs Hooper agreed without argument she was so surprised and relieved that it did not occur to her to wonder what lay behind such uncharacteristic obligingness.

Something at least of what lay behind it became clear when Mrs Hooper turned up that evening only ten minutes late, and accompanied by Tony, looking both bored and belligerent in a torn jersey and broken-toed gym shoes. His features were sharp and inquisitive, like a rather grubby sparrow, and he met Louise's glance of ill-concealed dismay with one of emotion even less disguised.

'I thought he might as well walk over with me,' explained Mrs Hooper hastily. 'It's such a nice evening. And, although my sister is so *very* fond of the children . . .'

'She meant that her sister has refused to stay in the house another night unless Tony is kept out of her way for a bit!' giggled Louise, as she and Mark hurried to the bus-stop, suddenly carefree in the evening light. 'That must be why she agreed to come to us this evening, so she could bring Tony with her. She daren't risk him annoying her sister so much that she leaves before the Sunbather's Weekend. Else she'll have to take the children to it with her.'

'I should have thought she'd want to take them,' said Mark; 'surely sunbathing is Natural, and Progressive, and all the things she approves of for them?'

'Oh yes – it is,' agreed Louise. 'But she'd have to look after them, you see. She likes her children to be progressive in all the ways that don't involve actually having them with her – look, shouldn't we wait for a 196? The trolley-bus only goes as far as the station.'

But the one who doesn't mind a half-mile walk is always in a stronger moral position than the one who does; and so Louise stepped meekly on to the trolley-bus behind her husband, wishing that her only pair of high-heeled sandals were smart enough to justify the discomfort they were causing. There is no proverb to comfort the woman who suffers and yet fails to be beautiful.

Mark had said that the film was one which Louise would enjoy; and before the end of it she knew that he was right. Not that she had managed to keep her eyes open for more than the first quarter of an hour – to sit on a comfortable seat in a darkened room with nobody asking her any questions was more than she had ever hoped to withstand. And yet, as she dozed guiltily in this unwonted peace and comfort, something of the film seemed to get through to her. Perhaps the mind, half sleeping, becomes receptive in some way to impressions that in full consciousness would be beyond its reach. Perhaps the emotions of the people sitting near were strong enough to act directly on such a mind – all these hundreds of people, each experiencing the same skilfully engendered emotion at the same skilfully gauged moment – did it add up to an emotion multiplied in power by hundreds? That would be powerful indeed – a terrifying power – no wonder if a sleeping mind should absorb it, just as a sleeping body can become tanned by the rays of the sun without ever being conscious of their warmth. No wonder that Louise, in her half-sleep, should be able to follow without conscious thought the story of the film. Should feel the mystery – the mounting tension – the impending tragedy – the tense, terrifying climax . . .

But where was the happy ending? Louise blinked, started up in her seat. But it was all right. There were the hero and heroine, alive and well, and just limbering up for that final kiss which one has learned to accept as a shorthand note for a chapter explaining that after that everything was all right for everybody. But why had the mass-telepathy broken off at just that point? Why were the deeper layers of Louise's mind still pulsating in the midst of the unresolved climax? Why had the feelings of relief in all those hundreds of minds failed to break through?

Or had the telepathy, if such it was, come to her not from hundreds of minds, but from one mind? A mind fixed not on the film, but on Louise; a mind that followed her day and night, waking or sleeping; a mind that never rested, that could contemplate no happy ending; a mind that could look forward as far as the climax of fear and hatred, but could look no further . . . ?

'Louise! My dear! Fancy meeting you here! Do let's go somewhere for some coffee, and have a real good talk.'

Louise had scarcely noticed that the film was over and that she and Mark were already making their way up the crowded gangway. For a moment she stared stupidly into

84

the pleasant, eager face with the frame of fuzzy honey-coloured hair that hadn't changed since the days of the Upper Fourth . . . Then: 'Beatrice!' she exclaimed, 'how nice. Why, yes, we'd love to. Where – is Humphrey with you?'

'Oh yes. That is, I've lost him for the moment – Oh, here he is.' Beatrice turned as they reached the foyer, and a stooping, intellectual figure with greying hair extricated itself from the crowd and hurried towards them.

'Ha!' exclaimed Humphrey triumphantly as he caught up with his wife. 'I *thought* you'd be on the watch for me. She watches me like a spider,' he added happily, addressing himself to Louise. 'She knows there was a nice little blonde just behind, and she won't take her eyes off me!'

Unfortunately for the success of this remark, Humphrey's wife had already taken her eyes off him to the extent of disappearing among the crowds that were surging out on to the rainy pavement; and by the time they found her again (which took some time, since both husband and wife held the theory that the best way to find someone lost in a crowd was to stand stock still and wait for *them* to find *you*) the little blonde was lost beyond recall. Louise felt sorry for Humphrey. Not because he had lost the little blonde – about that, she felt sure, he cared nothing whatever – but because he had lost the opportunity of keeping her in the conversation. Humphrey's real interests, she felt fairly sure, were restricted to his car, his work at the University and the installing of gimcrack improvements in his ugly but comfortable home in Acton; but in company he always felt it a social duty to display an unselective and non-stop interest in the opposite sex.

He wouldn't be seen out without it, just as another type of man won't be seen out without a rolled umbrella.

'And how is the lovely Louise?' he enquired, with painstaking archness, as the party settled themselves on stools in the crowded milkbar. 'Lovelier than ever, eh? I'll be getting myself into trouble, won't I?' he added hopefully, glancing at Beatrice. 'Shouldn't say that sort of thing with the wife listening—'

But unhappily the wife wasn't listening. She was hunting about in her handbag for a letter from an old school friend; and soon she was reading Louise extracts about someone called Muriel.

Muriel? Muriel? Am I supposed to have heard of her? And why is it so surprising that she should be living in Bristol . . . ?

At this point Beatrice seemed to sense that her hearer was not quite appreciating the story; for she abruptly laid down the letter.

'But of course!' she exclaimed. 'How silly of me! It's such ages since I've seen you, I was quite forgetting: I don't suppose you've even heard that Muriel was divorced?'

Nor that she was married, either, reflected Louise resignedly. Nor born, for that matter. She sipped her coffee uneasily; but before she was forced to admit her utter ignorance of all concerning the erratic Muriel, Beatrice fortunately began to follow up her second thread:

'Yes, it must be months since I've seen you,' she was saying. 'You weren't at the Fergussons' Christmas party, I know. And we get about so little now that we've given up the car . . . And then you know what it is with a house to run. All the washing, and the cleaning . . .'

'But Mrs Groves does all that, surely, Bee?' interrupted Humphrey in tactless bewilderment. He could never remember that his wife, while enjoying the leisure afforded by a full-time daily help, wished also to enjoy a picture of herself as a heroic, overworked housewife struggling to make ends meet. She frowned at her obtuse partner, and Louise hastened to change the subject.

'It's not *so* long since I saw you,' she said. 'Don't you remember, you came to see me in hospital when Michael was born? You and Humphrey both came, and brought me some marvellous peaches—'

At the sound of his own name Humphrey, drooping over the coffee that he feared would keep him awake tonight, brightened up again:

'Shall I ever forget!' he exclaimed, groaning in mock dismay. 'A *maternity* hospital! And all the nurses staring at me, wondering which baby *I* was the father of! They looked terribly suspicious!'

Louise could not help smiling as she thought of the busy, preoccupied nurses bustling past poor Humphrey without a glance; and she changed the subject quickly, even at the risk of being landed with Muriel again:

'How's Eva?' she asked. And Rhoda. And Alison. And the Heathcote twins. It was agreed that it was dreadful the way one lost touch with old friends; it was agreed, too, that the reason was that one was Too Busy. It struck Louise that most of the imperfections of life nowadays are attributed to being Too Busy, just as they were once attributed to the Will of God . . .

'Which reminds me,' said Beatrice suddenly – and it took Louise a moment to realise that Beatrice was not referring to the Will of God, but to some independent train of thought of her own: 'That reminds me – Did that woman ever get in touch with you?'

'What woman?' Louise was guarded. 'Do you mean the Old Girls?' she added suspiciously. Even when you hadn't belonged for years and years, the Old Girls always managed to track you down when it came to Appeals. New Wings; Enlarged Libraries; Another Hard Tennis Court; they loomed menacingly for a moment before Louise's eyes.

'No no. Nothing like that.' Beatrice was reassuring. 'No, it's a woman who – Humphrey, you remember, don't you? What was her name? That woman you met at an Educational Discussion Group, or something?'

Humphrey choked exultantly into his coffee, delighted at being accused of having met a woman his wife didn't know the name of – even though he couldn't remember her name either. To cover his ignorance he launched into an enthusiastic description of the lady.

'A fine figure of a woman,' he improvised manfully, ransacking his regrettably vague memory. 'Juno-esque, you know. Splendid shoulders – Bee will kill me for this, won't you, Bee,' he added, winking conscientiously at his wife, who steeled herself to smile at him in absent-minded encouragement – just as she might have steeled herself to say 'Isn't that nice, dear,' to a husband with a different sort of hobby – the sort that spreads glue and balsa-wood all over the sitting-room.

'That's right, dear,' she remarked patiently. 'But what we want to know is – what was her name? Don't you remember, you told me she asked you for Louise's address, and you couldn't think what she wanted it for? Well, I was just wondering if she'd got hold of Louise all right and – well – what it was all about?'

'I'll bet you wanted to know what it was all about,' interposed Humphrey, with ponderous innuendo. 'Doesn't do to tell the ladies everything, does it, eh, Mark?'

Mark blinked up stupidly from the discarded evening paper to which the boredom of the last twenty minutes had driven him.

'Doesn't what?' he was beginning unhelpfully, when Beatrice broke in:

'I've got it! Brandon. Vera Brandon. Of course. I remember wondering if she was any relation of the Brandon-Smith's, because of course they're only Smiths really, but she insisted on tacking her own name on to his when she married him because she's such a snob. So is he, of course, but he wouldn't have thought of it on his own because he'd been a Smith all his life and sort of got used to it—'

'If her name was Vera Brandon,' interrupted Louise gently, 'then she *did* get in touch with us. In fact, she's come to live with us – she has our top room. But I thought she was just answering our advertisement. I don't understand how she could have heard of us apart from that. Or why she should have asked you for our address. I don't understand any of it. *I don't understand.*'

Somehow her voice was suddenly much louder. Customers and waitresses alike turned to stare.

9

Mark didn't seem to think much of the Vera Brandon mystery as expounded to him by Louise on top of the 196 bus, damply rumbling through the hideous yellow lights of the suburbs. Why, he enquired obtusely, shouldn't Miss Brandon ask for their address and then answer their advertisement? Or, alternatively, why shouldn't she answer their advertisement and then ask for their address? Why, Louise didn't even know which she'd done first, he pointed out triumphantly.

'But either way it would be odd – don't you see?' protested Louise. 'If she'd seen the advertisement first, then she'd know the address. And if she'd asked for the address first, then what an extraordinary coincidence that she should come across the advertisement afterwards? And why should she *want* our address before she knew us? And if she didn't know us, how could she know that we knew Humphrey? How could she know that Humphrey knew— Don't you see, it makes nonsense.'

'Of course it does; that's just what I've been saying,' said Mark cheerfully as they stepped off the bus. 'Come on – that kid'll be yelling his head off by now, and Mrs H. will be applying the Natural Method with her feet up and a library book. Do you know it's nearly eleven?'

Now that they were off the bus it became even more difficult to explain. Louise had been on the point of reminding Mark that only a few days before he had remarked himself on the feeling that somewhere, sometime, he had met Vera Brandon before. She wanted, too, to tell him of her own fancy that she had recognised the blue suitcase up in Miss Brandon's room. And if she had only known, here and now, on this drizzling April night, with her sandals pinching so agonisingly – if she had only known how much might be at stake, then she would certainly have told him. Would have shouted at him – screamed at him – taken him by the shoulder and shaken him – until she had forced him to take her seriously.

But she didn't tell him; and the reason why she didn't was the street lighting. With its vampire glare it had sucked all the redness from her jacket, the whiteness from her sandals; and she knew that her face and hair were grey, as his would be too if she ventured to look at him. It was as if they were characters in a piece of Science Fiction: by merely stepping off a bus they had stepped across twenty years into a nightmare old age. How could she confide in this grey-headed stranger beside her? How could she encourage him to turn and look into her own grey and haggard face . . . ?

The lights of their own road were the old-fashioned kind that allow your blood to flow once more; and as Louise felt the ghostly mask of senility slip from her under their friendly brightness, she might have spoken. But by now she could already hear Michael screaming. The noise rang down the empty street; and as she rushed up the path to the front door she was dimly conscious of Mrs Philips' bedroom window closing, gently, but with shattering implications.

Michael was damp and scarlet with fury; and justly so, since it was more than an hour later than his usual supper time. A search through the house for Mrs Hooper, who had promised to keep him at bay with orange juice and boiled water, proved vain. Vain, that is, except for the discovery of Tony reclining at ease on Louise's bed, his sandshoes caked in mud, and manfully keeping himself awake with a volume on *Diseases of the Central Nervous System*, and a tin of pineapple from Louise's emergency store.

'Where's your mother?' demanded Mark sternly; and Tony paused in the midst of stuffing an unbroken ring of pineapple into his mouth. He stared at Mark in mild surprise. Fancy anyone expecting anybody to know where their mother was.

'Out,' he said at last; and then added, with a boy-scout air which might have been more convincing if he had had less pineapple in his mouth: 'I've been looking after the baby for you. Is it a boy?'

'Yes – Look here, this is a bit thick!' began Mark irritably. 'Your mother's got no business to walk off and leave you like this. You can't take charge of a baby at your age – and anyway, you've done damn-all about him. Anyone can see he's been yelling for hours.'

'It's not Tony's fault,' pointed out Louise. 'He's only a child—' She stopped, for it seemed that Tony was well able to conduct his own defence.

'I been in to him twice,' he claimed indignantly. 'But he kept right on yelling both times. So I reckoned that's what he'd do if I went in a third time,' he finished, showing such a confident grasp of one of the basic principles of scientific method that Louise couldn't think of anything to say in reply. Mark could, however, and said it:

'Get off that bed!' he ordered. 'And tell us how we can get hold of your mother. Is she proposing to come back here and fetch you? Has she gone home? Or what?'

Tony rolled off the bed, scattering mud from his sandshoes at every movement. He looked very small standing there in front of Mark and his eyes, with dark smudges of tiredness under them, were bright and excited in his pale face.

'I think p'raps it's something to do with the spy,' he hazarded, watching Mark guardedly to see how this suggestion would go down.

'Spy? What spy? What the devil are you talking about?' snapped Mark; and Tony hesitated, obviously torn between the incomparable joy of having a secret to keep, and the unspeakable rapture of having one to divulge. The decision was hastened for him by Mark's next remark:

'You've been dreaming!' he said witheringly. 'And no wonder – a little boy like you still up at this hour!'

'I've not been dreaming!' cried Tony indignantly. 'I've been awake every minute of the time. I've been on the watch, and a jolly lucky thing for you, too! I been keeping guard for you. D'you know you've got a spy in the house?'

He addressed this last remark to Louise, sensing (and rightly) that she was likely to prove the more sympathetic audience for such a story.

'Tell us about it,' she said gently, sitting down on the edge of the bed; and to Mark: 'No, dear, please! Leave him to me. Why don't you go down and ring up the Hoopers and ask what's happening?'

'*Ask* what's happening! I like that! I'll damn well *tell*

them what's happening. Letting us down like this! It's time someone told them a few home-truths, and I don't mind being the one to do it!'

Louise felt a moment's compunction about the un-offending sister who would probably answer the telephone and be taken for Mrs Hooper herself; then she turned her attention back to Tony, whose sandshoes were now being ground into the cushion of the armchair in which he was settling himself as elaborately as a cat.

'Tell me all about it, Tony,' she began. 'Who did you see? And what makes you think he was a spy?'

'It wasn't a *him*,' said Tony darkly. 'It was a *her*. And I didn't see her, not at first. I just heard her creeping around. She crept in at the front door, and then she crept in at the back door, and then she crept up here, into your bedroom. I heard her. That was before Mum – I mean Jean – went away,' he added awkwardly. Ordinarily Tony blandly ignored his mother's efforts to make him call her by her Christian name in the correct enlightened manner; but a confused feeling of loyalty often made him try to conform in the presence of strangers.

'So she might've heard it, too,' he concluded, rather vaguely.

'Well, why didn't you ask her, then – tell her about it?' asked Louise. 'If it sounded suspicious, I mean, and she was still here?'

Tony pondered this.

'I think Mum – Jean's – more interested in pottery,' he said at last, with an odd touch of dignity. Then he went on:

'So after she'd gone – Mum, I mean – I went on a tour

of inspection. All round the house, with silent tread. Do you know how to walk real silent?' he suddenly interposed, turning on Louise. 'Most people think the best way is to walk on tiptoe, but it isn't. Not indoors, anyway. You should always walk on the flat of your foot indoors. The whole flat of your foot – it distributes the weight, see, and then you're not so likely to creak a board.'

Louise acknowledged this piece of information with the respect due to it, and Tony continued his story.

'Well, I peeked into all the rooms, one after another, and into all the cupboards, until at last I came to your bedroom!' Here came a dramatic pause, during which Louise reflected that it was hardly a logical procedure to go to the bedroom last, when that was the very room into which the intruder had been heard to go; however, she recognised the artistic necessity of exploring the bedroom last, and waited with flattering interest for the denouement.

'I peeked in,' said Tony, 'ever so quiet, see, not a breath. I peeked in, and I *saw* her! Poking about in your bureau. In that thing with drawers, I mean,' he amended, scientific accuracy for the moment overmastering his literary style as he surveyed the nondescript piece of furniture which Mark and Louise shared as a 'desk'. 'Shared' consisted of Mark throwing all his letters and papers on top of it, and Louise at intervals bundling them pell-mell into whatever drawers would still hold them; while her own, more meagre, affairs collected dust on a corner of the kitchen dresser.

'She had all the drawers open,' continued Tony with gusto, for the moment forgetful of the fact that if all the drawers were open then only the top one would have been displaying its contents – 'and she was looking in and out of them all, shoving the papers about – *looking* for something. I knew at once that she was looking for something.'

'Well, yes, it does sound like that,' agreed Louise. 'But *who* was, Tony? You still haven't told me who this woman was.'

'*She was the one you keep upstairs*,' hissed Tony. 'The brown one.'

'Brown—? Oh, you mean that brown costume Miss Brandon always wears. But, Tony, I don't understand. What on earth did she want?'

'The papers, of course.' Tony's reply was unhesitating. 'The papers with the formulae.'

This expert diagnosis silenced Louise for a moment; and Tony continued: 'Mr Henderson's something to do with aeroplanes, isn't he? Well, it's his papers she's after, see. A blueprint for a new kind of jet. Or p'raps a new fuel. Is that what he works on?'

After ten years of marriage, Louise still had only the shadowiest idea of what her husband did in the offices of the aircraft factory by which he was employed; but all the same her womanly intuition told her that the documents for which he was responsible were unlikely to have much market value in the international underworld. And anyway, if they *were* important, they wouldn't be in the 'desk.' Presumably Mark had enough sense by now not to put in the desk anything that he ever hoped to see again. But all the same, what *had* Vera Brandon been looking for?

'I expect she'd lost something and thought I might have borrowed it,' said Louise casually. 'Don't worry, Tony' (just as if Tony had been worrying), 'I'm certain she's not a spy.'

Tony looked at her pityingly.

'I knew you wouldn't believe me,' he said simply – after all, no grown-ups in any children's book he had ever read ever believed anything that the children told them – 'but, you see, I *know* she's a spy. 'Cos I've seen her before.'

'When? Where?' Louise hoped that the little boy had not noticed the intensity of her interest. 'What do you know about her?'

'Oh, well, you see, she was at our house one evening. At one of Mum's meetings. Supposed to be, but of course that's not *really* what she'd come for. She'd come because she thought *we* had papers, too. I found her looking through Mum's desk, just like she was looking through yours. She'd come out of the meeting early, see, so's everyone else would be in the dining-room while she could have a look round. She didn't find any papers, of course,' he continued patronisingly. 'If *I* had any secret papers I wouldn't be fool enough to put them in a desk. I'd put them somewhere really unlikely. Like – like—' But, of course, to a real connoisseur in spy fiction, *every* place seems likely, not to say hackneyed, and so Tony, with an adroitness worthy of his mother, changed the subject:

'If I'd had a torch,' he announced, 'I'd have got a cast of her footprints for you. I had a look round out the back, but it was too dark. It's a swizzle, because there must have been some jolly clear prints. There's some super mud just by the back door.'

Eyeing the traces of the super mud on her counterpane, Louise could not disagree; but she did point out that if a footprint *were* found, it would only prove that Miss Brandon had been out to empty her rubbish that night.

Tony looked sceptical. This was just the kind of thing that the unenlightened grown-ups of children's fiction always did think of; but he was getting too sleepy to remember how the enlightened children countered it. His head began to sway.

'You wait and see,' he essayed darkly. The grown-ups always *did* see in the last chapter. Or maybe the last chapter but one.

IO

'Well, why on earth don't you *ask* her why she's taken the room, and be done with it?'

Like most men, Mark was not at his best while ransacking his drawers for a shirt with all the buttons intact, and Louise realised too late that she had chosen just the wrong moment for bringing up the subject of Vera Brandon again – particularly now that the matter had been further embellished by Tony's spy story. As might have been expected, Mark had dismissed this entire narrative with a single contemptuous grunt, and Louise knew that it would be useless to argue – even if there had been time for an argument at a quarter to eight in the morning, and the children still not dressed. She began to comb her hair, slowly, although it was getting so late. She had been sitting up with Michael as usual last night, but the effect on her seemed to be different. This morning she felt neither tired nor sleepy, only slow. Slow like an old woman. She stared into the mirror almost expecting to see the hair grey that the comb ran through; grey and sparse, and the comb would make furrows in its dead texture. The face would be lined, the eyes dull; the voice, when it came, would be querulous and thin:

'Why doesn't somebody attend to those children?' it would quaver. 'What are they doing in there, thump, thump, thumping? Why aren't they dressed? . . . Why

99

isn't breakfast ready? . . . That counterpane hasn't been washed for weeks . . . This house is full of confusion. Full of danger. Someone must come at once . . . Some bustling, motherly figure who will clean things, arrange things, quieten the children, ward off the danger . . . protect us all . . .'

The comb caught on a savage little tangle, and Louise gazed stupidly at the young woman in the mirror. A woman who was neither old enough nor young enough to hope for protection. A woman who must be her own bustling, motherly figure, cleaning, arranging, quietening. Tiredness would not get her out of it – nor inefficiency. Sometimes it happens that without skill a skilled job must be done; without courage, danger must be faced . . .

But what danger? Though her movements had grown so slow, Louise's brain seemed to have acquired a restless vigour of its own; like some hungry animal it prowled eagerly among the facts and guesses:

First, there was Tony's account of Vera Brandon as a spy. Well, of course, he *could* have made it up – or, more likely still, have lifted it bodily from Dead Hand Dick, or whatever was the current saga of his generation. But in that case, why were there no shots? No pools of blood? No heroic exploits by Tony himself? No matter how fertile a small boy's imagination may be, it could never, surely, en- visage a situation in which he (the small boy) took no more part in a drama of espionage than to peep through a key- hole for a few minutes and then lie on a bed waiting for the grown-ups to come home. Since such a story could not possibly be fiction, it must therefore – so Louise reasoned – be fact. Miss Brandon *had* been prying about in the desk.

But why? What was it that she had found – or failed to find?

Then there was the fewness of Miss Brandon's possessions – already remarked on by Mrs Morgan. No pictures – no ornaments – no souvenirs of her many travels. And no books to speak of, apart from school books – this seemed extraordinary in a woman who was obviously cultured, and who claimed to be a scholar of some distinction. There was the puzzle of the suitcase, too, and of Mark's feeling of recognition – which he had mentioned just once, and then never again. And now the address, so inexplicably sought from Humphrey. Didn't it all add up to something disturbing enough to be laid before Mark, as the responsible householder?

And if only the responsible householder had succeeded, even at this late stage, in finding a shirt with the full complement of buttons, Louise might have told him of her fears. As it was, the next five minutes were devoted entirely to Louise's shortcomings as a housekeeper, beginning with shirt buttons and ending with her having forgotten to get the mower repaired, and including en route the disciplining of the children, the losing of the spare front door key, and the repeated serving of cold meat and fried potatoes for lunch. At the end of it all Louise slunk off to prepare the breakfast full of rather blurred resolutions, such as: 'Always sew on your husband's buttons before starting an argument' and 'Never ask him questions before breakfast' and 'If he didn't agree the first time you said it, he certainly won't agree the second.'

Nor the third, of course. Mark would have to be left out of it for the time being. The obvious thing to do was for Louise to make some enquiries about Miss Brandon for herself.

Yes, that's all very well, she mused. 'Make enquiries' – it's a nice business-like phrase, but how do you start? Do you march into the headmistress's study at the grammar school and say: 'You've got a teacher here who calls herself Vera Brandon, and please is it an assumed name, and is there a Mystery in her Life?'

No, you have to find out where your subject used to live, and go and see her old landlady. It couldn't be difficult to find out the address – one might even get it tactfully from Miss Brandon herself without any direct question. 'How are you liking this neighbourhood, Miss Brandon? It must be a big change for you.' 'Oh no, Mrs Henderson [or 'Oh yes, Mrs Henderson,' as the case might be] I come from XYZ.' 'Oh, how funny, I've got a friend living in XYZ, I wonder if you were anywhere near her? . . .'

Yes, it could probably be done that way. Casually, the next time they met on the stairs. So long as Michael wasn't crying at the time, or Harriet asking questions, or something boiling over in the kitchen . . .

Bother! All the eggs would be hard by now, and Margery was the only one who liked them hard. Harriet liked hers soft, and Mark liked his *very* soft. As to Louise herself, she had long forgotten which way she liked them. It made the housekeeping that much easier if there was one person out of the five whose tastes didn't have to be considered. To neglect one's own tastes was more labour-saving than any vacuum cleaner, and it was a form of neglect about which no one would call you to account. Your husband wouldn't demand buttons on it – your children wouldn't hurt them-

102

selves on it, or be made late for school by it. It wouldn't pile up against you, like the dirty nappies . . .

Or would it? Louise set the saucepan with a clatter on to the draining-board, and as she did so the years of her future seemed to rattle menacingly about her ears. If you went on neglecting your own tastes like this, did you, in the end, cease to have any tastes? Cease, in fact, to be a person at all, and become merely a labour-saving gadget around the house? Less and less labour-saving, of course, as the years went by – ('My mother? – Oh, you mean that thing that used to do the washing-up so well? Daddy's thinking of getting a new one . . .')

'A new what, Mummy?'

With dismay Louise realised that she must have spoken the last sentence out loud as Harriet came into the kitchen. This was just what was liable to happen when one was half asleep like this.

'*What's* Daddy going to get new?' repeated Harriet inexorably, and Louise tried quickly to think of something reasonably likely – or, better still, something so utterly uninteresting that Harriet would forget the whole episode.

'A new washer for the tap,' she lied; an inspiration which fulfilled this last requirement so thoroughly that Louise herself as well as Harriet rapidly lost interest in the whole business. For at this time Louise had no reason to suppose that more than the last sentence of her thoughts had been spoken aloud. Still less could she have supposed that anyone but Harriet could have overheard.

The house was strangely quiet after the children had gone; and it seemed to Louise that the quietness was something more than that familiar tide of peace and relaxation which flows over any home when the door slams for the last time as the last member of the family departs for work or school, leaving the housewife to reign alone over her suddenly tranquil kingdom. Perhaps it was that Louise herself was sitting so quietly, her elbows resting on the kitchen table among the dirty breakfast things, her limbs heavy with the longing for sleep. Her eyes wandered distastefully over the unwashed floor, over the dresser littered with papers, plasticine, and miscellaneous woollen garments waiting to be put on, put away, or mended. And those eternal bits of broken crayon sprinkled all over the house like petals in spring-time; every time you tried to do anything one rolled off something on to something else. Strange that in the midst of such muddle it could still be so quiet.

So quiet that when Louise heard the heavy, measured footsteps on the stairs she gave a great swallow and jumped to her feet. Even as she did so, she knew that her alarm was foolish – it could only be Miss Brandon setting off for school – rather late for some reason, and walking more heavily than usual. The steps reached the foot of the stairs – moved nearer, and a moment later Miss Brandon was standing in the doorway, her small leather case in her hand, and a pleasant, unrevealing smile on her face.

Louise stood there beside the unwashed breakfast things looking – and feeling – as guiltily startled as if she had been one of Miss Brandon's own pupils caught red-handed with a crib to Thucydides; though what, exactly, she felt caught red-handed *at*, she would have found it hard to define. Her discomfort was increased by the knowledge that this was probably the ideal moment for that casual remark: 'How are you liking this neighbourhood' – etc. But how idiotic it would sound! How stilted – how carefully rehearsed! How on earth did real actresses manage to make their carefully rehearsed speeches sound natural? Well, for one thing, of course, a real actress would be playing opposite someone who had carefully rehearsed the appropriate answer. That must make it a whole lot easier . . .

'I'm sorry to interrupt you, Mrs Henderson, but I just thought I'd better let you know that I'm going out now and I won't be back till late. I have to go down to Oxford for the day, and then, in the evening, I'm giving a talk to the Archaeological Society. Quite a small affair, of course,' she interposed modestly. 'But the secretary tells me they were most interested by my article on Mycenaean architecture. And, of course, the recent finds have added to the interest. Perhaps you've read about them in the papers?'

Louise gaped at her visitor helplessly. Not because she knew nothing of the Mycenaean finds – nor, indeed, of anything else that had been in the papers during the last six months, except that headline about a woman who complained that her husband made her eat dog biscuits. No, her blankness was due not to ignorance but to bewilderment. Why should Miss Brandon be telling her all this – and have come into the kitchen specially to do so, too? Louise had an odd feeling that the whole speech had been rehearsed – just like her own still undelivered speech that began: 'How are you liking this neighbourhood?' A sudden absurd rush of fellow-feeling made her rack her brains for the appropriate response.

'I hope you have a nice time,' she said feebly; and was immediately aware that anyone playing opposite the

Senior Classics mistress should do better than this. She tried again:

'Have you broken up already?' she asked, and knew at once that this was worse than ever. Obviously Miss Brandon's school had broken up, or how could she be going to Oxford today?

But it was plain that Miss Brandon, like Nurse Fordham, had taught herself to suffer fools gladly. She answered patiently: 'Why, yes, we finished yesterday. Didn't your little girls—? Oh, no, of course; the Primary Schools go on longer, don't they? Right up till Easter, isn't it, this year?' Her voice, though civil, was preoccupied. She glanced first at her watch and then at the kitchen clock.

'I must hurry,' she said. 'It's twenty-five to ten. My train . . .'

She backed out of the kitchen, closing the door gently behind her. Louise again heard the heavy footsteps crossing the hall, and then the slam of the front door – a really terrific slam. The cups quivered on their hooks, and a fork rattled noisily from the draining-board into the sink.

Then silence. The same uneasy, waiting silence that had filled the house before. Louise went upstairs to make the beds with an odd feeling that she should be going on tiptoe. Should be pulling up the sheets slowly . . . slowly, not to make the slightest stir . . . The thud of Margery's velveteen pig as it slithered from among the blankets made her jump as if another door had slammed.

But it hadn't. Everything was quiet. Even Michael hadn't stirred, though it was past ten o'clock. Louise had put him out in his pram early this morning to catch the first glory of the April sun. Through the window she could see him now, his covers kicked off, his arms akimbo in such utter abandonment of sleep that the tranquillity of it seemed to fill the garden like the scent of some new, miraculous flower. The sunlight flickered through the leaves on to the magical texture of his skin – that texture which in a few months would be gone for ever, gone with the baby roundness of his cheeks and the plump, enchanting folds of his thighs.

Odd that she should be staring thus, with something near to worship, at her tormentor of so many nights. Odd, too, that she should just now feel that sweet and sudden pang of protective fear. He lay there so utterly relaxed, so utterly exposed and defenceless. What made him so certain that only the kindly warmth of the sun would be allowed to spread over him? Couldn't evil, too, pour down from above; flicker like sunshine through the young spring leaves?

Not from above. Evil traditionally comes from below. Doesn't it? Isn't that right? But what about the Evil Eye? 'Overlooking' – that must be done from above, the very word implies it. Why, it could be done by someone looking out of a window, with her elbows on the sill, just like this . . .

A familiar tingling warmth in her limbs warned Louise that she was nearly asleep again. Hurriedly she drew back into the room and finished making the girls' beds. Why did Harriet have to have *nine* soft toys in bed with her every night? And, not content with that, why did she have to feed them all on biscuits under the bedclothes, scattering crumbs far and wide?

The house was still quiet. Scolding herself for such

fancifulness, Louise nevertheless walked with unnatural softness down to the kitchen. The washing-up was waiting for her, and, really, it could be a delightful job if you were really tired. Plunging your arms into the blessed hot water, the next best thing to sleep, you could allow your thoughts to wander.

But they didn't wander. Like homing pigeons they flew straight back to Miss Brandon and her visit to the kitchen that morning. Was it just Louise's fancy that there had been something odd about that visit? That Miss Brandon's conversation had been somehow forced and over-casual? Miss Brandon was not a naturally garrulous woman; so why all those unsolicited details about her plans for the day? Wasn't there something too careful about the way she had brought them all in, one after another? Something purposeful, premeditated . . . ?

Those shining, steaming teacups were still hot to the touch and would be a joy to dry; but Louise was scarcely aware of them as her imagination gathered speed. Wasn't that just the sort of conversation one would engineer if one was trying to create an alibi? Tomorrow – next week – would Louise find herself saying to some police inspector: 'Oh, yes, she was here in the kitchen with me just at that time . . . Yes, I remember it was exactly 9.35. It happened that she looked at her watch and remarked on it, and I noticed that the kitchen clock said the same . . . Yes, it was certainly 9.35 . . .' And meantime some ticket collector or porter at Paddington would be confirming that a lady answering this description had got on to the 10.45 to Oxford – some ever-so-accidental little incident had fixed her in his mind. And, therefore, she couldn't possibly have been . . .

Been where? Doing what? To whom? All Louise's fears came surging back and the water wildly gurgling down the plug hole transfixed her with a senseless, babyish terror. This was how Margery must have felt when she made all that fuss about her bath a few years ago. For one second Louise could have wept for her lack of sympathy with the child at the time – could have wept and sobbed, knowing all the time that her tears were not tears of remorse or sympathy, but tears of fright – fright for herself, for her own skin, here and now in this grease-spattered scullery, with the spring sun wavering through the steam at the barred window.

Perhaps it was all nonsense. Perhaps this ridiculous panic was simply hysteria brought on by lack of sleep. But all the same, weren't you supposed to humour hysterical women; and since there was no one else to do it, she would have to humour herself. Humour herself to the extent of going up to Miss Brandon's room – now, this moment, while Miss Brandon was out – and nosing around like any music-hall landlady 'to see if anything was going on what shouldn't be going on' as Mrs Morgan had put it.

She thought again about Mrs Morgan's gruesome little story. An imbecile done up in a parcel – was that what she expected to find? What absurdity! What fantastic nonsense! She was simply curious to find out what (if any) papers Miss Brandon had taken from Mark's desk. She had a perfect right – indeed, a *duty* – to recover his property for him. Full of the courage of righteous purpose, she straightened herself and prepared to march boldly up the stairs – only to find that almost without noticing it she had already removed her shoes, and was tiptoeing guiltily, like a burglar in her own house. Irrelevantly, she remembered Tony's tip: 'Always walk with the flat of your foot, you're not so likely to creak a board. It distributes the weight, see . . . ?'

But perhaps it only distributes your weight properly if that weight is light, and irresponsible, and only nine years old. For Louise, the boards creaked at every step, and she was thankful when she reached the top landing with the door to Miss Brandon's room on her right, and the door to the lumber room on her left. At least there were no more creaking steps to climb.

And it was only as she reached out to try the handle of Miss Brandon's door that she suddenly knew why she had been creeping, tiptoeing about her own house in broad daylight. It was because Miss Brandon was still there. She was not conscious of having heard any sound inside the room; and yet, as clearly as if the door had been thrown open in front of her, Louise seemed to see the whole scene, just as she had seen it a few days before when she and her mother-in-law had burst in uninvited. Miss Brandon sitting at her table, motionless, with no books, no papers, no sewing. Just sitting there, waiting. Then, as now, Miss Brandon had elaborately and unnecessarily sought out Louise in the morning to tell her she was going to be out for the day. Then, as now, the front door had slammed with unnecessary violence . . .

What could it all mean? Could there be some rea- sonable, sensible explanation? Could Miss Brandon have planned to go out for the day, and then, with quite ex- traordinary suddenness, have changed her mind? Have gone to the front door – opened it – set her foot across the threshold – and then drawn back? Have shut the door with a noisy slam, and then tiptoed back up to her room? Yes – tiptoed – her usual confident stride could not possibly have gone unnoticed.

Her confident stride. Yes, Miss Brandon's movements were always confident. And firm, and powerful – even graceful in a large-scale sort of way – but they were not noisy. Not noisy like those heavy, over-loud footsteps that had come stumping down the stairs this morning. Why would anyone come down a flight of stairs as noisily as that? Because they wanted to be heard, of course. Because they wanted to be heard, and also because they wanted to emphasise in their own mind the contrast between this ostentatious descent and the silence and stealth with which they planned, a minute later, to creep back up that self-same flight of stairs . . .

Louise's hand never reached the handle of Miss Brandon's door; she did not even try to peer through the keyhole to confirm her suspicions. For a while she stood there on the little attic landing, her heart thumping, her mind clear as glass and boundlessly receptive, it was not a suspicion at all; it was a certainty. Her very bones knew that Miss Brandon was sitting silently inside that room, and the bones do not ask for confirmation. It was only long after she had fled downstairs on stockinged feet (on tiptoe or distributing the weight? – she never knew which) that it dawned on her that confirmation might be required.

I I

'My dear, how thrilling! Of *course* I'll try and find out for
you. What sort of things do you want to know?'

Louise hesitated. She hadn't meant it to sound thrilling
at all. In fact, she was already regretting the impulse
that had made her rush to telephone Beatrice. Her panic
was subsiding fast at this contact with a human voice –
particularly a voice as voluble and insistent as Beatrice's,
and as shrill with unsatisfied curiosity. Louise tried to remember exactly what she had first said after snatching
up the receiver and dialling Beatrice's number in blind
and ill-considered determination to find out something –
anything – about this woman she believed to be lurking
upstairs. She had hoped to say, calmly and with half-
humorous detachment, something like – 'Oh, by the way,
Beatrice. That Vera Brandon we were talking about last
night. I wish you'd tell me a little more about her. You're
always so good at getting the low-down on everyone—'
with a little laugh, of course, to show that this was meant
as a compliment, and that anyway the whole matter was
quite trivial . . .

But little laughs don't always travel well down telephone wires. They can sometimes sound more like gasps
of terror . . . Beatrice's unslaked curiosity twanged again
down the line:

'Listen,' she seemed to splutter, though that may have

been a fault at the exchange, 'listen, why not pop round right away and tell me all about it? I don't really know anything, but when you're upset there's nothing like talking it over with a friend.'

So she *had* given the impression that she was upset. Perhaps even that she was frightened. For a moment Louise contemplated confiding to Beatrice the whole story, even at the risk of making an utter fool of herself. To learn that you are being an utter fool can sometimes be very comforting.

She hesitated. She moved the mouthpiece nearer. She hesitated again.

It was the ghost of the Upper Fourth that tipped the balance. Already she seemed to hear Beatrice telling and retelling the story: ('Have you seen poor old Louise lately? My dear, when I last spoke to her she was in an awful state! No no, worse than that. My dear, she's positively seeing spooks!—') Mavis would hear it. Janice would hear it. That freckled little beast Pamela something would hear it. Yes, and the still unidentified Muriel sitting at her breakfast table somewhere in Bristol would lap it all up in her morning's post . . .

'No, no. It's perfectly all right, really—' she began; but it was not as easy as all that. Once upset always upset – or at least until Beatrice had at her fingers' ends the truth, the whole truth, and that satisfying little bit more than the truth. And it all ended in Beatrice and Humphrey's being invited to supper that night. If only Louise had been less preoccupied, she would have seen from the start that the telephone call could only end in this way. Since it was impossible for her to leave her children, her washing, and her stewing neck of lamb in order to pop round on the two-hour journey to Acton, then what more natural than that Beatrice should pop round to her? And since you can't ask people to pop that distance without offering them a meal at the end of it, and since you can't ask a wife to a meal without asking her husband too, if you know that he exists – well, it was clear to Louise (too late) that a full-scale supper-party had all along been the logical and only outcome. Perhaps, she reflected, the philosophers of Predestination had first been set on their heretical paths by just such humble episodes. Except that philosophers were nearly always men, and men just don't find themselves in these predicaments. If a man doesn't want people to supper, he merely doesn't invite them – it must be one of those few fields in which male supremacy has so far never been challenged.

Louise rang off, and began to think about the evening meal. The neck of lamb wouldn't do now. There wouldn't be enough, and anyway, it wasn't just Beatrice and Humphrey that she would be catering for. The whole of the Upper Fourth would be there in spirit; she could almost see them now – Janice – Winnie – Pamela – all the lot of them, hanging on to the ends of their telephones and listening to Beatrice's quite unnecessarily amusing account of the meal she had had with poor old Lou: 'Irish stew, my dear, and there couldn't have been more bones if she'd fished out the family skeleton for us!' . . .

Well, she'd have to get some mince and make one of those Italian-type dishes that are really the same as Shepherd's pie, only you serve them with macaroni all round instead of with mashed potato on top. They usually seemed to go down very well with one's middle-brow friends. Unless, of course, one had produced that very dish for those very same middle-brow friends the last time they came. And the time before that. Louise tried hard to remember what she had given Humphrey and Beatrice at their last visit. It was nearly a year ago now, and all she could remember of the evening was that the pair of them had missed their last train home, and had reappeared just before midnight to argue endlessly in the draughty hall about whether to ring up a taxi. Since they both appeared to be whole-heartedly in favour of the taxi, Louise did not see why the argument should have gone on so long. But then Humphrey and Beatrice always talked to each other like that, and apparently very happily. Like many husbands and wives, they never noticed how often and how closely they agreed with one another on almost every subject.

If the avowed purpose of the visit was to calm Louise's fears about her mysterious tenant, then it succeeded admirably. It had, in fact, already succeeded before it began; for while Louise, with Michael on one arm, stirred the mince and onion mixture, watched for the macaroni to boil over, and simultaneously tried to convince Harriet and Margery that it would be *much* more fun to have supper by themselves tonight instead of sitting up with the grown-ups – while she attended to these duties, it seemed to her that Miss Brandon's identity was no longer of any importance whatever. Let her be a spy – a lunatic – a murderess – *anything,* provided only that it didn't lead her to come into the kitchen at this moment to ask questions or argue.

Beatrice and Humphrey arrived a little before seven, in a brand-new car for which Beatrice at once began apologising. It was not, she explained, a *new* car at all, but one that they had picked up second-hand, incredibly cheap, and actually they hadn't paid for it yet, they were so absolutely broke.

Humphrey looked a little bewildered at this recital, as well he might, seeing that he had the receipt from the makers in his pocket at this very moment; but before he had time to spoil the story, Louise hastened to agree with Beatrice that it was impossible to afford *anything* nowadays. She understood better than Humphrey that Beatrice, with her flair for contemporary values, was grimly determined to be as bankrupt and poverty-stricken as a prosperous husband and a substantial private income would allow her; though her fur coat and diamond earrings sometimes made the role difficult to sustain. Louise tactfully bundled the fur coat away among the mackintoshes in the hall; admired the earrings in order to give her guest the opportunity, if she wished, of claiming that they came from Woolworths, and then left her visitors to Mark's reluctant care in the sitting-room while she hastened back to the kitchen.

The meal was a success – enough of a success, Louise hoped, to quieten the shades of Janice, Winnie, Hope and Pamela; though the total effect was somewhat marred by Harriet's four appearances for drinks of water – ('Nice little things, of course, but poor old Lou has *no* idea of controlling them. She never could, you know. D'you remember that time when she first went on cloakroom duty after she was made a prefect . . . ?')

It was just as they were returning to the sitting-room that the telephone rang. It was Mrs Henderson senior, who, after enquiring with grandmotherly solicitude whether the children would be out of the way by half past eight, announced her intention of dropping in at about that hour.

'But only for a few moments, dear,' she apologised. 'I have to go round to Hugh's, you know, he absolutely *insists*. He's entertaining some tiresome creature about a contract, and as it's bringing a wife, Hugh says I'd better be there too. I don't see that, do you?'

'No,' agreed Louise discouragingly; and then, relenting, she added warmly: 'But do come round. We've got some friends here actually, a Dr and Mrs Baxter. Do you remember them? – Anyway, they'd love to meet you.'

'Why are you talking like that? Do you mean they're in the room listening?' enquired Mrs Henderson cautiously; and then, less cautiously: 'What are they like? Are they as extraordinary as most of your friends?'

Louise found this a little difficult to answer. Mrs Henderson's voice was a carrying one, and it was quite likely that Beatrice and Humphrey had heard what the question was to which Louise would be saying 'Yes' or 'No.' Were people more likely to be offended if you said they were extraordinary, or if you said they weren't?

'I believe you've met them here before,' she compromised and rang off hastily before she should find herself launched on one of those descriptions which can only be sufficiently complimentary to one party by being incomprehensible to the other.

Whether Mark's mother had in fact met the Baxters was debated for some minutes; and the lady's arrival half an hour later did nothing to dispel the uncertainty. Both parties, to be on the safe side, assured the other that its face was familiar, indeed unforgettable, and that they had undoubtedly met somewhere; and with a certain blankness behind the eyes, each went through the motions of trying to identify the occasion.

Humphrey gave it up first. He was charmed by this new arrival, for not only was she old enough (despite earrings and eyeshadow) for him not to feel obliged to flirt with her (always an effort after a good supper); but she had the additional charm of possessing a car with which the very thing had recently gone wrong which he (Humphrey) knew how to put right. Knew better than any garage, and far, far better than the particular garage which had dealt with it for Mrs Henderson. Now, when *his* car had developed the same symptoms – not his present car, of course, but his dear old Vauxhall—

'Now he'll be happy for hours,' said Beatrice contentedly, as Louise came to sit by her on the sofa. 'That is, if your mother-in-law will put up with it. He loves talking about the inside of his car. It's a sort of substitute for talking about his operation,' she added vaguely.

Louise laughed. 'Oh, she'll enjoy it,' she assured Beatrice. 'Though I expect she'll soon get him on to his operation. She doesn't believe in substitutes—' Louise was talking at random, to fill in time. Out of the corner of her eye she had seen Mark sidle from the room with that air of belonging to a different planet with which men so effectively evade the visitors who bore them. Six months ago, thought Louise, I'd have winked at him as he left the room, and he'd have winked back. But now my eyes – my eyelids are too stiff, too sleepy. Sleep has captured me – is parting me from him – as ruthlessly as any lover . . .

118

Beatrice's voice caught her attention again. It had dropped to that piercing whisper which both shows proper respect for your secrets and also allows everyone else in the room to enjoy them:

'The first thing I did,' she hissed, 'was to pump poor old Humphrey about the woman, but you know what he is. She impressed him tremendously, except that he can't recall her name; he had a wonderfully interesting talk with her, except that he can't remember what it was about; he thought she was exceedingly attractive, except that he doesn't know what she looked like; he was determined to keep in touch with her, except that he never asked for her address; in fact, if he only knew her from Adam, he'd be having an affair with her right now!'

Louise laughed. 'I know – that's all very well,' she said. 'But he must have known more than that to start with. Didn't he tell you *anything*? – At the time, I mean?'

'Only her name,' said Beatrice thoughtfully. 'He'd written it down, you see, in his pocket book. He always writes people's names down in his pocket book – he gets into the way of it because of the new students each year. And the name stuck in *my* mind because, as I told you, the Brandon-Smiths – Besides – well – names just *do* stick in my mind.'

This was perfectly true. Beatrice could still recite the names of every girl in every class that she and Louise had ever been through – with the addition, now, of the said girls' employers, children, husbands, ex-husbands, and co-respondents. Her mind, reflected Louise, must be like a telephone directory, only with little notes appended to each name:

Abbotts, Joanna . . . Married insurance clerk with glass eye.
Mortgage on bungalow not yet paid off. Garden a mess.
Ashley, Penelope. Still looking after old mother. Not filial
duty, just no good with men. Failed typing course . . .

'. . . And so all I can *definitely* get out of him,' Beatrice
was saying, 'was that it was she who picked *him* up, and
not the other way round. She came up to him after the
meeting, and congratulated him on something he'd said in
the discussion – no, don't ask me what, it cramps my style
if I have to talk in words of more than six syllables – and
how she led the conversation round to *you,* Louise, I can't
imagine, since all the rest of it seems to have been about
terribly intelligent subjects—'

'It was *me* then, not Mark, that she asked for the address
of?' asked Louise quickly, wondering why this point had
never struck her before.

'Why, yes – that is—' Beatrice hesitated. 'I *think* that's
what he said. Or did he? Did he say "Them" perhaps? Oh
dear, if only Humphrey wasn't such a fool!'

His own name hissing across the room like an escape of
gas could hardly fail to attract Humphrey's attention, and
he looked round amiably.

'Now, now, now!' he chided. 'What are you ladies saying
about me? Nothing very flattering, I'll be bound.'

'No, dear,' said his wife, also amiably. 'We're just saying
what a fool you are. I've been telling Louise it's no good
asking you, because you never remember anything, but
what we want to know is: When that Brandon woman
asked you for the Hendersons' address, whether it was her
or Mark she asked you for it of?'

This sentence baffled Humphrey for a moment; but experience of the unseen translations of his first year students stood him in good stead, and he was soon able to reply:

'Why, really, I simply can't remember——' And then, like a good soldier answering the call of duty, he roused himself to grin coyly at Louise:

'Aha! Aha!' he enunciated with scholarly precision. 'So that's the way the wind blows! The little lady thinks Hubby may have a secret! Could be, could be. Husbands *do* have their little secrets, don't they, Bee? Now admit it!'

'I never said they didn't,' said Beatrice impatiently. 'I'm not accusing you of being faithful, only of being forgetful. Now, do try to *think*, Humphrey. What did she *say*? What words did she use? Did she say "The Hendersons"? Or did she say "Louise Henderson"? Or "Mark Henderson"?'

'Well, now,' said Humphrey, wrinkling his brows obligingly, though not as if he thought the smallest enlightenment would result. 'When I think about it, I think she must have said "Mark." Or "Mr," was it? – not that that makes any difference. Yes, that's what she said. Must have done, because I remember now it made me madly jealous to think that no sooner had she met me than she wanted the address of another man.' He turned and challenged his wife, a trifle absent-mindedly: 'Didn't I come home seething with jealousy that evening? I'm simply asking you – didn't I?'

'Yes,' agreed Beatrice equably, 'but that was because Dr Wilcox had managed to get out of taking the Second Year seminar and you hadn't. But are you *certain* that she said——'

Here Mrs Henderson senior, who had been following the

conversation with the amused tolerance of a grown-up at a children's tea-party, broke in with mock dismay:

'Children, children! Why can't you be more modern? Why can't any of you be up-to-date? Though I've noticed before that no one under fifty ever is – I suppose up-to-dateness takes all that time to learn. Between you, you seem to be trying to make a triangle out of this Mark-Louise-and-Violet-What's-her-name— Oh, all right, Vera, then— Out of this situation. A *triangle!* Don't you know that Triangles are absolutely out? *Out*, I tell you. Like the Sack Look. Besides, Mark's far too lazy to get into much trouble. Always has been.'

Beatrice surveyed her interrupter without amusement. She was not sure on whose side this outburst was supposed to be, but she was in no doubt about one thing – that it had broken the thread of what was promising to be a first-class story.

'Well, you know Mark best, of course,' she allowed grudgingly. 'But all the same, I think it's funny that she should have sought out Humphrey simply to ask him for an address that she couldn't know that he knew—'

'Who says it *was* simply to ask me for the address?' began Humphrey indignantly; and simultaneously Mrs Henderson raised her hand beseechingly:

'Please – *please!* Haven't we been through it all enough? Why did who tell whom what about which – really, any-one would think we were investigating a murder—'

Everybody heard the front door slam. Suddenly, thunderously, as if it was intended to arouse the whole street. But it was only Louise who imagined that she had heard another noise first. The faintest, faintest shuffle of a sound . . . down the stairs . . . and across the hall . . . It was only Louise who now trembled and felt her face grow stiff and expressionless as the loud, ostentatious footsteps sounded across the hall and towards the stairs. Now, now, if she only dared to grasp it, was her opportunity to confront Vera Brandon with Humphrey; to stand over her, as it were, demanding: *Why* did you ask him for our address?

To the surprise of her guests, she jumped to her feet and ran to the door. Flinging it open, she called into the dim hall: 'Come in, Miss Brandon; won't you come in and meet some friends of mine?'

Was it her fancy that Miss Brandon did not look as if she had just come in from outside? In spite of her tweed coat, her hat and her little case, she did not have the cold, brisk look of a person who has just walked up a windy street; she had the look of a person who has been sitting, hunched in a chair, all day long . . .

'I think you've met Dr Baxter before,' said Louise clearly; and watched the two faces. For a moment, both were devoid of expression; and she blundered on: 'Dr Baxter tells me it was he who gave you our address. I'd no idea. I thought you'd got it from our advertisement . . .'

She had not meant it to sound like an accusation. Strange how so slight a deviation from a conventional introduction should sound so ill-timed, so aggressive . . .

Miss Brandon was looking at Louise now with slightly raised brows and that painfully tolerant smile ('You've committed a fearful gaffe,' it seemed to say, 'but I, with my superior poise, will do my best to cover up for you'). She held out her hand to Humphrey.

'I'm afraid Mrs Henderson is mistaken,' she said pleasantly. 'That's the trouble about having a namesake in my own field. It's always leading to this sort of confusion. However, I'm delighted to meet you *now,* Dr Baxter.' She gave him a distant, conventional smile, looking straight into his face. Louise looked up into his face, too, and watched it slowly growing red. Red from collar to hairline, from one greying temple to the other. Embarrassment? Humiliation at not being recognised? Or was there something more?

12

It was Michael's sudden and opportune protest from upstairs that helped to tide over the moment of speechless embarrassment. Louise leapt thankfully to her feet, and left to her mother-in-law the task of reviving some sort of conversation. Mrs Henderson rose to the occasion with cheerful efficiency:

'Nice to see you again, Miss Brandon,' she said composedly. 'Keeping busy as usual?'

'Pretty busy,' replied Miss Brandon, a little guardedly. 'Term's over, of course, but I do quite a lot of lecturing in the holidays. And then, I'll be going abroad quite soon.'

Louise hovered in the doorway, hoping to hear more. Did Miss Brandon mean that she was leaving them altogether, or did she just mean she was going away for the Easter holidays? But before Miss Brandon could say anything more – if indeed she intended to do so – Beatrice had intervened:

'Lucky you! Where are you going? We went to France last year, but everything was terribly expensive. We had to sleep out most of the time.'

'But it cost more to sleep out in one of those chalets than if we'd stayed in the main hotel,' objected Humphrey, his discomfiture of a few minutes earlier apparently forgotten. 'The whole idea of the chalets—'

Louise smiled, and slipped out of the room. Poor

Humphrey was always inadvertently frustrating his wife's attempts to keep down with the Joneses, just as she was always frustrating his attempts to appear as a wolf. It was almost as if it was some game they were playing between them, neither of them aware of the rules, and yet both enjoying it. As she went up the stairs she could still hear Humphrey's voice droning on about some meal they'd had in Paris. The wines and the sauces were forming a sort of bass accompaniment to Beatrice's shrill claims to have lived on nothing but bread and sausage.

When Louise came back she was greeted by that sudden silence which meant that they had all been talking about her. Miss Brandon, she was thankful to see, was no longer there, and in her place sat Mark who had either condescended to reappear or else had been dragged out of the kitchen by some over-zealous guest. Probably the latter to judge by his expression of gloomy non-existence.

'We've just been telling your husband how lucky he is,' observed Beatrice brightly, but without evoking the faintest flicker of response from the glum figure in the armchair. 'And,' she essayed, hoping perhaps that this would sound more plausible: 'We were saying what a lovely baby you have. What a pity we haven't been able to see him this time.'

'I'll bring him down if you like, he isn't asleep yet,' threatened Louise, which had the effect of rousing at least one of her guests to a sense of the passing of time. Mrs Henderson's headlong departure was followed by the rather more leisurely withdrawal of Beatrice and Humphrey. This unhurried manoeuvre began at 10.45 in the sitting-room, with an account of Flora Curtis' emigration to Australia (complete with her chastened return eighteen months later). It ended at the front gate, an hour later, with Sybil Pratt's failure to run a mink farm in Berkshire. It was nearly midnight before the final details of Lydia Carver's miscarriage had faded on the night air, and Louise returned to the sitting-room. To her surprise, Mark was still there. He looked up as she came in, smiled not quite into her eyes, and then watched her face in an odd, strained sort of way, as if trying to learn something.

'I'd never thought of you as a jealous woman, Louise,' he suddenly jerked out, the clumsiness of both words and manner giving an aggressive quality to the situation which had not been there before. 'I do think,' he went on, gaining confidence as men do from the cleansing introduction of anger into any situation, 'I do think that you might talk to *me* before you discuss our affairs with the whole neighbourhood. Haven't *I* any right to know what you're thinking?'

Louise stared. 'What do you mean?' she faltered, too sleepy to burst out with the anger that might have brought her close to him. 'What do you mean? What have they all been saying?'

But she knew, of course, what they would all have been saying. Humphrey, with conscientious persistence, would have been labouring with untiring coyness at his thesis that Louise had been making enquiries about Vera Brandon because she suspected her of some past intrigue with Mark. Beatrice, in the interests of many a future telephone conversation with old school-fellows, would have been encouraging this point of view as much as (and probably more than) was decently possible. Mrs Henderson, with her airy and up-to-date reluctance to take her own child's part about anything whatever, would have been displaying an absent-minded sympathy with her daughter-in-law which could only make matters worse. Altogether they would between them have given Mark the impression that she, Louise, had been making a jealous scene and accusing Mark, behind his back, of some sort of liaison with Vera Brandon. Perhaps, indeed, he had been imagining for some time that she was jealous – that she was resenting the classical interests that Vera Brandon could share with him and that she, his wife, couldn't. Perhaps, if it came to that, she *was* jealous. Not that she had ever felt jealous – she could not remember having felt anything about Mark's tête-à-tête conversations with Miss Brandon other than the vague satisfaction that any wife feels when her husband is happily occupied with something that doesn't spread glue or sawdust all over the sitting-room carpet. But don't they say nowadays that what you think you feel doesn't count for anything? In fact, if anything, it only goes to prove that you are really feeling the exact opposite. If you don't feel jealous of another woman, it simply proves that subconsciously you are feeling so madly jealous of her that you just can't face it. But surely there must be a limit to this theory somewhere? If you don't feel interested in stamp collecting, or netball, or the annual rainfall in Turkestan, does it really prove that you are so desperately interested in these things that your conscious mind simply can't face it . . . ?

'Louise! Can't you *say* something? Don't just stand there, as if you were asleep!'

Louise blinked. She *had* been nearly asleep, of course. She was nearly asleep most of the time nowadays. It would be no wonder if Mark *did* find some other woman better company. *Any* other woman. 'What has she got that I haven't got?' 'Just that she can stay awake while he speaks to her. Nothing else.'

Again Louise forced her eyes open. She was swaying a little as she stood, her elbow resting on the mantelpiece, and Mark's figure looked huge and blurred; his voice sounded painfully loud.

'It's impossible to discuss anything with you!' he seemed to be shouting. 'Anyone would think you were half-witted!' If there was anxiety as well as exasperation in his words, Louise did not hear it, and she made no attempt to recall him as he slammed out of the room. She only wanted to go to bed. Wanted it so much that as she sank into the armchair in front of the fire, she half thought that she *had* gone to bed. That the light had been switched off, that all her tasks were over, that she was free to fall into a deep, deep sleep to last for hours – for days – for weeks . . .

At first it did not seem like a dream. It seemed more as if her thoughts were marshalling themselves with a brilliant, rational clarity which they never achieved in waking life. 'Of course he is attracted by her,' they began. 'And that is why he is so annoyed when you keep on puzzling about who she is and where she has come from. She has come out of his past. That's why he half remembered her at first. She has been searching and enquiring for him for years, and at last, through Humphrey, she has tracked him down. But for what? To start a new love affair? To blackmail him about an old one? Has she some hold over him? Was that why she was searching his desk last night – to get possession of some document with which she could threaten him? Or was she seeking some photograph – some love letter – with which to revive past memories – past obligations – past love?'

'But she's not attractive enough for that sort of thing.' 'Oh, but she is. Your busy, preoccupied daytime mind doesn't see it, but your sleeping mind knows it well enough. By day you see her as a middle-aged schoolmarm; too intellectual – too muscular – too efficient for romance. But now, in the vividness of sleep, you know that her intellect is a feminine intellect; and if it has grown powerful through great learning, then its femininity has grown powerful too. Her big-boned body is strong indeed, but not with a masculine strength; rather with the strength of a tigress . . .'

A tigress. Why should Louise be thinking about tigers? There were no tigers here, in these narrow, shadowy streets. It was tiring, too, pushing the heavy pram. It confused her thoughts, just when they had been growing so clear. What miles she had walked through these mean streets, for hours and hours, with never a break in the small, dull houses, and with never a soul passing by. It was growing dark, too, and her back was aching with the weight of the pram. No – not aching – what was this feeling? Right in the small of her back? She had never felt it before, but she recognised it quickly enough, for it was the most ancient feeling in the world – the feeling of the hunted. The feeling that warns you when eyes are watching from behind; when stealthy footsteps are following . . .

But you must not run. For the sake of your very life you must not run. Indeed you *cannot* run; the weight of the pram is like lead; the pavements are soft like dough, and the wheels sinking slowly in. The baby in the pram is screaming now; you cannot see his face because of this glaring redness before your eyes, you can only hear him. He is screaming – screaming – screaming . . .

13

It was several seconds before Louise was sure that the redness before her eyes was only the redness of the dying fire; longer still before she was sure that this feeling in the small of her back was only the ache and stiffness that comes from falling asleep in an armchair. But there was no mistake about the screaming. Louder and louder it sounded from the floor above, and still half-dazed Louise looked at the sitting-room clock. Two o'clock, of course. She struggled to her feet and stumbled upstairs to Michael's room.

He did not seem to have woken anyone yet. Mechanically, as if she had pressed some button to set this maternal robot of a self in motion, Louise scooped him out of the cot and carried him downstairs to the scullery.

While she fed him he was quiet, eyeing her impassively over the curve of her breast, and he sucked down the milk in great satisfied gulps. And then, when he had finished, he began to cry again.

How he cried tonight! Worse, it seemed to Louise, than he had ever been before. Struggling, kicking, threshing about on her lap; pulling himself up, as if with desperate purpose, into a standing position against her shoulder, and then, once there, crying more desperately than ever. He did not seem to be exactly angry – nor frightened – nor in pain. His crying had that senseless, timeless quality that she remembered from the occasional bad nights of Margery and Harriet's babyhood. If only they could *tell* me what's the matter! she remembered thinking, and now, at eight and six, they *were* able to tell her what was the matter. Able, and indeed willing, to tell her for hours on end and with scarcely a pause for breath. And how blessedly comprehensible it all was. How utterly different from this senseless, soulless noise which seemed to destroy all possibility of human contact. When a baby was like this, nothing could be got across to him, nothing at all, not even the warm primitive contact of hugging him to her breast . . .

Louise became aware of a sharp, insistent knocking on the wall. It must have been going on for a minute or more, but she had at first drowsily supposed it to be the dripping tap; now, with sickening certainty, she knew what it was. It was Mrs Philips. Mrs Philips, who was having a new hot-water system put in upstairs, and who would therefore be sleeping in the downstairs back room – the one that adjoined Louise's kitchen. Now, for whatever length of time that leisurely, chain-smoking plumber chose to spend on the hot water system, for so long would Louise's kitchen and scullery cease to be a refuge at night.

The knocking grew more insistent; and, with no plan in her head other than to get out of range of Mrs Philips, Louise blundered with her baby through the kitchen and into the hall. The sitting-room? But that was directly below hers and Mark's bedroom; within five minutes he would be down, distracted and irritable, to bombard her with that mixture of ill-timed criticism and impractical advice which was the last straw on these weary nights. And

Miss Brandon's door would be heard, opening and shutting reproachfully . . .

Louise looked this way and that, like a cornered rat, and her eye fell on the pram.

Well, why not? An outing in the pram always soothed Michael by day – why not by night too? And here she was, already dressed after falling asleep in the armchair. Only her coat to put on, and in two minutes she could be out of hearing of Mrs Philips – of Mark – of Miss Brandon – of all the censorious lot of them!

The night air was cold and exhilarating. Louise felt suddenly awake – vividly, poignantly awake, as she had not felt for weeks. Michael was quiet now; he stared wide-eyed at the wonder of the street lamps as they passed above his face. How wise he looked, how ageless under the ageless night! Louise could scarcely keep from running, so light, so strong had she grown through sleeplessness. The pram was no burden to her; it seemed endowed with a half-life of its own as it raced along before her. She could have imagined that she wasn't pushing it at all; that instead it was pulling her along the sleeping streets. But that, of course, couldn't be happening; it would be against the laws of nature.

Yet the laws of nature seem different at night, when there is nothing – nothing at all – between you and the Milky Way. At such times the laws that rule the movements of the stars come very close; and yet their very closeness may make them unrecognisable – as a much-photographed celebrity might be if he suddenly walked into your kitchen. For a moment it seemed to Louise ridiculous to doubt the existence of miracles; how could any

sane person imagine that a power that could set the neb-
ulae in motion should be unable to push a pram along a
suburban road without Louise's help . . . ?

All at once, the disembodied lightness, the sense of vi-
sion, were gone, and Louise looked about her, shivering
and a little scared. She had not come so very far after all
– that skimming, birdlike swiftness of movement must
have been mostly imagination – but she was approaching
the main road already. Any moment now she might meet
somebody – a policeman maybe – who would ask her what
she was doing, taking a baby out at this hour of the night,
and then what would she say? That the baby wouldn't
sleep – that he was disturbing the neighbours? But that
sounded ridiculous – people just don't take babies out
in the middle of the night for such a reason. Yet it had
seemed at the time a sufficient reason – it still seemed
so. How could she have ignored Mrs Philips' knocking?
How could she have allowed her own household to be kept
awake all night? Taking the baby out in the pram had been
the only possible thing to do. She had been driven to it.
She had had no alternative.

In that case, why did she fear having to explain it to a
policeman? If her action was really sensible and necessary,
why should it sound so silly? More than silly; mad. Perhaps it *was* mad. Perhaps this was just the way mad people
did feel – that they were being logically and inevitably
driven to their crazy actions; that they had no alternative.

Louise stood still, and with her hand resting lightly on
the handle of the pram she gazed up at the night sky,
which held no faintest glimmer of dawn. Wasn't it during
the hours before dawn that sick people were most likely to

die? Perhaps it was during those same hours, too, that sane people slipped over into madness . . . ?

She was roused by a fretful wail. Michael had no intention of putting up with a motionless pram any more than a motionless cot; and Louise obediently jerked herself into movement once more. She was deadly sleepy again now, and she did not notice in which direction she was going. She knew only that she must keep walking about, walking about, until Michael should fall asleep . . .

But what was the matter? Why was he that ghastly colour? With a little moan of sheer terror, Louise lunged forward – and then began to laugh, weakly, and without amusement. For he was all right. It was only the lights. Those ghastly, bloodless lights of the main road that sucked all the colour from everything. Even after she had realised this, Louise could still scarcely bear to look at the grey, corpselike pallor of the child's face. She hurried him along, in absurd distress, until she came to a side turning. And it was as she plunged up this turning, heedless and unseeing, that she first became aware that she was falling asleep. Falling asleep even as she walked, and that it was beyond her control.

It was tiring, pushing this heavy pram. What miles she must have walked through these mean streets, for hours and hours, with never a break in the small dull houses, and with never a soul passing by. Her back was aching with the weight of the pram. No – not aching – what was this feeling . . . ?

Just as in her dream, Louise dared not run. Neither did she dare to stand still. Nor to turn round.

'It's a dream!' she told herself wildly. 'Just a dream. The

same dream all over again, and in a moment I shall wake up. In a moment the pram will become too heavy; I shall see that red light before my eyes, and it will be the sitting-room fire dying down. Or am I asleep in the scullery, my feet on the mangle, my head leaning against the draining-board? In that case, I shall wake up and see that barred window. It will look like teeth at first, but I must remember it's not teeth, only bars. Nothing to be frightened of. Not teeth, only bars . . . Not teeth, only bars . . .'

The bars were in front of her now, black and clear. 'Not teeth,' she repeated triumphantly. 'Not teeth' . . . and waited for that sweat of relief that breaks out at the moment of waking from a nightmare.

But there was no sweat of relief. Neither were those the bars of the scullery window. They were railings, iron railings, fencing off a patch of shadowy waste ground where the newest of the discarded sardine tins gleamed faintly in the light of the street lamp.

And yet Louise felt that she *had* woken up from a dream. That feeling of hostile eyes boring into the small of her back was gone now. Her knees were weak, as if she had been just roused from sleep. And now, for the first time, she realised that she did not know where she was, nor in which direction lay her home. And she was tired; so tired that she no longer had any fear of the darkened street; so tired that for a moment she thought of sitting down, here on the pavement, with her back against the railings, and falling asleep.

Was that a footstep? No, it couldn't have been, there wasn't a soul in sight, up or down the street. But the sound, whatever it was, had roused Louise to a sense of absurdity. If anybody *should* come, what would she look like, pram in hand, lolling against the railings, aimlessly, in the middle of the night?

She set off again, and she never knew whether it was a long time or a short time before she came to the little park. No, not exactly a park; it was just a paddling pool really, surrounded by grass and gravel paths, and a few flowering shrubs. And seats. Blessed, miraculous seats! Seats with *backs*! Louise bumped her pram across the soaking grass, across the gravel path, and sank gratefully on to the nearest seat. She would rest here, for just a few minutes, and collect her thoughts. A little quiet consideration would soon show her which direction to turn for home, and then she must set off at once. Why, Michael was almost asleep at last, there was not the slightest reason for staying out any longer.

The light from a street lamp shone faintly on the dark bushes, whitening here and there the great pale clusters of blossom. Beyond the bushes the pool gleamed silently, without a ripple, still as the blade of a knife. It was quiet. Too quiet. The bushes, particularly, were too quiet. It would have been a relief to hear the faint stir or chirrup of some small night creature, or even the disembodied rustle of the night breeze.

And yet, when there *was* a rustle, faint as a breath, from a dark overhanging shrub on her right, it was not relief that Louise felt. Instead, her heart began to pound, and she stared, straining her eyes into the darkness until spots and lines began to whirl in front of them, and she was obliged to look away towards the glinting water, towards the pale blossoms, to get the darkness out of them.

How sweet the scent was from the flowering shrubs. What kind were they, those flickering dim blooms? Lilac? Too early for that – at least, the lilac in her own garden was scarcely in bud yet. She could not tell the colour of the flowers before her; they gleamed so whitely against the dark background of the leaves, but then any colour would do that – any of the soft, pastel colours of spring-time, that is to say. The scent seemed to grow stronger, and it was strangely out of place in the bleak darkness of the night. It was the scent of sunshine; of sunshine on that first day of summer when you put on a cotton dress and walk down to shops, dizzily conscious of the warmth on your bare arms. It was the scent of childhood, when you set off for school half drunk with happiness because tennis was beginning this term. And farther back still, back and back to those regions where the waking memory can never reach, it was the scent of a narrow woodland path, where the cowpars-ley and the great teasels almost met above your head. It was quiet in that path, and yet not quiet at all, for round your ankles, even as far as your knees, there hummed and twittered and rustled the real owners of the earth in un-named, uncounted millions. It was good that there was a large grown-up hand to hold your own, and that a pair of heavy booted feet were clearing the way, subduing for a few moments the owners of the earth so that your own bare legs and sandalled feet could follow safely. The sun was hot, hot as it had always been on those golden, endless afternoons of childhood; hot, surely, as it could never be again. The path seemed endless, too, winding in and out among the trees, twisting into sudden clearings of parched grass and the purple glory of willow-herb . . .

'Watch out for that child. There may be snakes.'

The sick terror of that moment was undimmed, and the words snapped like a pistol shot across the years. Louise struggled to open her eyes, to move her body on the hard damp seat. One movement would be enough to wake her; one tiny movement. Even her little finger. If she could just move one joint of one little finger . . .

But everyone knows that a snake's eyes are hypnotic eyes. Once a snake is staring at you, you can never move again. You may hear it slithering up behind you, but if its eyes are fixed on you, you cannot move. You will feel its malignant stare boring through your spine, and from your spine travelling up the great nerves that feed the brain; and you will sit still, and wait for your brain to grow numb and senseless even as your body is numb and senseless now . . .

It was the rattle of a passing lorry that woke Louise, and for a moment she stared blankly, stupidly at the lightening sky. Her coat – her shoes – her hair were drenched with dew, and she was so cold that at first she did not even wonder how she got here. Then slowly, slowly, like a hibernating creature roused from its winter sleep, her mind began to work again. Michael. She had taken Michael out because he was crying. She had lost her way. She had sat down on a seat, and must have dropped off, and now it was morning. She must get him home quickly; in that uncovered pram he must be almost as wet and chilled as she was herself.

And it was only then that Louise saw in the growing light that the pram was gone.

14

At first she did not believe it. She closed her eyes quite calmly, confident that when she opened them again the pram would be there. And when it wasn't, she still, some-how, could not take it in. I must be sitting on the wrong seat, she thought stupidly; and it was only after she had risen stiffly to her feet to peer through the icy mist at the neighbouring seats, that she realised the implications of this supposition. She might indeed be sitting on the wrong seat; but if so it meant that she, herself, either sleeping or crazily awake, had moved during the night from the right seat to the wrong one. Had moved purposelessly, without sense or consciousness, leaving her baby behind.

Or taking her baby with her – where? For what pur-pose? How far might you wheel a baby as you wandered sleep-walking through the night? Where might your brainless body put him while your sleeping mind, far off in some other world, dreamed, perhaps, that it was pushing him comfortably home?

'No – no! I can't have taken him far! Just to some other seat? – Behind the next bush—?' In mounting panic she staggered on her stiff, chilled limbs from seat to seat, from bush to bush, and stood finally in the pinkish chill of dawn at the water's edge.

It must be a shallow pool, surely. That steely, silent expanse of water, motionless as a slab of metal in the cold morning light, was meant for children to play in; to paddle and sail toy boats. It couldn't – Oh, God! surely it couldn't! – be more than two feet deep even in the middle. Far too shallow for a runaway pram to disappear in without trace. The handle would be sticking up out of the water. The hood. Or the wheels, crazily askew . . .

'It *must* be shallow, I *know* it's shallow!' she muttered, and she knelt down and thrust her arm over the low stone rim.

It was even shallower than she had expected. Not even up to her elbow. Far, far too shallow to engulf a pram. The idea had been absurd.

Yet still the idea persisted. It was as if the idea was not her own at all, but had been forced upon her by some out-side power. As if it had been left, like a booby-trap, for her to stumble into by the side of this metallic pool . . .

The police! The police will find my baby! The thought was suddenly, overwhelmingly reassuring. Of course they would find him. The police were finding lost children every day. All she had to do was to look for a policeman . . .

For the second time that night it seemed that a miracle was perfectly right and natural. She had only to think of the word 'policeman' and, of course, a policeman would appear at her side. Naturally, a rather young and embar-rassed policeman he was, who said, 'Excuse me, Miss,' and then seemed unable to get any further. But Louise would not have let him get any further anyway.

'You've found my baby!' she cried, almost incoherent with joy. 'You've found him!'

But the young policeman looked blank. His embarrass-ment increased.

'I didn't have no instructions about a baby,' he said helplessly. 'They didn't say nothing about a baby at all,' he proceeded, gaining confidence at the recollection of 'Them.' 'They just sent me along to enquire if – well, what you was doing sitting in the Gardens at night. If you was ill – that kind of thing,' he finished placatingly.

'Who sent you? What do you mean?' asked Louise, still convinced that all this must in some way refer to the discovery of Michael. 'Has someone seen the pram?'

But the young policeman, it seemed, hadn't had no instructions about a pram, either. It appeared that up at the Station they had had an anonymous phone call from some passer-by who had seen a lady sitting alone on a seat in the small hours, and had thought, not unreasonably, that something might be wrong. But this baby business, he didn't know anything about this baby business, and hadn't she better come along to the Station?

At the Station they seemed less bewildered than the young policeman, but not very much more helpful. No, the anonymous caller had made no reference to a baby, nor to a pram; the police officer who interviewed Louise was positive about this, and he seemed a little disappointed that Louise was in no way placated by this assurance, even when it was confirmed by his notes. He listened to her story with grave and kindly attention, though with an irritating air of having heard this sort of thing dozens of times before – irritating, that is to say, if she had been calm enough to notice it. Possibly he thought she was drunk; and indeed, the frantic and incoherent manner in which she related her implausible tale would have justified such a supposition.

'I'm sorry, Mrs Henderson,' he said at last (he had asked for her name and address by this time, and had written them down in his ominous great ledger), 'I'm sorry, but I can't really follow your story at all. I think the best thing we can do is to telephone your husband and see what he can tell us. No – no, if you please, Mrs Henderson, don't trouble, I would prefer to make the call myself.'

Through the closed door Louise could hear the ping of the receiver as he lifted it; and, a long, long time later, it seemed to her, she heard his voice, muffled and expressionless. She could not hear what he was saying, but he seemed to be talking to Mark for a very long time. What could they be saying to each other? Had Mark, perhaps, some notion of what could have happened to Michael? Some clue on which to base the search—?

Abruptly the door opened, and the police officer reappeared, a faint, pitying smile on his face:

'Exactly as I thought. Your husband tells me that your baby is asleep in his cot, and the pram is just where it was last night, in its usual place.'

15

It was hardly to be expected that a young matron of this neighbourhood should be able to return home at six in the morning under police escort without rousing comment.

Louise did not expect it. She was not surprised when, a few hours later, while she was manoeuvring her basin of washing round the dolls' pram which was blocking up the back door, she saw Mrs Morgan's brown wrinkled face and neck stretching out over the brick wall like a tortoise from its shell.

Louise nearly ducked back into the house again; but two things prevented her. One was the knowledge that the longer the episode was left to Mrs Morgan's unaided imagination the more horrific it would become: the other was the dolls' pram, whose hood had now become entangled with the strings of Louise's apron. Before she had managed to dissolve this ill-timed union, all hope of retreat was gone, for Mrs Morgan was already calling out, with piercing solicitude:

'You feeling better, dear?'

'I'm all right, thanks,' called back Louise noncommittally, wrenching at the knot in her apron.

'It's your nerves, that's what it is, dear,' bellowed Mrs Morgan sympathetically. 'That's what I said as soon as I heard, I said "It's her nerves, poor thing, they're all to pieces, and it's no wonder—"'

At this point the apron string gave way, and, with her apron dangling uselessly, Louise hurried across the grass before the three gardens on either side should enjoy any more of the story.

'You're looking proper poorly, dear,' continued Mrs Morgan, examining Louise's face enthusiastically. 'Proper poorly. What you need is a real good rest. That's what I've been telling everyone: I don't want to listen to no spiteful gossip, I've been saying; all Mrs Henderson needs is a real good rest.'

This was clearly Louise's cue to contribute something to the conversation. It was her opportunity, too, to think quickly of some dull, respectable and perfectly credible reason for such a melodramatic return with the police. But it was too difficult. She could think of very few credible explanations at all, and those she could think of were neither dull nor respectable. Anyway, it was important first to find out how much Mrs Morgan did in fact know.

'Why, what have people been saying?' she asked innocently. 'I didn't know anyone was talking about me.'

Mrs Morgan gave her usual precautionary glance at the tufts of grass behind her, and at the small, cheeky dandelions which by now really did seem to have an inquisitive, eavesdropping air; then she leaned forward excitedly:

'I won't mention no names,' she began. 'No names, no trouble, that's what I always say. Besides, it was a wicked thing to say about anyone, and I wouldn't be repeating it, dear, you know that, without I thought you had a right to know. That's what I said to her, I said it's not right to talk about Mrs Henderson like that, not behind her back it isn't. There's many good reasons, I told her, why a per-

146

son might be paddling into a pond at four in the morning, and crying her eyes out with it. You don't want to jump to the aspersion that she's out to do herself in, do you, now? That's what I told her, I told her straight: You don't want to jump to aspersions, I told her, it's wicked. Never mind if they do bring her back in a police van, I said, it's none of my business, no more than it's none of yours. A nice, respectable young woman like Mrs Henderson, I said, she wouldn't do no such thing. It's just her nerves, that's all it is, I told her.'

She paused expectantly, and Louise knew that the dull and credible story must be produced now, immediately, or the chance would be lost for ever. The possibility of telling the truth did cross her mind; but, as often happens, the truth seemed more fantastic when put into words than all the colourful inventions that were flocking into her mind.

'So silly of me,' she improvised hastily. 'I was out at my – at some friends, you know – and I missed the last train back, so I had to walk. I lost the way, and so I asked a policeman, and he very kindly brought me back all the way. Very nice of him, I thought. Very considerate.'

'Very considerate they are, some of 'em,' conceded Mrs Morgan agreeably, and with unqualified disbelief of every word Louise had been saying. 'Very civil. What was the pond, then, Mrs Henderson, what you stumbled in in the dark? You didn't hurt yourself, did you? I heard you come home all wet.'

'Oh, just my sleeve,' said Louise lightly. 'One of those paddling pools, you know. The lighting wasn't too good.'

Mrs Morgan considered this with tolerant incredulity.

'A shame,' she summed up at last; and, astonishingly,

the phrase held in it genuine warmth and sympathy, in spite of the disbelief with which it was uttered. It was the same warm, genuine sorrow that an author can feel for his heroine when he is about to plunge her into yet worse disaster.

'A shame,' proceeded Mrs Morgan. 'A proper set-to, eh? And the kiddie, and all. Must have given him a scare, didn't it?'

Louise was startled. Mrs Morgan's talents were truly astonishing. Neither the police nor Mark had believed for one moment that she had really taken Michael out last night – with the child safely asleep in his cot and the pram in its usual place, why should they? The police probably assumed that she had been drunk; Mark that she had been dreaming, or sleep-walking, or both. Louise herself was by now inclined to agree with Mark. The memory of last night seemed now nothing more than a confused nightmare. How then could Mrs Morgan, even with all her skills, guess that Louise had – or had imagined that she had – taken Michael with her on her queer journey?

'What kiddie?' she asked stubbornly. 'I was by myself. Naturally.'

'Naturally,' agreed Mrs Morgan happily. 'That's what I said. Mrs Henderson'd never do a thing like that, I said, not take the kiddie out with her for such a purpose. Not that time of night, giving him a chill in the night air. It's your nerves, duck, that's all it is, you want to watch your nerves. My husband's sister, she used to suffer with her nerves. They found her lying in the kitchen one day with the gas full on – all three of the rings, and the oven too. And the grill.'

'And was she—?' enquired Louise hesitantly. 'I mean, did she—?'

Mrs Morgan shook her head regretfully.

'They was sharing the kitchen, see, with another young couple. Makes things difficult, you know, sharing. Two women shouldn't try to share a kitchen, that's what I always say, it's bound to lead to inconvenience.'

Louise could see that this was indeed probable, particularly if one young woman's suicide attempts coincided with the other's need to prepare breakfast; and she expressed guarded agreement with the principle. Then, feeling that this shifting of attention from herself to Mrs Morgan's husband's sister was to be encouraged, she led Mrs Morgan on to a further recital of that lady's career, including her gentleman friends, her varicose veins and her final demise without a burial insurance.

By this time the church clock was striking half past twelve, and Louise hurried indoors. She had been late with everything this morning, and now lunch would be late, too. It had been a mistake to go to bed at all when she came in at dawn this morning; but the temptation had been very great. She had been encouraged, too, by the reflection that as school had finished yesterday it wouldn't matter what time the children got up; and had been bowled over completely by Mark's touching but impractical suggestion that she should stay in bed all day. And so she had fallen into a heavy sleep from which she had been roused by Margery, wearing a pyjama jacket and one bedroom slipper, at a quarter to ten. Mrs Philips was at the door, Margery explained, and was asking did her mother know that the baby was crying again, and could she, Margery, start the new packet of cornflakes because the old one was all crumbs?

Foolishly blind to the implications of this last request, Louise was naïvely saying 'Yes' to it when a babel of shrill protest arose from half way up the stairs. It's not *fair*, Harriet pointed out, with all the unanswerable righteousness of a foghorn; Louise had *promised*, she'd absolutely *promised*, that Harriet should have the next one of Bimbo the Boxer. Margery had already had *three* Bimbo the Boxers, and—

All this, of course, had somehow to be side-tracked for long enough to get a civil message delivered to Mrs Philips, still glowering on the front step. Louise had no intention of facing Mrs Philips herself, particularly in a dressing-gown. It was bad enough that Mrs Philips should see that the children weren't dressed by this hour in the morning, without revealing to her the still more disgraceful fact that Louise wasn't dressed either.

Now, three hours later, things seemed to have achieved a temporary lull. Mrs Philips had gone out shopping, and might, if Louise was lucky, be meeting a friend at the Kosy Kuppa, which would keep her out for some time yet. Margery and Harriet seemed to have reached some amicable agreement which had resulted in Bimbo the Boxer and his surrounding coils of cardboard covering the whole of the kitchen floor, while paste and more snippets of cardboard littered the table. Both children were now quietly engaged in writing in their new fourpenny exercise books, bought with last Saturday's pocket money. They were very quiet and quite absorbed, and Louise was surprised at the number of pages they seemed to have covered. Margery's would probably be a hideously derivative story about a pixie, and Harriet's would consist entirely of rhyming couplets – or triplets – or quadruplets – according to how long it was before her vocabulary gave out. There once was a frog, Louise found herself thinking as she sorted out the large potatoes which wouldn't take so long to peel – Who sat on a log, And saw a dog, And fell into a bog – Really! Who was it said that motherhood automatically rots a woman's brain? One could see what he meant . . . It would have to be chips, of course; they were quicker than anything else, and besides, if there were chips perhaps there wouldn't be any fuss about the cold meat that was to go with them . . .

'Mummy, how do you spell "Recknergizzled"?'

Bother, she hadn't even put on the chip pan to heat yet, and it was nearly one o'clock. Now it would be at least twenty minutes before—

'*Mum-mee!* How do you spell "Recknergizzled"?'

'What, dear?' Louise hastily lit the gas under the pan. 'R-E-C-K—' she continued mechanically, and then pulled herself up. '*What* did you say, Margery? What's the word you want?'

'Recknergizzled,' repeated Margery patiently. 'How do you spell it?'

'But, darling, there isn't such a word. Where did you hear it?'

Margery looked helpless, and Harriet broke in cooperatively:

'It's in the Spy Book. I know how to spell it. R-E-C—'

In spite of the chips, and the preternatural speed with which the hands of the clock always revolved as lunch-time drew near, Louise was becoming interested.

'What *is* this word?' she asked. 'I've never heard of it. What does it mean?'

Both children stared at her, and Louise felt apologetic for having introduced so superfluous a complication into an already difficult problem. She went on hastily. 'What's the Spy Book? I don't remember it. Is it from the library?'

'Oh *no*!' said Harriet, wide-eyed. 'It's not a printed book at all. It's a written book. Spy books always are, Tony says.'

'Is it a book of Tony's, do you mean?' asked Louise, light (she thought) beginning to dawn. 'Something he's written about spies?'

'*No!*' said Harriet again, a little impatiently. 'Tony didn't write it, he's only copying it. At least,' she added cryptically, 'we're copying it for him, because he can only do it if you ask him to tea a lot. It's only us who can get into the Rubbish Room.'

'You're not to call it that—' began Louise automatically; and then, realising the implications of Harriet's words, she became suddenly alert:

'Do you mean it's something of Miss Brandon's? A story she's shown you?'

'Oh no,' said Harriet placidly. 'She hasn't shown us. It's a secret, you see. We go when she's not there and copy it out for Tony. He says we've got to, it's very important, but it's miles long, and we've still only done four pages, haven't we, Margery?'

'*You've* only done three and a bit,' corrected Margery. 'Because you got that page with only two or three words on it. I'm on my fifth—' She pointed proudly to her new page, where the words: 'She knows nothing. I am washing my time' were clearly written.

For a moment Louise was mystified. '*Washing* my time'? – was this a code message to delight Tony's heart? Then she realised that the word must be not 'washing' but 'wasting' – a mistake easily explained when she saw the untidy, crumpled piece of paper from which Margery was copying.

'You see,' Harriet explained proudly, 'we have to copy it quickly – you know – anyhow – while we're up there, and then we rush down and copy it properly into our Record Books. Tony says we mustn't *ever* take the Spy Book itself away, even for a minute, or she might come in in that minute and notice. That's why we have to copy it twice.'

Evidently this refinement of technique had taken a lot of explaining by Tony, and Harriet was proud to have mastered it.

'And it's all a deadly secret cross my heart,' added Margery, rather belatedly. 'That's why we can't tell you about it, Mummy. Mine's much tidier than Harriet's, isn't it?'

Louise studied the proffered page, hoping that she was not betraying too much interest. But the text, twice copied by Margery, was too garbled to convey much at a brief inspection. 'The apple in M's eyes' – did that mean 'the appeal'? And what about this word that Margery was struggling to spell? 'Recknergizzled.' Once written down, the derivation was clear. 'Recognised,' of course. Miss Brandon had been writing something about someone being (or not being) recognised . . . The document appeared to be something in the nature of a diary . . .

'Mummy, you're *reading* it,' accused Margery, with gentle reproach, after watching her mother studying the page closely for the best part of five minutes. 'I told you it was a secret. Tony said we weren't to let anyone see it except him.'

'But you *showed* it to me, darling,' pointed out Louise, though not with much hope that such reasoning would carry any weight with her audience. 'And,' she added, feeling that it was about time that the ethics of the whole business should be given an innings: 'It was very naughty of you both – and Tony too – to pry about in Miss Brandon's room like this. This must be her private diary, and you've no business to touch it. Or to go in her room at all, for that matter, without being invited. That room is her home, don't you see. How would you like it if people just walked into our home without knocking or anything?'

'We *didn't* walk in,' objected Harriet; and Margery amended: 'We *can't* walk in, because she always locks the door now. But she keeps the Spy Book behind the broken ceiling, you see, inside the cupboard. We can get to it under the roof from the hole in the other attic. Tony showed us. It's where we used to keep the Regulations and the Password of the Explorers' Club. That's how we found it, you see, because we were looking for the Regulations again, because I said we'd done them in red ink, and Harriet said we hadn't, and so I wanted to just *show* her. I *knew* we must have done them in red ink, you see, because—'

Louise remembered the Explorers' Club very well. It had enjoyed its week and a half of glory about six months ago, during which period Tony Hooper, two other exceedingly dirty urchins, and a rather bigger and considerably less dirty little girl with straw-coloured plaits, had appeared regularly after school to consume immense quantities of bread-and-jam and rock-buns. The party then repaired to the attics, where they bumped suitcases about, argued and dropped things until Mrs Philips sent in a message about her head, and Louise had to put a stop to it all. Louise had known, vaguely, about the holes in the plaster of the attic cupboards; but she had not realised the uses to which they could be put – or, indeed, that either of them were big enough to crawl through at all. Nor had they been, it now appeared, until the resourceful Tony had greatly enlarged the one in the lumber room with his pocket knife; though it was Harriet who thought of shifting a slate above their heads so that there should be a crack of light sufficient to read by.

For a moment Louise thought wistfully of those modern children who are said to do nothing but watch television in their spare time. Then she turned her attention back to her duty as a parent:

'You're not to do it any more, do you understand?' she said severely. 'It's very dishonest to read people's private diaries—'

'But we weren't reading it; we were only copying it,' protested Margery; and, in view of the utter lack of intelligence of Margery's transcription, Louise could not but feel that the distinction was valid.

'Well – anyway – you're to stop it,' she concluded, perhaps a shade weakly as she contemplated the guilty eagerness with which she herself would be studying those exercise books as soon as the children weren't there. 'You'd better give me the books, and—'

But this raised a storm of protest. The exercise books were *theirs*; they had spent *fourpence* on them. Besides, it was a *secret*, and the books must be kept in a special, ever-so-secret place, Tony had said so.

Louise had to give in for the moment, for the fat in the chip pan was beginning to smoke. In any case, she felt sure that the ever-so-secret place would in practice turn out to be the kitchen floor, among most of their other belongings.

16

The kitchen floor it was. Louise found the two exercise books after lunch, as she swept up the crumbs, the bits of chalk and the remains of Bimbo the Boxer. There seemed to be a certain lack of finesse about Harriet's and Margery's methods of guarding their deadly secret, and Louise could not but be touched by Tony's apparent faith in his two colleagues. She shook the crumbs off the books and carried them guiltily upstairs to her bedroom – though whether the guilt was due to her intention of extracting the secrets from another woman's diary, or to the fact that she ought at this moment be washing the bathroom floor, she could not tell. A housewife's sense of moral values is often blurred by this sort of thing.

In Louise's case, it was blurred even more by the fact that she could make almost no sense at all of Margery's careful transcription – failure to achieve dishonesty often seems the next best thing to honesty itself. Although the writing itself was careful and neat, the meaning of what she was copying had clearly been far beyond Margery's comprehension. She had copied one word after another as best she could, parrotwise, and only here and there did a phrase stand out which had been within her grasp, and had therefore been copied legibly. 'M's cheek against mine' was one of them; and 'M and I' recurred three or four times, the bold, straightforward capitals standing out unequivocally amid the surrounding gibberish.

'M and I.' 'M and I.' Louise felt illogically and immediately certain of two mutually contradictory ideas. First, that it was impossible that the 'M' of the diary should refer to Mark – that he couldn't – wouldn't – deceive her in such a way. Second, that it couldn't refer to anyone else, and that right from the beginning she had known and expected just this. And who could blame him? He had been getting little enough from his wife these past months – none knew that better than Louise.

'And yet he knows I *really* love him,' she thought wildly. 'He must know it. It's like the happiness – it's just put away in a drawer for the time being until I have time – energy – to take it out—'

But can love live in a drawer? And for how long? And if it can – if it is tough – resistant – can take anything – still, how can anyone but the owner of the drawer know that it is still there? How can you expect the neighbours to know that you possess a mink coat if you never wear it?

Louise felt her heart beating in heavy panic. Was it already too late to open that drawer . . . ?

Trembling, she pushed the book away from her, and in doing so knocked Harriet's book on to the floor, in company with two cotton reels and an unemptied ash-tray. The book had fallen open at the second page, and even before she stooped to pick it up, Louise could read the three words which straggled across the middle of the page in black, uneven capitals:

'M IS DEAD'

For a moment the shock deprived her of all sense. Like a puppet on a string, she jerked round to stare at the double bed, half expecting to see her husband's body, stiff and white, stretched out on it. Her next impulse was to rush down to the telephone, to ring the office, to find out if Mark was well, to tell him to be careful, terribly careful . . .

Then her intelligence began to work again, telling her over and over again that of course Mark was all right; it couldn't conceivably refer to him; that Vera Brandon must have dozens of friends of whom Louise knew nothing; for all she knew, the whole lot of them might have names beginning with M. Maurice. Mervyn. Mickey. Monty. Oh, heaps of them. Martin. Manfred. Marmaduke . . . The need to think of names beginning with M was taking on the quality of an obsession. It was becoming irrational . . .

Irrational? Well, of course, the whole thing was irrational. Her intelligence had told her at least twenty times that she was being a fool to worry about any of it. Yet still those black, ill-formed capitals stared up at her in purposeful silence. 'M Is Dead.' The message was for her. She knew it. An instinct, older and more compelling than any intelligence, warned her that she would neglect that message at her peril. Though the words had been copied by Harriet's unskilled hand, they were not Harriet's words. They were someone else's words, born of such savage intensity of feeling that they had grown like plants, with a life, a power of their own. They were Words of Power, belonging by rights in a darker, younger world than this . . .

Another second, and Louise was herself again; civilised, rational and inquisitive. Oh, terribly inquisitive. All guilt, all hesitation gone, she studied Harriet's exercise book as if it held the key to all earthly happiness and security.

In a way, this book was more satisfactory than Margery's, for instead of copying blindly and senselessly as Margery had done, Harriet must have skimmed through the original for words and phrases that she could understand. She had written them all down in block capitals in a disjointed list, which had an oddly apocryphal effect:

'NO SENSE OUT OF HER'
'WIND AND HAIL BETWEEN THEM'
'HARDER TO FIGHT A FOOL'
'FILL IN MORE FORMS'
'IT SEEMS I MUST HATE IN TRIPLICATE'

Louise wondered that Harriet had tackled 'Triplicate' so successfully; and then she remembered the ball game that Mrs Philips had been complaining about only last Saturday:

'Careful Kate
Climbed the gate
Take it down in triplicate.'

At the word 'Triplicate' the player had to twirl round while the ball was still in the air, and then catch it, and this, with shrieks of joyful frustration, the children had consistently failed to do; it was this, combined with the thud – thud – thud of the ball against her side wall that had roused Mrs Philips.

Louise turned a page.

'RE DORSANDY'

What a peculiar name – if it was a name? Or a place? Not much use trying to guess – Harriet had probably misspelt it anyway. Louise read on, and was surprised to find herself confronted with two carefully printed though badly spaced addresses:

61ELSWORTHYCRESCENT N2
10 MORT LAKEBUILDINGS N17

61 Elsworthy Crescent. 10 Mortlake Buildings. Neither address conveyed anything to Louise, but they seemed perfectly plausible. Might not one or the other of them be the address she had been seeking – the address of someone who might be able to throw some light on the past life of this Miss Brandon? That previous landlady, perhaps, from whom Mrs Morgan said Louise ought to have obtained a reference?

Louise was suddenly reluctant to do anything about it at all. It was one thing to lament the fact that she knew nothing of Miss Brandon's past; it was quite another to be confronted suddenly with a perfectly simple means of finding out something.

'M IS DEAD'

It was as if the page had spoken aloud, repeating the message peremptorily; demanding the answer. Snatching up the exercise book Louise ran downstairs to the telephone.

No, the operator explained, she was sorry, there was no telephone at No. 10 Mortlake Buildings. There was one at 61 Elsworthy Crescent, but what was the name, please? To Louise's tentative suggestion of 'Dorsandy' she replied with a momentarily nonplussed silence; and then, after a little delay, suggested obligingly that perhaps Louise meant 'Palmer'?

Louise agreed to this at random and at once, and was forthwith given the Palmers' telephone number.

After all, she reflected, as she dialled this number, I'm only a voice on the telephone; it doesn't matter if it all sounds terribly silly. They'll only think I've got a wrong number . . .

'Hullo. Frances Palmer speaking. Who is it, please?'

The voice was young and self-possessed; and before her self-confidence drained away completely, Louise plunged into her enquiry.

Miss Brandon. Yes, Frances Palmer did know a Miss Brandon – *had* known her, rather. Yes, Vera Brandon, that was right. There was a hesitancy, a lack of ease, about the previously confident voice. The owner seemed to be searching for words; to be afraid of saying too much, and yet anxious not to close the conversation.

'Oh. You mean she's living with you right now? Oh.' Again the voice hesitated. 'Listen,' it went on, hurrying a little. 'Listen, could you possibly come round here? Now? I – well, it's rather difficult talking on the telephone, isn't it? If we could meet, I might be able to tell you – that is, to ask you – I mean, I don't know you, do I?' the voice concluded rather lamely.

Louise was reassured. The speaker was not, after all, as

self-possessed as she had seemed at first. And she seemed interested – indeed, she had sounded as if she was anxious in just the same way that Louise herself was anxious. A meeting between them might clear up a lot.

It was not until she had agreed to this proposal and had rung off that she began to face the question of how she could walk out of the house at four o'clock in the afternoon with no one to look after the children, no tea ready for them and no idea what to cook for supper when she got back.

She decided to try Edna Larkins. If she was home from work (and, after all, it was Good Friday tomorrow, she might easily be finishing early today) there was a very good chance that she might be lured, knitting and all, from the sofa of her aunt's front room to be re-deposited on the corresponding sofa of Louise's front room.

It all worked perfectly. Edna was only too delighted to come once she heard that Louise had a pair of No. 8 needles she could lend her for when she came to the end of the ribbing; and she was soon happily settled on the sofa, with a brand new pair of No. 8 needles and an assurance that Margery would be a *great* help over getting the tea, won't you, darling?

'What?' said Margery discouragingly; but Louise felt that the moment had come for her to escape without further argument. She always clung hopefully to the theory (based on observation of other people's children) that her family behaved better when she, their mother, wasn't there.

17

No. 61 Elsworthy Crescent was one of those little red brick houses so smart and clean that you would think it was kept indoors. The front garden was discreetly ablaze with almost unnaturally healthy flowers; and on a tiny patch of closely-clipped grass stood a pram so new and shining that Louise expected to see an equally new baby in it. She was surprised to observe that the child with the clean white frock and the clean pink face was at least as old as Michael. And it wasn't crying, she noted enviously. Its mother was expecting a visitor, was anxious for a quiet talk with her and it *wasn't crying*.

The mistress of all this perfection, in a starched cotton frock and really white sandals, greeted Louise with a sort of guarded warmth, and led her into a white-painted chintzy sitting-room, where the only evidence that a baby belonged to the household was a new fluffy Teddy bear with a red bow round its neck. No nappies. No bits of chewed rusk. Louise sighed, and wondered if she should ask the girl how she did it. But it wouldn't be any use. These competent mothers never could tell you how they did it. The clean, quiet babies, the unsticky Teddy bears, simply seemed to happen to them.

Frances Palmer, competent though she might be, was clearly worried. No sooner had she produced tea and a plate of nicely browned little cakes, than she began to question Louise. How, she wanted to know, had Louise heard of her? Had Vera Brandon spoken of her? What had she said? Had anything seemed – well – odd in any way?

Louise could not answer any of this very satisfactorily; she could only ask other questions in her turn, and very soon Mrs Palmer was recounting all she knew.

It had all happened, apparently, one day last autumn. There had been a ring at the front door, and when Mrs Palmer answered it, there was this tall, distinguished-looking woman, carrying a little case, and announcing that she had seen Mrs Palmer's advertisement for a housekeeper.

'I was utterly mystified, of course,' continued Frances Palmer, 'because I'd never advertised for a housekeeper at all. Why should I, with this tiny house, and I'm not working or anything. She had the cutting with her, she said, and she began fishing about for it in her case. Well, I felt I had to ask her in – it was so awkward for her, I mean, standing there on the doorstep trying to look through this case full of papers. So I brought her in, and we had a cup of tea – she still couldn't find the cutting, by the way, and I told her it must be Elsworthy *Avenue* she wanted – people are always getting us mixed up with them – though actually I found out afterwards that they hadn't advertised for a housekeeper, either, and anyway this woman never called there at all. Well, anyway we got talking, and she stayed quite a long time. I got a bit fed up with it, honestly, because of course I'd only expected her to stay for a few minutes, and I'd got a lot to do. I didn't even get the impression that she was enjoying herself, either. She was sort of *making* conversation, if you know what I mean – as if – how shall I explain it? – as if she was waiting for something. As if she had to fill in time. She kept glancing about the room – glancing at the clock – glancing at me when she thought I wasn't looking. I don't know – I began to feel very awkward; and what made it more uncomfortable still was that I had an odd feeling that I recognised her. That I'd seen her before somewhere, only I couldn't for the life of me think where—'

'But that's exactly how *we* felt,' burst out Louise impulsively. Briefly she described Mark's first reaction to seeing Miss Brandon, and also her own qualms about the suitcase. Frances Palmer had gone a little pale.

'You see what *that* means, don't you,' she said, her voice quivering slightly; and then, recovering herself, she went on: 'But of course – how silly – I haven't even told you what happened yet! Well, as I was saying, there she sat, and I kept dropping hints to make her go. I told her we were going out that evening – all sorts of lies – but it was no use, she wouldn't take any notice. After a bit I simply had to feed Lesley and put her to bed, and then Tom came in wanting his supper; and that *did* seem to shift her at last. She was full of apologies for having stayed so long, and off she went. I don't suppose I'd have thought anything more about it, only, later that evening—'

Frances Palmer paused, and offered Louise another cup of the now cooling tea. She seemed to have lost the thread of her story; almost to be deliberately transferring her uneasiness to the problem of the tea: was it hot enough? strong enough? Did Louise want more sugar? Or didn't she—?

'Later that evening—?' Louise prompted gently; and Frances Palmer started, flushed a little, and then continued:

'It sounds so stupid really,' she apologised. 'I mean, Tom was quite sure I was imagining it all, but anyway, this is what I *thought* I saw. We'd been out, you see – just for a stroll, after supper. We often do, just for half an hour, when we're sure Lesley is settled. We usually go as far as the canal and then back along the Avenue; but this time, for some reason, I felt anxious about Lesley. I don't know why; she'd been perfectly well all day and had gone off to sleep as good as gold. But I kept worrying about it, and Tom kept telling me not to be silly; and at last I got so worried that I said I must go back. He was furious about it – he's Irish, you know, real redheaded Irish, and men like that *do* flare up easily, don't they? He said it was crazy to turn back like that; and then when I began hurrying he was crosser still, and wouldn't try to keep up with me. So I got home by myself, and the minute I stepped into the hall I had that feeling – you know – that there was someone in the house. I told myself it was silly, but all the same I was almost too scared to move. I was so frightened I actually took my shoes off and tiptoed around peeping into every room. It was in my bedroom that I saw her, Tom says I didn't. Tom says I was imagining it all because of my fright, and because it was getting dusk by then and I hadn't dared turn any lights on. But *I* know I wasn't imagining it. She was there. There's a mirror, you see, a big mirror on the wall facing you as you go in, and I saw her reflection in it. Just her back view, bending over the little table by the bed, but I knew it was her. Something in the way she was standing – I'd have recognised it anywhere. Not only from seeing her that afternoon, you understand, but from having seen her somewhere before. I had that feeling even more strongly then than I'd had it earlier. That's what frightens me, really. Why do I recognise her? And why do *you* recognise her—'

'But wait —' said Louise. 'What did she say? Didn't she explain what she was doing – why she'd come back into your house—?'

Frances Palmer looked rather shamefaced.

'No – that was the ridiculous part. I ought to have gone in straight away and challenged her. Of course I ought. But I was frightened, you see. I wanted Tom to be with me. I just scuttled down to the front door to look for him, and when he came – it can't have been more than half a minute later – we went up to the room, and she'd gone! Absolutely gone. That's what I can't understand. That's what makes Tom say it's all my imagination. You see, she *couldn't* have come down the stairs behind me as I stood at the front door. Well, I mean, you've seen our tiny hall – she'd have been barely two yards away from me. Of course,' she added a little wistfully, 'if only there'd been something missing it wouldn't have seemed so queer. We looked through my jewel case at once, of course, and at Tom's silver cups – everything. And the watch on the bedside table where I'd seen her standing – it's an old-fashioned silver one, you know, it belonged to Tom's father. Tom never wears it, he has a wrist watch, but it keeps very good time, and I suppose it's worth a few pounds. Anyway, she hadn't taken it. Nothing seemed to have been touched at all.'

'Perhaps,' said Louise slowly, 'she hadn't time. I mean, if she was going round examining things and making her plans, and then *you* came in – well, naturally she'd give it up and make a bolt for it.'

'But how?' protested the other girl. 'I *know* she didn't come down the stairs. I told you.'

'Through a window, then,' suggested Louise, though without much conviction. The chances that a respectable tweed-costumed lady could climb from an upper floor window in a street like this without being observed by the local Mrs Morgans seemed small indeed. Frances Palmer was speaking again:

'I puzzled about it for ages,' she said. 'And for weeks I was scared of coming back into the house by myself. And then, when I'd just about stopped bothering about it, *you* rang up. You really scared me, you know. When I first heard your voice I thought it was *her*; but then when you went on talking, I realised the voice was quite different, and I knew it couldn't be. So then I thought she'd been asking about me – trying to track me down again – or something—'

Frances Palmer's voice trailed away uncertainly, and Louise hastened to reassure her.

'No, no. Nothing like that. She's never mentioned you. It was just that—' It was Louise's turn to hesitate. She could hardly confess to this comparative stranger that she had been prying into her tenant's private diary. 'I – she left a paper about with some addresses on it,' she lied feebly.

In spite of her agitation, young Mrs Palmer managed to put up a most courteous show of believing this, and was quickly rewarded with an only slightly edited account of Louise's own fears and suspicions about Miss Brandon.

'You know what all this adds up to, don't you?' said Frances slowly when Louise had finished. 'You and I both recognised something about her. And your husband too.

It's too much of a coincidence that we should all of us have met her by chance on some previous occasion. The only explanation is that she must be some public figure. Don't you see? Someone we've all seen photographs of in the papers.'

Louise did not immediately grasp Mrs Palmer's full meaning.

'You mean she's a film star or something?' she asked, puzzled. 'Honestly, I don't think . . .'

'No no – nothing like that!' corrected Mrs Palmer, a trifle impatiently. 'Other people beside film stars can get their pictures into the papers. Criminals, for example. Murderers.'

Louise swallowed.

'But that's nonsense!' she exclaimed, a little too quickly. 'I mean,' she added foolishly, 'she doesn't *look* like a criminal—'

Didn't she? Who's fears was she trying to quieten, her own or Mrs Palmer's?

'I don't see that,' Mrs Palmer was saying. 'I mean, a murderess who *looked* like a murderess would have been caught in the first place, wouldn't she? That's why she's still at large. That's why she can still prowl about in other people's houses —' The pretty, capable little face suddenly crumpled: 'She's here now! I'm sure she's here now!' she cried. 'Oh, I'm so frightened! Please don't go! Oh, please stay until Tom gets in.'

Louise was surprised. This sudden collapse into panic seemed out of keeping with all that enviable housewifely competence. Or was housewifely competence a more limited quality than one usually supposed; something that didn't stand up to much strain? However, there was no time now to dwell on the comfortable corollary to this theory – namely, that domestic incompetence such as Louise's must necessarily denote other, more sterling qualities – for something must be done, and quickly, to soothe this frightened young woman.

'There's nothing for *you* to be frightened of,' she pointed out. 'Whatever brought her to your house last autumn – well, she hasn't done anything more about it for six months, has she? Why should she suddenly start being interested again now? It's *me* she seems to be interested in now. Or my husband. *I'm* the one who should be frightened, not you.'

Louise observed, a little wryly, the look of relief that spread over her companion's face at this not very comfortable deduction. But, after all, why should this girl worry overmuch about Louise, who was still, when all was said and done, almost a stranger?

'I'd better be going,' she began; but at this all Mrs Palmer's alarm seemed to revive. 'Oh – *please!*' she exclaimed, 'not till Tom comes in. *Please!* I know it's absurd, but this has brought it all back to me so, you can't imagine! I've got an awful feeling that when I go upstairs I shall find her in my bedroom bending over that table, just the way she was—'

'But I *must* go!' protested Louise. 'It's nearly six, and—'

Her companion broke in agitatedly:

'Oh! I know. I mustn't keep you. But please – before you go – I wish you'd just come up to the bedroom with me and look. I know it's all nonsense, of course, but if you'd just do that before you go, then I think I'd feel all right again.'

'Very well,' said Louise resignedly; and a minute later she was following her hostess up the neat little staircase with its white painted banisters.

The bedroom had the same clean, dolls' house prettiness of the rest of the house. The walls were painted pale pink, a pink floral counterpane covered the bed, and clean white curtains hung crisply at the windows. The tidiness of it all could have made Louise weep as she thought of her own bedroom at home. Mark's second oldest suit thrown over a chair to remind her (so far unsuccessfully) to take it to the cleaner's. Books and papers on every available surface. And shoes. Where on earth did other women keep their husband's shoes? In this room, not a shoe was to be seen – nor, indeed, any garment of any sort. All the polished surfaces of the furniture were bare except for a few neatly placed lace mats, and, on the small bedside table, a pair of silver-framed photographs of Mrs Palmer's snub-nosed baby and her astonishingly similar snub-nosed husband.

And, of course, the room was empty. No mysterious figures leaned over tables or cowered in wardrobes. To set her hostess's mind still further at rest, Louise explored the rest of the little house with her. Everything was quiet and in perfect order.

A sudden thought came to Louise.

'Listen,' she said. 'I think I can see how she got away. While you were at the front door, watching for your husband, she could have slipped into one of the other upstairs rooms; and then, when you and he rushed up to the bedroom – naturally you'd go there first – she could just have walked across this landing here and down the stairs, while you were searching the wardrobe, or something. Or did one of you keep watch on the landing?'

Frances Palmer shook her head helplessly.

'No – oh no. I stayed right by Tom all the time. I was frightened. I – I suppose – Yes, it *could* have happened that way. How odd I shouldn't have thought of it before.'

It seemed odd to Louise, too; but after all, one must make allowances for the girl's panic at the time. Why, she was looking quite white and strained even now, at the very memory of it. Louise cast about for some way of reassuring her.

'As a matter of fact,' she remarked, as they made their way to the front door, 'it's just occurred to me – there can't be anything very sinister about the woman's past – I mean, your idea that she's a notorious criminal or something. If she was, she'd never have given you her real name. And it *is* her real name, I know. She teaches at our local grammar school.'

Mrs Palmer looked dully at Louise, her delicate pink and white features looking less young than they had earlier in the afternoon.

'How do you know?' she said heavily. 'Have you actually seen her teaching there? Or gone there to enquire if it really *is* her name?'

'Well – no,' said Louise, rather taken aback. 'Actually, I haven't. But, I mean, it would be such an easy thing to check up on – she'd never dare tell lies about it.'

'But that's probably just what she's counting on!' exclaimed Mrs Palmer. 'Just because it *is* so easy, that's the very reason why nobody will bother to check up. They'll all think just the way you do.'

'I can't help feeling that's a bit far-fetched,' observed

Louise. 'Besides – I told you. She writes books. Homeric archaeology. That sort of thing. Terribly learned.'

'Have you *read* them?' persisted Mrs Palmer inexorably. 'Have you ever even set eyes on them?' And when Louise did not answer, she concluded, not without a certain complacency: 'You've only got *her* word for it that she's ever studied the classics at all. Hers – and your husband's.'

18

Louise stepped out into the tranquil bustle of a suburban spring evening. Threading her way through the hurrying husbands and the tricycling children, the setting sun blindingly in her eyes, she made her way back to the bus stop.

But which bus stop? Which bus? There was still that other address, not more than a quarter of an hour's journey away. It was after six already; by the time she got home it would already be too late to cook a proper supper, and the children would be whining, Mark aggrieved. Things would be bad enough; but would they be any worse if she stayed out another half hour? She tried to think how she could explain her absence. After last night, she couldn't possibly confess that her errand was in any way connected with Vera Brandon. Already Mark – not to mention his mother and the Baxters – suspected that Louise was jealous. Looked at from their angle, this expedition would seem like suspicion and jealousy run mad, and no amount of explanation could be expected to alter this impression very much. That was the trouble about jealousy; once the word had been spoken between you, then everything you did or said was liable to be interpreted in that hackneyed but hideous light. Well, don't say anything then, except that you've been having tea with a friend . . .

The trolley-bus which could have taken Louise homewards drew up by the stop. She stepped forward. Two youths pushed in front of her. She stepped back.

'Hurry along, lady, cantcher make up your mind?' yelled the conductor; and the two youths, discerning – or feeling that they ought to discern – some sort of feeble innuendo in the remark, began to guffaw half-heartedly.

Louise drew back. Even when wearing her best things, she was never quite sure whether such guffaws were meant in compliment or in mockery; today, in this four-year-old cotton blouse and winter skirt, she felt that there was no doubt at all.

Well, that settled it. There wouldn't be another trolley-bus for twenty minutes, so it would be almost as quick to go to Mortlake Terrace as not. Besides, if she didn't go now, she would only go some other time, and have to explain things to Mark all over again. Why have two rows when one would do? she thought philosophically, and moved across the road to the other bus stop.

The façade of the great block of flats was grey and forbidding. Lines of washing filled every balcony, and the now sunless courtyard was full of screaming children. Dirtier children than those in Elsworthy Crescent, but just as many of them, were mounted on tricycles, and Louise rubbed her shins ruefully, and dodged as quickly as she could into the stairway that led to No. 10.

Four flights of surprisingly hygienic-smelling stairs led her to the door she sought, and at her second knock a heavy, adenoidal child of about seven appeared, and stared up at her with a blankness only faintly tinged with suspicion.

'Is your Mummy – your Mum – in?' asked Louise.

The suspicion in the face seemed to fade a little, but the blankness increased. Two more heads appeared round the door – no, three, for the skinny little ten-year-old was peering out from behind a large and doughy baby who looked much too heavy for her.

"'Ts a lady,' she diagnosed at last, shrilling the words into the dark passage behind her; and then, when there was no response: 'G'ahn, Em. Tell Mum there's a lady to see her.'

'A lady,' screamed the adenoidal child obediently, without taking her eyes off Louise's face; and a voice in the darkness behind took up the cry: 'A lady!' 'A lady!' echoed again from behind some closed door in the recesses of the dwelling; and at last, with a flurry of slippered footsteps and shrill admonitions, Mum herself appeared, patting her faded, gingery hair with a damp, steaming hand.

Miss Brandon? No, she didn't think she'd heard of no Miss Brandon. Not to remember it, like.

Some time ago, perhaps? Louise prompted, remembering that Mrs Palmer's adventure had taken place last autumn. Six months ago, or thereabouts?

Six months ago. Mum considered this. That would be just about the time she'd come out the hospital, and there'd been no end of ladies round then, naturally. There'd been the lady from the Welfare; and the lady about the milk vouchers; and the lady about Em's special boots on account of her toes turned in, and of course being in hospital she hadn't been able to get her along to the clinic, not that month. Then there was the lady about the Registrations, and the lady from the School Attendance, because of course she'd had to keep Lil at home from school to help, being that she was only just out of hospital. Ever so kind, that lady had been, ever so sympathetic, and she'd written off for a form what'd put it all right, and the form hadn't come, but it was all right, because they hadn't heard nothing more about it, not a word, had they, Lil?

Louise could not help wondering what tiny fraction of all these ladies' salaries would have solved Mum's problems for good without any more bother to anybody; but aloud she only asked if Mum could remember any *other* lady? Had there, she hazarded, been one wearing a brown costume?

Well, yes, to tell the truth, Mum thought that there had. In fact, now she came to think of it, most of the ladies were wearing brown costumes. Quite smart, too, some of them. Quiet, you know, but smart. But then, most of the girls *were* smart nowadays, there'd been a big change since the war, didn't Louise think so?

It was Louise who wilted first. Of course, it was she who was confronted with the five unblinking pairs of eyes ranged alongside Mum, and under their gaze she found it difficult to pursue the enquiry intelligently. Besides, among this multitude of brown-costumed ladies there seemed little chance of identifying Vera Brandon by her appearance; and as to her conversation or activities, these would have had to be very odd indeed for Mum not to have thought resignedly that they came legitimately under some Schedule or other.

'Well – thank you very much, Mrs – Um – Er—' began Louise, and was a little disappointed that Mum should accept this title so contentedly – she had hoped that she might learn the woman's name without having to ask for it point blank. Not that it mattered: it was hard to imagine that this woman could have any important connection with Vera Brandon's affairs.

'Thank you so much,' she said again; 'it's been very kind of you – I must have mistaken the address.' She backed to the stairs, awkwardly, and it was not until she reached the third flight that she felt herself really free of those twelve eyes.

The last streaks of sunset were fading as Louise hurried up the road towards her house, guessing uneasily at the time. Would Edna still be there, and would she have done anything about the children's supper? Or would Mark be coping with everything—?

'Good evening, Mrs Henderson. I'd like to speak to you, if you don't mind. It's not that I wish to complain, you understand, but—'

What, Louise wondered, would happen if she simply said to Mrs Philips: 'No, of course you don't' and walked on up the path? Was that what the Keepers of Themselves to Themselves would do? She thought enviously of these technicians of suburban living who figured so large in Mrs Morgan's anecdotes – those heroines who succeeded in keeping Themselves to Themselves in the face of murder, suicide or rape. Had it taken them years of study and practice to perfect their arid skill? Or had it been born with them? Were they simply endowed by nature with the chill genius needed to pass Mrs Philips without a word – to move unscathed through their front gardens like Daniel through the lions?

'I'm so sorry, Mrs Philips,' she said hurriedly. 'I've been out, you see. I was – er – called away in a hurry, and I had to leave the children. I'm terribly sorry if they've been disturbing you.'

Mrs Philips regarded her woodenly.

'I didn't say they'd been disturbing me, Mrs Henderson,' she observed. 'They've been bouncing their balls again, of course, those two older ones, but then that's only to be expected, brought up wild the way they've been, no consideration for anybody. I'm not expecting consideration, Mrs Henderson. I've given up *looking* for consideration. But all the same, I feel I ought to tell you, there are limits. There are limits beyond which flesh and blood can't endure, and the time has come, Mrs Henderson, when I must speak to you about your baby.'

It seemed to Louise that this momentous pronouncement would have carried more weight if Mrs Philips hadn't been speaking to her about her baby roughly three times a week ever since he was born. However, she hastened to apologise:

'I'm terribly sorry if he's been crying this afternoon. I left instructions about his bottle, but perhaps . . .'

Mrs Philips interrupted.

'No, Mrs Henderson; it's not that. I'm not complaining about this afternoon. As a matter of fact, your baby has been very quiet while you've been out – I haven't heard him at all. I suppose he's been properly looked after for once. No, Mrs Henderson, it's the night-time I'm talking about. Last night I didn't get a wink of sleep, not one wink, with all that crying through the wall, right by my head. Never stopped all night long, it just about drove me crazy—'

'But that's impossible—' Louise was beginning; and was

about to add that Michael had been out in his pram most of the night, far away from the house. Then she thought better of it. There was no point in stirring up yet more gossip about her outing last night; and it wasn't as if Mrs Philips was ever mollified by explanations, or even listened to them. For, after all, Mrs Philips was in the right, and the person who is right doesn't need to listen very much.

'If it goes on,' Mrs Philips was continuing, 'if it goes on, Mrs Henderson, I'm warning you, I'll have to go to my doctor about it. Really I will. *He* knows that my nerves won't stand that sort of thing. I've been under the doctor for my nerves for twenty years, ever since my poor husband died. *He'll* tell you that I need my night's sleep, don't have any doubt about that, Mrs Henderson. *He'll* tell you that I can't stand this sort of thing.'

Louise recognised this threat as a trump card. For minor annoyances, you threatened your neighbours with the police; for major ones, you brought in the doctor. Not, Louise fancied, because the doctor was the more alarming bogeyman of the two, but because he was the more power-ful. From the doctor's surgery emerged potent little scraps of paper which could subdue the milkman into giving you milk at half price; which could get you off work for weeks on end; which could conjure out of thin air lini-ments, spectacles and artificial legs. Surely from this shrine a piece of paper could also be summoned which would stop Louise's baby crying at times when Mrs Philips wanted to go to sleep?

'I'm sorry,' said Louise for the third time; but before she could say any more (if, indeed, there was anything more to be said) she was interrupted by an explosion of sound from the house. The front door burst open, and Margery and Harriet were down the steps and flinging themselves upon Louise in imbecile rapture, as if she had been away for months, for years.

'Mummy!' they shrieked. 'Mummy! Mummy!' Their welcome was as warm and noisy and senseless as that of two puppies. And if only they *had* been two puppies, Louise reflected, how different the conversation with Mrs Philips would have been. How her face would have softened; how she would have beamed, and admired, and sympathised; how patiently she would have put up with the shrill yapping . . .

'Funny time for children to be out of bed, I must say,' Mrs Philips observed bleakly, and as loudly as was becoming in one whose nerves couldn't stand noise; and then, louder still, to be heard above the commotion: 'Of course, it's all what you're brought up to . . . Some neighbourhoods . . . Playing and screaming in the streets till ten o'clock at night . . .'

'Where've you *been*, Mummy?' Harriet was squealing. 'We haven't had any supper, and—'

'Yes, we have,' contradicted Margery. 'Oh, Mummy, why—?'

'No, we haven't, Mummy. And—'

'Hush, darlings, hush! One at a time! Listen: Isn't Daddy in?'

'No,' said Harriet; and 'Yes' simultaneously said Margery.

Louise tried again. 'Well, where's Edna, then? Is she still here? And is Baby all right?'

Fatal, of course, to ask two questions in the same breath.

182

'No' shrilled into one ear while 'Yes' pierced the other; and Louise tried to manoeuvre her clamorous escort up the path and into the house. A little sense began to emerge from the babel of contradictions. Yes, Daddy had come in, Margery explained, and had given them supper (No, not *supper*, only *baked beans*, Harriet contributed aggrievedly) and had then gone up to the Rubbish Room.

'To have supper with the Spy Lady,' elaborated Harriet, in tones likely to edify two-thirds of the street. 'And she's cooked him a *much* nicer supper than us. I can smell bacon, and cheese, and kippers, and—'

'Not kippers,' corrected Margery. 'I know it isn't kippers, because—'

'It is,' snapped Harriet.

'It isn't!'

Louise could see that both children were overtired, and no wonder. She interrupted hastily: 'Is Daddy still up there with Miss Brandon?'

'Yes,' said Harriet resentfully. 'And I think he's going to be there for *ever*! He didn't put us to bed, or anything. He went up there hours and hours and *hours* ago!'

'No, he didn't,' said Margery. 'It was only—'

'Yes he did.'

'Didn't.'

'Did!'

19

Louise hastened first to Michael's room. Yes, he was all right. Edna must have fed him and put him to bed most efficiently, for he was rosily asleep with a well-fed, well-bathed air that was unmistakable. Louise was surprised. She had left Edna with only the sketchiest of instructions about giving him a bottle, and none about putting him to bed; and Edna was not a girl who was given to using much common sense or initiative – particularly where common sense and initiative would involve getting off a sofa and walking upstairs. Edna must be changing – waking up. Well, seventeen was the age for changes. Any day now she might stop knitting. And stop baby-sitting, too, thought Louise ruefully; the two no doubt went together. That was the whole difficulty about baby-sitting. The very qualities that made people willing to do it were just those qualities which also made them no good at it.

Outside on the landing she paused. She had expected Mark to call down to her when he heard her come in; to hurry down and ask her where she'd been, what had made her so late. But he must be too much engrossed with Vera Brandon up there. She could hear their voices, faintly. A short laugh. The scrape of a chair. Voices again. The flavour of Miss Brandon's cooking still lingered faintly on the air, and Louise considered that Harriet was most decidedly wrong about the kippers, and probably about the cheese and bacon too. The smell was a far more subtle one, far more exotic. Mushrooms, perhaps, and little cubes of veal fried in butter, with the faintest dash of garlic . . .

'Mummy!'

'What, darling?' Resignedly Louise gave up her speculations and turned into the girls' room. 'What's the matter, Harriet?'

'Mummy, I can't go to sleep.' The words were spoken with a smug, trump-that-if-you-can sort of air that was both irritating and endearing. Louise sat down on the bed and waited for more.

'Mummy, I'm too hot, and I can't have my blanket off because if I do a big hen might come and peck me while I'm all bare.'

If only Harriet and Socrates could have met, thought Louise wistfully. It would have done them both good, particularly Socrates. He who had argued so many learned philosophers out of their cherished convictions, would *he* have been able to convince Harriet that there wasn't – there couldn't be – a hen in the room? Or would he, too, after half an hour's fruitless struggle on behalf of reason and sanity, have resorted to the non-Socratic method of promising to take her to the fair tomorrow if she was a good girl?

Harriet's transports of gratitude at this offer made Louise feel quite ashamed – as if she had bought her victory in this idiotic argument with counterfeit coin. Because, of course, she had been going to take them to the fair anyway, some time during the weekend. She always did on Bank Holidays. Indeed, how could she ever hope to do otherwise, when it was only such a short journey to Hampstead Heath; and when the children saved their pocket money with such touching and infuriating fervour for weeks beforehand; and when *all* the other children go, Mummy, every single one, and Milly and Patsy White go three times, on the Friday, *and* the Saturday, *and* the Monday.

Downstairs, the kitchen was silent, and full of crumbs. The remains of the baked bean supper still littered the table, and the corner of a piece of burnt toast jutted out from under the grill. A blob of tomato sauce had joined the streak of jam under Harriet's chair, and Louise glanced at the clock. Would there be time to give the floor its long-overdue scrubbing tonight? If Michael stayed asleep till half past ten – and if Mark continued absorbed upstairs—?

The ringing of the telephone put an end to these speculations; and when she heard Beatrice's voice she knew at once that the kitchen floor would wait another day. What with Kathleen's mother having her face lifted; and Muriel's not being able to hold down a job because of Bristol being so provincial and narrow-minded; and Laura's going to a psychoanalyst at last, in spite of what she'd always said about them – and what her husband had always said about them – and what, come to that, Beatrice herself had always said about them – well, by that time it was after ten, and Beatrice had honestly only got a moment left to tell Louise what she was really ringing up about.

'Your Vera Brandon,' she buzzed happily down the wire. 'I've had my spies out, and I can tell you *one* thing about her, anyway. I don't know if it's relevant, and of course keep it under your hat, because the girl who told the sister of the woman who knows Humphrey's friend's wife said it was in strictest confidence – well, anyway, there's been a bit of a scandal about her. Last summer. That's why she couldn't take up the University job she was supposed to be starting last October. It was bad luck on her, Humphrey says – well, of course, he *would* – but anyway, it seems she'd actually been taken on for this lectureship or whatever it was – I'm not very up in these things, you know – with Humphrey's friends talking about them all the time of course I make my mind a blank. Well, this Something-or-other-Ship – it seems she was turned down at the last moment because of the scandal.'

'What sort of scandal?' asked Louise, and was aware of a momentary surprise at the other end of the line. Of course; Humphrey was Beatrice's informant, and to his painstaking judgment there could be only one sort of scandal.

'You mean who was the man?' asked Beatrice, recovering herself. 'Truly, my dear, I don't know, and Humphrey doesn't either, though of course he tries to look as if it was himself, poor darling. But I wouldn't worry, Louise, really I wouldn't. I don't believe she's Mark's type a bit. As I was saying to Pamela this afternoon—'

'I don't mean that,' interrupted Louise. 'I only meant are you sure that the scandal wasn't something – well – worse—'

She found it hard to be more explicit. Frances Palmer's talk about notorious criminals and the picture papers had seemed credible at the time – in fact more than credible – alarming. But how would it all sound at second hand? And down the telephone? And, above all, what would it sound like retold to Pamela – to Muriel – to Janice? ('Poor old Louise, she *is* cracking up! Do you know, the last time I rang her up . . .')

'Worse? Oh – I see what you mean.' Beatrice seemed suddenly enlightened. 'Well, as a matter of fact, I wouldn't be a bit surprised if you're right. Humphrey didn't actually *say* so, but after all – well, she could easily be just the sort of fool to get herself into a jam like that. These academic types, they're absolute *infants* when it comes to coping with real life, aren't they? Don't I know it, after living with one for nine years! Still, you must hand it to her, if there *was* anything of the sort, she's managed to hush it up pretty cleverly—'

Louise was finding it hard to follow the sense of all this. She had heard Miss Brandon's door upstairs opening, and now she could hear voices on the stairs. Mark's voice. Vera Brandon's low, cynical little laugh. Somehow the conversation with Beatrice must be hustled to a close before the two newcomers came near enough to gather the subject of it.

'Well – I'm so glad you're both well,' she called unconvincingly into the mouthpiece, and hung up ruthlessly. She turned and walked towards the stairs just as Mark and Vera Brandon rounded the bend of the landing.

She looked up at the two of them, their faces dim where the light from the hall almost failed to reach. She could just see that Miss Brandon was smiling; and in the half darkness she fancied that the woman's eyes were bright as she had never seen them before. Shining, dancing, with some secret triumph.

'Hullo, Louise; had a good time?' It was Mark who broke the silence. His voice was bright and cheery, and yet somehow uncomfortable. Louise stared up the dim length of the stairs, uncomprehending. Where did Mark think she had been, then? Why wasn't he asking questions? Why wasn't he surprised – put out – that she was back so late? Whatever sort of message could Edna have given him? He went on speaking, still with that uneasy cheerfulness:

'Hadn't you better go to bed now? Have a rest, I mean – or something? Vera says – that is – I'm afraid I've only just realised how much you've been – overdoing things lately.'

Was Louise imagining the glance of mocking triumph with which the older woman looked down at her out of the shadows? Now she spoke, as if from a pedestal far above Louise's head:

'Yes, indeed, you should go and rest,' she agreed, in a voice of grave concern which was imperceptibly edged with some other emotion which Louise could not identify. 'You must have a real, long sleep tonight. Prolonged lack of sleep – it can become – well – dangerous.' She shot a swift, sidelong glance at her companion, and added inconsequently: 'We've been having another talk about the *Medea*, your husband and I. He's managed to convince me at last that the psychology of it is sound. Haven't you, Mark?'

She spoke with a curious air of recklessness that seemed quite inappropriate to the subject; and it seemed to Louise that she watched Mark closely for his response. He looked oddly bewildered and uncomfortable.

'Yes – just about,' he assented awkwardly; and then, with an evident wish to change the subject: 'Is one of the kids still awake, Louise? I thought I heard a sort of scuffling up there—?'

189

'Yes, it's Harriet,' said Louise, relieved to encounter at last something that she could understand in this top-heavy conversation down the length of the stairs. 'She's been restless all the evening. I told her we'd go to the fair tomorrow, Mark. Is that all right? It'll save us going on Monday, and it may not be so crowded.'

'What a hope!' groaned Mark – and Louise was thankful to note that the artificial brightness had left his voice; he seemed to have thrown it off as a healthy man throws off a fever. 'What a hope!' and then, with cautious optimism: '*I* don't have to come, do I?'

'Well – no,' said Louise reflectively. 'Actually, it might be more help if you stayed at home with Michael—'

'No – well, perhaps I'd better come,' Mark hastily corrected himself. 'It's nice to see the kids enjoying themselves,' he added virtuously. 'And we needn't start till the afternoon, need we?'

There was no doubt about the triumph in Miss Brandon's eyes now. Was she thinking, with scornful pity, that *she* wasn't going to spend her Easter holiday dragging three fretful, exhausted children through the crowds and the noise, settling their arguments, consoling them for the prizes they didn't win, wiping ice cream off their faces . . . ?

Once in the hall, Miss Brandon moved to the front door. She had, she said, to slip out and see a friend for an hour or so, and might be back rather late . . . But, of course, she had her key . . . She waved it at them reassuringly; and, avoiding Mark's eyes, she gave Louise an odd, cold little smile, and disappeared into the darkness.

Mark followed Louise into the kitchen. Together they

surveyed the debris which still remained from tea and supper.

'I'll give you a hand with the washing-up tomorrow,' said Mark cheerfully – tomorrow, in Mark's opinion, was always the best time for washing-up. And then, surveying the cold baked beans, he added, a trifle unnecessarily:

'She's a marvellous cook, our Vera. Very simple ingredients, you know – just some oddments of vegetables and a little meat, and she turned out a meal fit for a king. She's one of those cooks who uses real imagination.'

'Real butter, you mean, I expect,' retorted Louise ungenerously. 'You can afford it when you're only cooking for one or two. But Mark—' She hesitated. She had been on the point of asking him where he thought she had been this evening – what message Edna had given him? But what would be the point? Since she felt unable to tell him the whole truth, surely it would be better to leave well alone?

'What did you say?' But Mark did not pursue the matter, for by now he was peering into the cupboard for something palatable to spread on the piece of crispbread he had fished out of a tin.

20

It wasn't the noise itself that was so exhausting, Louise decided, as they pushed their way through the crowd towards the Caterpillar. It was the strain of trying to hear what your family were saying to you through it all. Margery into one ear, Harriet into the other, and Mark contributing incomprehensible advice from a foot or two behind. And you couldn't, as you could at home, simply say to them all: 'Yes, dear,' 'Of course, dear,' and 'How nice, dear,' at random, because they couldn't hear you, either. 'What, Mummy?' they would scream; 'What did you say, Mummy?'

'I said "How nice, dear,"' Louise would bellow patiently, only to hear in reply: 'What, Mummy?' 'What's nice, Mummy?' 'What did Margery say was nice, Mummy?' 'Who said nice?' 'You said nice.' 'What was – ?' 'I didn't.' 'You did—'

Michael's collapsible canvas push-chair wasn't a success, either. He was too young for it, of course; but the pram was too big to get on the train, and anyway the idea had been that Mark should carry him most of the time. But now it had turned out so hot, all the coats had to be carried instead of worn; and there was that awful plaster ballet dancer that Harriet had won on the Spot-the-Dots; and the bottle of Tizer still wasn't finished. What with one thing and another, you couldn't expect Mark to carry the baby as well.

Anyway, by the time they had reached the queue for the Caterpillar, Mark had disappeared. His technique of staying a pace or two behind so that the children wouldn't catch sight of him and scream 'Daddy' instead of 'Mummy' must have overreached itself, and he had lost sight of them altogether. Never mind; he was well out of it. He had just about reached the limits of his endurance, and a few minutes of being lost would make a new man of him.

Now for the ever-recurring problem. Should Louise stay with Michael and the push-chair, and watch with her heart in her mouth while Margery and Harriet whirled round alone on this heaving, dizzying monster; or should she go on the monster with them, and watch with her heart in her mouth to see if Michael was still all right left alone in his push-chair whenever he came giddily, intermittently into sight?

It was Margery who decided the question. No sooner was she settled on her seat in the unnerving vehicle, than she came to the shrill conclusion that she couldn't – wouldn't – go on the Caterpillar. But neither could she possibly get *off* the Caterpillar, because she had already paid her sixpence, her very own sixpence that she had saved out of her dentist shilling, and if she lost that sixpence, then she could only go on *two* other things, because there weren't any threepenny ones, at least only ones for babies, and—'

The Caterpillar was already trembling into motion when Louise silenced this tearful recital by leaping into the seat with Margery and taking her on her lap. Michael would be all right, surely, strapped in his push-chair. She would have a glimpse of him every ten seconds, and anyway the whole ride would take barely two minutes.

Slowly the fantastic vehicle began to revolve. The rails looked terribly narrow for the width of the cars; but after all, thousands of people had ridden safely on the thing already. In her lap, she could feel Margery's body tautening with mixed joy and apprehension. From the seat behind Harriet's voice, so confident and yet so babyish, could just be heard over the blare of the music:

'Look, Mummy! I can do it without holding! Look, I'm not holding! . . .'

'You *must* hold on, Harriet,' Louise admonished over her shoulder, knowing all the time that her voice was being carried uselessly away into the tumult of the fair. 'You *must* hold on, it's going to go faster than this.'

It *was* going faster. Louise tightened her grip on the warm steel bar with one hand, while with her free arm she gripped Margery more tightly. She turned to see if Harriet was holding on, but her head seemed almost to swing from her shoulders at this attempt to face backwards against the mounting speed. She tried to get a glimpse of Michael as the faces whirled past; but always her eyes seemed to come into focus a moment too late, and he was gone.

Faster, faster. Was Harriet holding on? Did this speechless stiffening of Margery's body mean real terror? And why couldn't she somehow get a glimpse of Michael . . . ?

Louise remembered how she had always enjoyed these absurd rides – and it was with a little shock of dismay that she realised, not that she no longer enjoyed them, but that she no longer noticed whether she enjoyed them or not. Her soul was no longer in her body as it dipped and whirled; it had divided into three. One part was with Margery, bolstering up her waning courage; another part was with Harriet, radiating authority and will-power sufficient to prevent her doing anything rash; the third part was with Michael, willing him to sit still – assuring him that she would be back in a minute. Not one particle of it remained in the body of Louise Henderson to register either joy or fear at this rollicking caricature of travel.

And then the canvas hood came heaving over their heads, covering them in, and they surged on in a greenish, flickering twilight. A menacing wail from the loudspeaker joined with the shrieks of the passengers. Noise seemed to obliterate even speed, and Louise could no longer even tell if Margery were screaming.

Daylight again. The canvas hood had withdrawn itself, and the machine was slowing down. The single blur of the crowd resolved itself into separate thousands, and Louise scanned their ranks giddily for Michael's blue knitted coat and leggings.

But they must have stopped on the other side – there were no landmarks that you could hope to recognise in this ever-fluctuating wall of faces and summer dresses. Ignoring Harriet's fervent shrieks of, 'Let's go on it *again*, Mummy!' (echoed with inexplicably equal fervour by the green and shaking Margery), Louise hurried the two of them round to the other side of the roundabout. Still no Michael. He must be *this* way, Louise told herself. No, *that* way . . . She had circled the area completely three times before she allowed herself to realise that he wasn't there.

But it was all right. Of course it was all right. Mark must have found him – after all, Mark couldn't have been more than a few yards away really, hopelessly vanished though he had seemed. Mark must have found him – crying, no doubt – and would be wheeling him around to cheer him up until they got off the Caterpillar. In a moment he would come back and find them. The thing to do was to stand still and wait.

But, as often happens with this resolution, the time comes when you begin to wonder how *long* you should stand still and wait. To you, it always seems that the only rational, the only possible thing for your partner to do is to come and look for you here. He *must* know you are here. You couldn't be anywhere else.

But Louise had been married long enough to know that this simple reasoning doesn't work. Although in fact you couldn't be anywhere but here, your partner always has some obscure reason for being positive that you are at some spot hundreds of yards away. Some spot where you never said you would be – never dreamed you would be – couldn't by any laws of sanity have ever contemplated being. There he will wait for you, growing more bad-tempered and puzzled with every passing moment; and no amount of arguing and explaining afterwards – not hours – not days – not weeks of it – will ever solve the mystery for either of you.

Louise knew all this; and therefore, after a few minutes' wait, she set off to explore the fair-ground.

Oh, but the crowds! The surging, pushing millions of them! How could one hope to find anybody in such a crush? It was impossible.

Well, impossible for Louise. Some people seemed to be luckier:

'*Just* the person I've been looking for!' shrieked Mrs Hooper into Louise's ear. 'I wonder, my dear, could you possibly help me out? You see, Tony's so anxious not to miss anything, and I don't see how I can take Christine all round with us, especially the Big Wheel, and that sort of thing, so I wondered—?'

'Can't Tony go round the fair by himself?' enquired Louise, eyeing Christine without enthusiasm; while Christine, her face smudgy with tiredness, eyed her back.

'Well – no, not really. I mean—'

Mrs Hooper was flustered, as progressive mothers are apt to be when caught out taking proper care of their children. 'That is to say,' she amended, 'of course he'd be all right but I always feel that one's own attitude to one's child's interests—'

She stopped, feeling, perhaps, that the subject was one she could not do justice to at the top of her voice. She returned to the essential point: 'So if you could stay with Christine for just a few minutes? I mean, since you've got Michael—'

'But I *haven't* got Michael.' Louise seized her chance to break in. 'I can't find him. Or my husband. You haven't seen them, have you?'

Mrs Hooper looked blank. Other people's affairs often had this effect on her. Then she made an effort.

'They must be somewhere,' she suggested helpfully. 'Now, if you stay with Christine, right here by the yellow dolls—'

But Louise had escaped. Past the Lucky Numbers. Past the *goggling* clowns' heads with mouths agape to receive ping-pong balls. Past the swings. Past the Big Wheel which rose with strange dignity into the quiet sky. Out, at last, on to the stretches of heath where the picnic parties were more widely scattered, and where the grass showed green between the paper bags. And still there was no sign of Mark and the baby.

How long had they been searching? An hour? Perhaps more. Surely Mark would have given up looking for her by now, and would have taken Michael home. Well, of course he would . . .

'Mummy, look! There's Edna!'

A little incredulous, Louise wheeled round. Such a devotee of the sedentary pleasures of life as Edna would surely not have subjected herself to the exacting physical disciplines of the Bank Holiday fair?

Edna nevertheless it was. Plump and placid in her new pink dress, she sat on a hummock of dusty grass, licking an ice-cream cornet. On her left lay her knitting bag, half open to reveal a bundle of mauve Quick Knit, and on her right sat a bespectacled youth who was gazing at her with dumb devotion. Unfortunately the dumbness seemed at the moment to be getting across to Edna more effectively than the devotion, for she looked just a trifle bored, and was beginning to steal longing glances at the knitting bag. Louise longed to call out to her to leave it alone – to stuff it out of sight – to throw it under the wheels of the Bumping Cars. Did the girl not know that it is far more important to hide one's knitting from a new boyfriend than it is to hide one's past love affairs?

'Mummy, can *I* have an ice-cream cornet?' began Harriet piercingly, and Edna looked up.

'Hullo, Mrs Henderson,' she said, a little awkwardly,

and with a sideways, doubtful glance at her companion as if he was a piece of luggage that she wasn't sure if she could carry. 'This is Al,' she explained laconically. The youth stumbled shyly to his feet, murmuring some inaudible greeting. Louise responded equally unintelligibly, as seemed most conducive to the comfort of all parties, and turned back to Edna.

'Have you seen Michael?' she asked. 'With my husband? He's dressed in a blue knitted suit – the baby, I mean – and we've somehow missed each other—'

Edna shook her head slowly. 'Not in a *blue* knitted suit,' she observed, as if debating in her leisurely way whether Mrs Henderson might not be prepared to accept a baby in a pink knitted suit instead, if it was presented tactfully. 'Not in a *blue* knitted suit. But I think I saw Mr Henderson,' she added, more brightly. 'Down by the station. Where they start the pony rides,' she elucidated, in a fresh burst of helpfulness.

'Down by the station? Are you sure? Then they must have gone home,' exclaimed Louise in relief and then, with a tiny stirring of doubt: 'But he *did* have the baby with him, didn't he?'

Edna looked bewildered. 'He must have done,' she said, 'if they were together. Al—' She turned suddenly to her speechless admirer. 'Al, that gentleman we passed down by the station. Did he have a baby with him?'

Poor Al, bubbling over with wordless desire to be helpful, looked rather at a loss – as well he might, since they must have passed several hundreds of gentlemen, with and without babies, down by the station. However, he was not a boy to give in easily:

'Um!' he contributed eagerly. 'I reckon so. Um!' Further speech seemed to fail him, but this was enough to satisfy Edna.

'That's all right, then,' she said comfortably; and the boy glowed with pride. 'I hope you didn't mind, Mrs Henderson,' she went on. 'Last night, I mean, when I had to go early? You'd said you'd be back by half past six, you see, and besides, the little girls told me their Daddy would be in any minute. I hope you found everything all right?'

'Oh yes, splendid,' Louise assured her. 'That was quite all right. I didn't even know you had gone early. And thank you so much for feeding Baby and getting him to bed so nicely.'

But Edna was looking blank again. Was she perhaps wondering if anything could be done to induce her mono-syllabic admirer to attempt another sentence? Or was she making calculations about the decreasing for the armholes of that mauve garment in the bag? Either way, there seemed no point in prolonging the conversation; and Louise was soon hurrying her two charges towards the station.

The journey home, ordinarily accomplished in fifteen minutes, took well over an hour today, and it was nearly six when the three straggled wearily up the garden path.

'Where on earth did you get to?' Mark greeted them cheerfully. 'I couldn't find you anywhere. You said you were going to the whelk stall.'

Tired though she was, Louise controlled the impulse to point out that not a word had been said about the whelk stall the whole afternoon; that never, in all these years, had any of them bought, or even suggested buying, any whelks; that it was the one place in the whole fair-ground where neither she nor the children could have any motive for going.

'I'll make some tea,' was all she said; adding: 'Was Michael all right coming home?'

'I've made some,' said Mark proudly, with a flourish of the hand in the direction of the kitchen. 'I just about needed a pot of tea, I can tell you! I expect it's still warm,' he added, rather deflatingly, as Louise turned towards the kitchen. Then, suddenly, the last half of her speech seemed to register:

'Michael? What do you mean?' he exclaimed. 'He was with you. You had him!'

Husband and wife stared at each other in absolute silence. Sensing disaster, though she had not listened to a word her parents were saying, Harriet burst into noisy sobs, and Margery into non-stop enquiry: 'What, Mummy? What's happened, Mummy? Who, Mummy? What is it, Mummy?' – over and over again.

'We must phone the police at once,' exclaimed Mark, when he had heard the essentials of Louise's story. He moved towards the telephone. Stopped. Looked at Louise. It was as if he had said, in so many words: 'How can we? It's less than forty-eight hours since you went to them with a cock-and-bull story about a lost baby. They'll merely think you're crazy. And, really—'

Aloud he said, gently: 'You stay here and get the girls to bed. I'll go back to the fair and make enquiries. Don't worry, I'll find him.' And giving her a pat on the shoulder meant to be reassuring, but conveying, somehow, nothing but pity, he strode out of the house.

It was barely half an hour later when he telephoned to say that he had found Michael straight away, in the Lost Children tent. No, the man didn't know when he'd been brought in – nor by whom – since he had only just come on duty. Yes, the baby was perfectly well, a bit hungry and fretful, that was all; and they were both coming home immediately.

21

It was exactly as if they had been giving a party that evening. All the world seemed to have heard of this second mislaying of the Henderson baby, and one after another they came ringing on the bell to make anxious enquiries. Mark's mother; Mrs Hooper and Magda; Miss Larkins and Edna; Miss Brandon; one after another they had to be invited into the sitting-room, assured that the baby had been found, and offered cups of tea to atone for this anti-climax. And then they had to be told, over and over again, the same bald, inexcusable story. Louise felt that she could have repeated it in her sleep: 'I left him in the push-chair for a minute while I took the children on the Caterpillar. I thought I'd be able to keep an eye on him, but it went too fast . . . When I got off, he wasn't there . . .' At intervals, Mark would intervene obstinately with: 'You must have left him by the whelk stall'; and at intervals, too, Margery and Harriet, still not effectively in bed, would say: 'Who did, Mummy?' or 'Which Caterpillar?'

'Well, all's well that ends well,' remarked Miss Larkins brightly. 'Isn't it, dear?' She appealed to her niece, who was frowning dreadfully over the spacing of the buttonholes in the front ribbing.

'What?' said Edna; and it was all Louise could do not to say, 'Go to bed, dear,' to her, likewise.

'Psychologically, of course,' pronounced Magda, stretching out her rather dirty toes with their chipped scarlet nails, 'psychologically, it's been proved that nothing is *ever* lost by accident. It's always because, subconsciously, the loser *wants* to lose it.'

She stared challengingly at Louise, and Mrs Hooper looked on admiringly. Both waited, with tongues poised to counter the expected protests with a few well-chosen polysyllables. But Louise was silent. For one thing, she knew the rules of this one-sided game too well to play into their hands by protesting; and for another, her attention had at that moment been distracted. Glancing across the room, she had intercepted a look from Miss Brandon – a look meant not for her, but for Mark. A long, meaning look. 'What did I tell you?' it seemed to say. '*Now* do you believe me . . . ?'

For a second Louise felt a little sick. But Magda was speaking again, reduced by Louise's silence to supplying the indignant protests for herself:

'Of course,' she was saying, 'most mothers are terribly shocked when you show them that subconsciously they hate their children and long to get rid of them. They won't believe it. They just won't face up to their subconscious dislike and resentment.'

'I don't see what's subconscious about it,' put in Mark's mother cheerfully, 'particularly during the holidays, or on Sunday evenings. And as for a baby like that, who keeps everyone awake all night – well, if I was Louise I'd curse the day I had him.'

'Mummy found him under a gooseberry bush,' put in Harriet brightly, feeling that she had been left out of the conversation long enough, and knowing very well how best to shock the modern adult. 'She did. She found him under a gooseberry bush!' She was rewarded by a gasp of horror from both Mrs Hooper and Magda.

'Do you mean to say you haven't *told* her?' they both breathed in unison to Louise. 'You mean to say you've kept the Facts of Life from her—?'

'Not kept them,' explained Louise patiently. 'I've told her the truth any number of times, but she won't believe it. She just says it doesn't sound a bit likely. What can you do?'

'And how right she is!' exclaimed Harriet's grandmother. 'That's what I've always said myself – that there's not a single one of the Victorian nursery myths that doesn't sound a lot more probable than the truth. Even after I'd had my own babies, it still seemed terribly unlikely. Don't you agree?' She appealed to her rather unresponsive audience – unresponsive, that is, except for Harriet who, enchanted by this easy way to notoriety, began pirouetting round the room, chanting:

'They found him under the gooseberry bush
    The gooseberry bush,
    The gooseberry bush;
They found him—'

Her voice trailed away, and she came to a standstill. It was so rare for Harriet to be embarrassed about anything that for a moment Louise thought she must have stubbed her toe on a chair leg. Then she, too, became aware of the dark, almost maniacal excitement with which Miss Brandon was staring at the child.

'How's that for subconscious insight?' she cried, in a shrill voice quite unlike her usual measured, scholarly tones. Then, suddenly, she recovered her usual manner, and turning to Magda began talking quietly, competently, about the works of Jung.

Quietly. Competently. And with evident acquaintance with her subject. And yet Louise knew, with a certainty that she could neither explain nor reason away, that Vera Brandon was talking at random. Talking mechanically, barely conscious of the apt and well-turned sentences which her training enabled her to pour forth so fluently and with such an appearance of interest. Talking to gain time; talking to cover up some gross and disastrous slip . . .

Frances Palmer's words yesterday afternoon echoed suddenly, peremptorily, in Louise's brain: 'I had the feeling she was waiting for something.'

Yes, she's waiting for something. Ever since she came here she's been waiting for something, and now the waiting is nearly over. How do I know it is nearly over? How do I know that there is an excitement rising inside her that she can barely control? Is it the brilliance of her eyes tonight? Is it that glance of triumph that she throws at my husband every now and then? She glanced at him like that last night, too, as they stood above me on the stairs. What was it she was saying then? Something about the *Medea* again – she seems obsessed with the play; is it just because her fifth form are doing it for their exam? What is the wretched play about, anyway? Medea. Was she the woman with snakes in her hair – no, that was Medusa. Anyway, Jason comes into it somehow; what can I remember about Jason? Jason-and-the-golden-fleece. That's all I know. Eleven years spent at school, and all I can remember about Jason is Jason-and-the-golden-fleece . . .

'I *must* get these children to bed!' she burst out suddenly, unceremoniously. 'Come along Margery – Harriet . . .'

She hurried from the room. Hurried without a glance behind to see if the children had taken any notice of her (which they hadn't) – upstairs and into the bedroom. Mark's Dictionary of Myth and Legend would tell her the story of Medea . . .

So Medea had murdered her two children in a fit of insane jealousy against their father. That was the sense of those last two paragraphs of blindingly small print at which Louise was staring.

But she was no longer seeing the tiny, long-winded sentences. She was seeing instead a pram mysteriously wheeled away from her as she lolled asleep on a bench. She was seeing a push-chair whisked out of sight amid the heat and crowds of a Bank Holiday fair. She was seeing a woman sitting in silent hatred staring down at the children in a sunlit garden throughout a whole long afternoon. She saw again a dozen hints and glances which she had barely noticed at the time.

Not that it made any sense; for where was the faithless lover? Where the jealousy that could drive a woman to murderous madness? Where was there any clue at all as to what it could all mean?

Under the roof, of course. Under the roof, where Tony, Margery and Harriet had crawled with such unflagging purpose, and with so sadly unintelligible results. Under the roof, where now, if ever, it would be safe to explore, while the party, including Miss Brandon, were settled drinking tea in the sitting-room, their voices comfortably rising and falling, continually, like gusts of day-long rain with no stir of change.

22

The fading light of the spring evening still shone through Tony's gap in the slates, and after the choking, dusty darkness through which she had crawled, it seemed to Louise quite brilliant. The stout little notebook was within easy reach among the shadows, and beside it gaped the dark, jagged hole in the plaster which led into the top of Miss Brandon's cupboard.

The book was grey with dust, but of course that didn't mean it hadn't been handled recently. Dust was thick everywhere; it scattered down in little pattering showers every time you moved. Louise's heart beat quicker, just as the hearts of her three small predecessors must have beaten quicker as they reached their enchanting spider-haunted goal. Her thoughts, too, followed that same thrice-beaten track: first, the impulse to take the book away and read it elsewhere in physical comfort; second, the realisation that if she did so then there would be no way of putting it back in a hurry should Miss Brandon be heard coming upstairs. The only difference was that the children, telling themselves that they were in deadly earnest, had known in their hearts that they were only playing a silly game; whereas Louise, telling herself that she was only playing a silly game, knew in her heart that she was in deadly earnest.

Hurriedly, under her absurd little skylight, Louise opened the book and began to read. At first the dust in her throat and the ache of her cramped limbs seemed more important than that slashing, sloping writing before her; but before she had reached the bottom of the second page her discomforts were forgotten. She was no longer aware of the dust pricking and scraping in her throat, nor of the cobwebby darkness that moved in ever closer as the line of evening light grew fainter. She was aware only of a winter wood, the dead leaves thick and silent on the ground, and the snow not yet come.

'*Jan. 13th*,' she read. 'Today I am certain. How can I be certain so soon? I am not a young woman. No, that is no longer true. In the last week I have been growing younger, and that is why I am so sure. That, and this strange new feeling in my breasts, and this new, springing strength in my legs as I stride uphill, and neither mud nor brambles nor the treacherous ditches can slow me down. Hermes skimming over the sea at the bidding of Zeus must have felt like this. No, *was* like this, for now I too am a messenger of the Gods, a bearer of great meanings.

'But what will Edgar say? I wish I could tell Edgar now, today, while I sit on the damp leaves inches thick, and the sun grows red and low and the mist comes up from the ground. If I told him now I could make him understand; I could; I could! and he and I, a pair of staid middle-aged schoolteachers, would dance for joy among the tree-trunks, hand in hand, leaping and laughing, while the red light fails and the twigs grow sharp and black against the sky.

'Don't be silly. It's *Edgar* you're talking about; remember? *He* will only see the problems, the difficulties, just as he has always seen them during these twelve long years. Twelve years of living in sin so cautiously, so respectably, that respectability itself must surely blush! He has a microscope, has Edgar, through which he examines life most minutely, and analyses all its tiny problems. Of course, it's only the tiny ones which will go on to a microscope slide.

'"It's impossible!" he's always said when I've told him I want a child. "It's absurd!" he's always said; and "It's not as if we could get married," he's said. And: "What about your career?" he goes on; and "You'd be ruined" and "You could never keep it dark." "Mad." "Ridiculous." "Out of the question."

'Poor Edgar. Poor, quaking Edgar. I will tell him on Saturday.

'*Jan. 16th.* Edgar horrified. Edgar terrified. Stumbling over problems left and right, as he always does, like a man with hobbled feet, when one good stride would clear the lot.

'Why can't I make him see the wonder of what he has done?

'He is like a child I had in my class once, years ago, who could draw such birds and animals as I've never forgotten. Enchanting, brilliant little creatures, that seemed almost to spring out of the paper with their life and movement. And always she would crumple them up, tearful and frustrated. 'But it's not *like* a camel!' she would wail, thrusting some little masterpiece into the wastepaper basket; or: 'I haven't got the legs right'; or 'I can't do the ears.' She wanted to get things *right,* that child; and so does Edgar. Neither of them will ever know the wonders they created.

'*Jan. 20th.* So Edgar wants me to get rid of it! The only sensible thing, he says. He's heard of a man, he says . . .

'Get rid of it!' Get rid of the sun because it could fade the carpet. Wipe away the sea because it might wet your feet. Blast all the vegetation from the face of the earth because a twig might scratch your face. Blot out the stars because it gives you a crick in the neck to look at them. Wipe out everything; destroy everything; trample down everything, and then you'll be safe. That's Edgar. Why did I suffer it for twelve long years?

'But why am I bothering about him? Already I have gone a long way beyond Edgar. I can go further; and I can go alone. I have the strength; I have the skill. Strength and skills are coming to me across ten thousand years, they are foregathering inside me now, I can feel them, every day and every night.

'*Jan. 22nd.* Term has begun. I can walk with pride among the girls at last, no longer the withered, barren schoolmarm. If only they knew! If only everyone knew! I would have liked to shout it aloud in the staff-room, on the hockey-field, but I must bide my time. It will be many months yet before anyone notices. When they do, of course, I will be dismissed. Dismissed into paradise; condemned to life! It will be my day of triumph, and even while they pretend to be shocked and pitying, my colleagues will know it.'

Conscious now that the light was fading fast, Louise skimmed through a number of pages until she came to the entry for June 19th:

'Half term here already!' she read, 'and still no one has noticed anything. Or, at least, no one has said anything. Silly to be disappointed – the longer it remains a secret the longer I can go on earning, and that is very important from

212

a practical point of view. But how can I look at it from a practical point of view? Does an explorer, as he nears the top of Everest, start looking up the trains to Victoria ready for when he lands back in England?

'Yes, it *is* like exploring. Millions of women have been here before, and yet their reports are so vague, so false. Why did none of them – not one – ever tell me of the mighty strength that comes with pregnancy? This sense of being immortal – invulnerable – of being irrevocably on the winning side?

'And yet, somehow, I have always known it would feel like this. In the past I have heard the sickly, puny women of my acquaintance moaning and complaining about their pregnancies: "We feel sick," they whine: "We can't sleep . . . We get cramp in our thighs . . . You don't know what it's like!" they whimper.

'Well, now I *do* know what it's like, and I shall be able to tell them. I shall no longer have to listen to their complaints in the abject silence of the barren; I shall be able to turn upon them; to unleash the glorious truth like a tiger among that whimpering throng.

'*July 7th*. At last someone has noticed. Gladys has noticed. Maybe because she's PT mistress, or maybe because she shared a flat with me once and knows me better than the rest. Anyway, she's noticed, but she assures me that no one else has. *Assures*, if you please, as if I didn't *want* them to notice! They just think I'm putting on weight, she says, and they congratulate themselves on their own diets and exercises. It's because I'm big-boned, she says, it never shows so much then. Are these bits of information part of the PT training?

'She is full of sympathy and broad-mindedness and what am I going to *do*? And what is Miss Warwick going to say? And what are the Board of Governors going to say?

'I mustn't snub her, she is kind; but why should she think I need her sympathy and broad-mindedness when my whole body pulses in unison with a Mind broader than she has ever dreamed? Why should I give a single thought to the ant-like squeaks of the Board of Governors when the whole of Evolution prances behind me, laughing and triumphing?

'*July 22nd*. Term finishes today. "My secret is still safe," as Gladys insists on putting it. Really, she is growing tiresome with her concern for my future. Where will I go? What will I do? I have ruined my hopes of a post as headmistress. And what about that University job I was applying for?

'Well, what about it? Hopes, indeed! She doesn't know what the word means! I tell her I will get a housekeeping job, there are plenty such, and she throws up her hands in horror. A wicked waste of my powerful brain, she cries. Has she never thought to notice the wicked waste of my powerful body all these years?

'Well, in two–three months' time I will come back and see them all. On some late September day, I will walk into the staff-room without notice, with my baby in my arms. I will watch their mouths fall open and their eyes grow round with envy while the red ink dries on their pens.

'*Sept. 1st*. It is coming. Nearly a month early, but I suppose he is grown too strong, too impatient to wait any longer. My suitcase is already packed – has been for some days, and labelled, too, in block capitals. I suppose I was hoping that someone coming into the room would notice it, but no one did. And if they had, I suppose they would only have tried to sympathise with me, like poor Gladys.

'And yet, now, I wish I had never booked up at that hospital at all. I don't need them, I would know what to do. I feel so strong, so wise, and these mountainous surges of feeling – I can't call them pains – are making me wiser. No, more than that; they *are* wisdom, and I am their High Priestess. They come every few minutes now, they seem to suck away my strength like a wave sucking back over the beaches, leaving my limbs helpless as a starfish on the sand. And then, suddenly, the strength is there again, and twenty times as great, mounted in exact perfection . . .

'*Evening*. My son is born; but why did they whisk him away so fast, before I could even see him? A flash of shining flesh, streaked with black like a little seal, and he was gone, and they still haven't brought him back.

'I think they are angry, because I would not do what they told me. I would not lie this way and that way and breathe in their footling anaesthetic. 'Let me enjoy it!' I cried; 'I know what to do!' They are used to women who cringe, and cling, and call for help. Help, indeed, at a moment when you possess in your own body more strength and skill than the whole staff of them rolled into one.

'But they look at me so queerly. They are annoyed, I think, because I won't call myself Mrs. They've got dozens of unmarried mothers here, of course, but they like them to call themselves Mrs. But I won't. Why should I? Why should I pretend to be ashamed when I am half swooning with pride?

'I shall call him Michael.

'*Sept. 2nd*. Still they won't bring Michael. They say there won't be any milk yet. They say I need rest! Rest, when I'm bursting with energy and joy! I shall go along to the nursery for myself. I shall speak to the doctor. I shall knock some sense into them!'

Louise did not want to turn the next page, to the evening of September 2nd. She knew what she would see, for she had seen it once already, in Harriet's clumsy capitals. She did not want to see it again, in the naked agony of the original:

'M Is Dead.'

She moved to close the book. This would be the end. No one could continue such a record beyond this.

And yet there was some more. Pages and pages more. The light was so dim that Louise had to move her face to within a few inches of the page to decipher the next words, blackly and boldly though they were written:

'They have tricked me!' she read — and the date, she could just see, was Sept. 5th. 'They have tricked me! Somehow I feel that I must have known this all along, or I would not have gone on living. That puny, limp little dead baby that they so grudgingly let me see — that was not *my* baby. My baby is alive and well, and somewhere in this hospital. One of those smug, self-satisfied mothers is feeding him at this moment — *my* baby!

'I know they have tricked me, and I know why they have tricked me. "Unmarried mother," those officious, pigheaded nurses must have said to themselves. "Unmarried mother, she'd be thankful to have a stillborn baby, so let's do the poor thing a good turn and give *her* the dead baby, and give the live one to that nice, respectable married woman who would really be very upset to learn that she had lost *her* baby."

'That's the way they think. Haven't I seen it, haven't I heard it, in all their half-hearted condolences?

'"*Isn't* this a piece of luck for you!" they all but say aloud; and that's how I first began to guess that they were tricking me.

'Useless, of course, to accuse them. They just shake their heads pityingly and give me a sedative, and if that doesn't work they give me an injection. They have the answer to everything, these competent fools, with their bottles and their syringes.

'Sister tells me that my baby had a defective heart, and would never have grown up normal even if he had survived the birth. She doesn't know that her story only makes me the more certain that the baby they showed me wasn't – couldn't have – been mine. I – *I* in such strength and triumph to have borne a defective child? No. No. Only perfection could have come from such power as I was aware of then. I know it. I know it. My baby must have been big and strong, not wizened and undersized like the poor little wretch they showed me. Premature, they said. Defective, they said. And, in addition to everything else, it had ginger hair! Ginger – when I am dark, when Edgar is dark! How can they think I am such a fool?

'However, they have managed in spite of themselves to give me a clue. The mother who has stolen my strong, dark baby is likely to be a woman with ginger hair. Or her husband is likely to have ginger hair. By that very clue, perhaps, I will track her down. Tomorrow I am officially an "Up" patient, and on one pretext or another I will prowl from ward to ward, from bed to bed, until I find her. I shall listen to the shrill, timorous gossip: "Never again, my dear." "Eleven hours of agony . . ." "Too weak even to sip the tea she gave me . . ." I shall listen to it all, and its thin cowardice will be threaded through with facts; with names; with times of births. I shall listen; I shall learn. And wherever that woman is, she will see me passing through her ward, up and down, on this or that innocuous errand, and she will not know that a pursuit more relentless than that of any bloodhound is beginning.'

And, of course, Louise had not known. But then, like many of the mothers, she had gone home on the fifth day, when the pursuit could hardly have been begun. She could not recall the dark, agonised figure that must have roamed like a ghost between the beds in her ward; but everything else became clear to her. The blue suitcase, with all its bold, foreign labels that had looked so out of place among the heavy, apprehensive young mothers in the Receiving Ward . . . The brief glimpse Mark must have had of Miss Brandon as he hurried past at some visiting hour, scarcely registering on his mind at all at the time . . .

So clear was the whole story becoming that Louise scarcely knew now how much of it she was wresting from the gathering darkness of the pages before her, and how much was unfolding of its own accord in her own mind. She saw the list of names and addresses slowly, painfully assembled from ward gossip – from cautious questioning. She saw one name after another eliminated as it became clear that the baby was born too long before or after; or that it resembled one or other parent so closely as to rule out any doubt. She saw the short list of parents one or other of whom had the right coloured hair – 'Red or Sandy' it was headed. 'RE DORSANDY' – of course. She saw the bitter search intensified as Vera Brandon left the hospital, and felt the precious milk drying irrevocably in her breasts; she saw the visits to different homes; the desperate pretexts resorted to in order to stay long enough to study both baby and parents. The sham application for a job at Frances Palmer's, and the hope that was abruptly ended by the sight of the photographs in the bedroom, which proved beyond all argument the likeness between father and child. The pilgrimage to Mortlake Mansions, and the instant rejection of the doughy, unintelligent-looking infant displayed in the arms of Em. The meetings at Mrs Hooper's, where Christine's dirty but brightly intelligent little face had roused a spark of hope. Several other homes she had visited; and then, when hope seemed dim indeed, there came the discovery of the Hendersons. Vera Brandon had known that there was a ginger-haired husband whom she had not yet traced – she had noticed him in a blank unseeing way one evening before she had begun to suspect that her baby was still alive. Later, she could find out nothing about him. Louise had left the hospital by then, and neither she nor her husband seemed to have left any traces on the ever-dissolving annals of ward gossip. Vera Brandon could only remember that this redheaded father had been in the company of another man – a man whose tall, stooping figure and intellectual face had caught her attention. It was by a wonderful chance that, six months later, she had caught sight again of this stooping figure at a lecture. Cautiously she had scraped acquaintance with him, learned that his name was Dr Baxter, and extracted as much information as she dared about his redheaded friend. Further enquiries about the Hendersons in their own neighbourhood had revealed the fact that they were actually seeking a tenant for their top room. Here was a ready-made entrée into their house, with an opportunity to stay and study parents and child for as long as she pleased.

And then, oh then, how hope had piled on hope! A lovely dark baby boy, big and strong; unlike his parents and sisters; a mother who seemed unable to understand and manage him as a real mother would surely have done. And, of all things, his name was Michael! Not that that had any logical bearing on the matter; and yet it seemed, somehow, like the hand of Fate.

And then the planning, the considering. Would it be best to challenge the Hendersons outright, to convince them that he was not theirs? Perhaps some detail on his birth certificate would incriminate them, if it could be found? Search their papers, then, while they are out. But it seems in order. What next? A direct challenge, without proof? But if that fails, then there will no longer, ever, be any hope of taking the child by stealth. His future disappearance would at once and inevitably be traced to Vera Brandon, and there would be no corner of the world where she could hope to hide him. But if no one knows that Vera Brandon feels any interest in the child . . . If no one suspects . . . If no one has the slightest inkling . . .

'*April 6th*. But *does* she suspect? *Has* she any inkling?

'I heard her talking to herself this morning in the kitchen, and it sounded, somehow, as if it might be about me. All day today I will sit in my room, silent, never scraping a chair, never creaking a board, for I feel certain that if she suspects anything she will come and search my room today. She thinks I am out. I have told her I am going to Oxford today – told her with so much circumstantial detail that she cannot but believe it. Though it seems I was wasting my time – she didn't even know that our term was over – she thought I was going off to school as usual! Subterfuge is wasted on fools – I must remember this in future.

'I will leave my door unlocked. I would like her to just walk in.

'And if she does? If I find out that she does indeed suspect something of what I intend? Why, then, I shall confront her with my certainty – and who knows, she may simply give in! She gives in to everyone else, after all – "Yes, Mrs Philips," "I'm sorry, Mrs Philips" . . . Why not "Yes, Miss Brandon," "Here he is, Miss Brandon"? Why, it'll be child's play! I could reduce her to pulp in thirty seconds!

'Reduce her to pulp! What a lovely phrase. It lingers on my pen. I watched her clumsily delving in that attic the other night, puffing and worrying over one of her footling little incompetencies. I stood in my doorway and watched her, and I thought how easily her little skull could be crushed – crushed like an ant in the midst of her joyless scurrying, and her snivelling little suburban life snuffed out.

'For I watched her, that first evening, feeding my baby from her dreary, insensate breasts, with no joy in her face; while I stood there watching, my breasts seemed to tingle again even after all these months with a return of milk. The next night I tried to feed him, for I felt my milk had miraculously returned. But it was too late. He turned from my dry breast, sobbing and crying, and I too ran sobbing and crying up the stairs.

'*April 7th*. She did not come. Once I fancied I heard the stairs creak but no one tried the door. I think she is not suspicious after all. I must be careful for a little longer, till after I have started my housekeeping job. I have told them that I have a baby; I must manage somehow that they see him soon.

'I am glad now that I never went to the hospital authorities and accused them outright. What would they have done? Given me another sedative? No, that is the panacea for people in bed. What is the panacea for people who come bothering round the offices?

'A form, of course. They'd have given me a form to fill in. "How many babies have been stolen from you?" "On what dates?" "What was your grandfather's occupation?" . . .

'No I am well clear of them, and my concerns are such as can find no place in their filing system. Black hatred need not be listed in Column A. Revenge need not be filled in in block capitals. Murder need not be stated in triplicate and countersigned by a responsible householder. I have stepped tonight into a world that is still free.

'*April 9th*. Such a fool for an enemy; such an incompetent fool! Once I thought it was hard to fight a fool — for who can calculate how or when they will fight back? But now she has played right into my hands. The whole neighbourhood knows that she sits up with the baby half the night and is so dazed with sleep that she scarcely knows what she is doing; and now I have seen to it that the police know it, too. She took Michael out in the pram last night. I watched them, I followed them, for I was afraid of what crazy thing she might do with him. But she only fell asleep on a park bench, and I might have taken Michael then and there; but I cannot risk him and myself disappearing at the same time. I have a better plan than that, a plan which will divert suspicion entirely. So I simply wheeled him home and put him to bed! What a fool she must have made of herself when she made all that outcry about him, and then he was found safe at home! Who will ever trust her testimony after this? What will the police think when, in a few days' time, she claims that her baby has disappeared again? I have dropped a hint to her husband, but he is an odd, inattentive sort of fellow; I doubt if he took in my real meaning. So I had recourse to Mrs Morgan – an inspiration, that! Just a word about poor Mrs Henderson and her nerves . . . about her being found by the edge of a lake gabbling about a drowned baby. Good Mrs Morgan – I couldn't leave it in better hands!

'My little Michael; he must never know of all this. And yet, in my heart I hope that when he is a grown man he will somehow read these words, and know how his mother outwitted the whole fumbling, insensate lot of them!'

23

Slowly it dawned on Louise that these last paragraphs, at any rate, were not the recollections and deductions of her own brain. She had been *reading* them. Reading them, though the light through the slates had faded to almost nothing half an hour ago. Reading them with no trouble at all, clear and black on the white paper . . .

How long, then, had the sharp yellow light been shining up through the hole in the plaster? Not, certainly, the whole time she had been here. When she had first reached for the diary, the hole had been a jagged blackness by her elbow. While she had been crouching here, absorbed – maybe half dreaming in the grip of that accursed drowsiness – someone had switched the light on in the room below. Someone had opened the cupboard door; had peered, perhaps, right up into Louise's unconscious face; and had then silently crept away, leaving the cupboard door open, the light on.

Or had she crept away? Could she still be there, silent as a beast of prey, somewhere in the blaze of light below?

Louise lay very still. A few minutes ago she had been feeling such an ache of pity for this woman, it was odd that now she should be feeling such fear. Or was it odd? It's something to do with her feeling she is so strong, thought Louise, with a confused sense of having hit upon some eternal truth; and then a little flutter of falling dust made her check all further thought; as if even the movements of her brain might make a sound that could be heard from the room below.

For the room below was so quiet. Quiet as it would be if someone waited there, alone and purposeful. But quiet, too, as it would be if no one was there at all. As it would be if the occupant had simply gone away; gone downstairs to Michael's room, and was even now wrapping him furtively in a blanket . . .

But when Louise reached his room, panting and half-choked with dust, she found Michael still in his cot, asleep. Beautifully, arrogantly, asleep, an utter abandonment of trust displayed in every outspread limb.

Dare she leave him, even for a moment, to go downstairs – to find Mark? But suppose Mark didn't believe her – as he hadn't believed her about the lost pram? Suppose he thought she had been dreaming again? Was overwrought – crazy? What a fool she had been not to have brought the diary with her as she clambered back over the rafters; but at the time there had been only one thought in her mind: to get to Michael.

Footsteps. Voices. Vera Brandon and Mark walking up-stairs together.

'Isn't it a bit late?' Louise heard Mark say; and then Vera Brandon's voice, too low for Louise to hear her words, though the mounting, barely suppressed excitement was unmistakable.

Louise's first impulse was to rush out on to the landing and pour out the whole story to Mark then and there, re-gardless of his companion. But even as she moved towards the door, she caught sight of herself in the mirror. Plaster in her hair. Black streaks of dust all over her white face and rumpled dress; her eyes wide with fear. She looked like a mad woman. Whatever doubts Miss Brandon was instilling into Mark's mind about his wife's sanity would be reinforced a thousandfold by such an apparition. She hesitated . . .

They had reached the landing now.

'Oh – well – just a few minutes, then.' Mark's voice came clearly to her. 'Your coffee is something I can't resist'; and a second later the footsteps had begun to mount the attic stairs. Miss Brandon's door closed behind them.

Well, it was too late now. Anyway, it was far better to wait for a chance to talk to Mark alone. It would be well-nigh impossible to make the story sound plausible, let alone convincing, in Miss Brandon's hostile presence.

Indeed, it was beginning to seem implausible even to Louise herself, now that the first shock was wearing off. Could she, somehow, have made some idiotic mistake about it all . . . ?

She caught sight of herself once again in the mirror. Clearly, the first thing to do was to make herself fit to be seen; to wash her face, take off these dusty, plastery clothes. In fact, she might as well get into her nightdress and wait for Mark in bed. Their bedroom was right underneath Miss Brandon's, so she would hear at once when Mark came out of her room. She could straight away run out and call to him. They would fetch Michael and settle him in the safety of their own bed, and then, secure from Miss Brandon's denials and explanations, they could decide what to do.

Louise felt suddenly at peace as she reached this decision; and it was only after she had got into bed to wait for Mark that it dawned on her to wonder what, exactly, Vera Brandon would do now.

For she knew, now, that Louise had read the diary, there could be no doubt about that. Would she simply destroy the document, and then hope to convince Mark that Louise had made up or imagined the whole thing? That it was all part and parcel of her odd behaviour lately? But Mark surely would not simply take her word for it against Louise's without at least some sort of investigation? Besides, how could she destroy the diary – a stout, sturdy little volume – either now, with Mark up in the room with her, or later in the night when, having heard the story, he would certainly be asking and searching for this vital proof?

Well, what *would* she do, then?

As Louise lay there, listening to the murmur of voices and the faint padding of footsteps above her head, she felt a curious stiffening of her muscles – a something less than a throbbing in her head, and she knew that she was afraid.

But it was silly to be afraid. Soon Mark would know the whole story, and they could act together. Meantime, nothing could happen, not while he was himself upstairs with Vera Brandon. All the while she could hear voices through the ceiling, she was safe, and Michael was safe. There was nothing to worry about at all.

And the talk from up above showed no signs of ceasing. On and on it went . . . rising . . . falling . . . jolting up and down . . . up and down . . . like a carriage on a stony road . . .

Louise woke with a curious roaring in her ears, and her first thought was that there was a storm, and she was listening to the dying away of thunder. But no; it was only Mark, snoring beside her in the darkness. Snoring heavily – noisily – it was most unusual for him, and Louise lay listening stupidly, half-dreaming, and wholly forgetful of what had passed before she fell asleep. Forgetful and yet still somehow uneasy . . . what could be the matter?

Michael crying, of course. Michael crying because it was two o'clock in the morning, and the long night's ritual must begin.

Dressing-gown. Stairs. Feed. Scullery. Louise had gone through the whole performance almost in her sleep before she began, slowly, to recall the events of the previous evening. Her feet propped on the mangle, the tap dripping behind her, she began gradually to realise not only the danger, but also the absurdity of her situation. Upstairs, her avowed and deliberate enemy was planning who knew what; and here was she blindly, mechanically putting herself to great trouble to ensure that enemy a good night's sleep! For that was the original point of these kitchen vigils – not to disturb the new tenant!

Ridiculous, then, to sit in this dank, tealeafy cold. She would take Michael upstairs at once, and soothe him in warmth and comfort . . .

Louise's head had fallen forward a little as she reached this decision. Her shoulder, leaning against the draining-board, twitched slightly as she fancied herself reaching out for the banisters with her free hand. Her foot on the mangle stirred as she dreamed she set it on the first step of the stair. The tap dripped; the dim square of the barred window outlined the mistier darkness of the night; and if there was a sound from beyond the kitchen door, if there was the faintest whisper of an indrawn breath, then Louise did not hear it; for by now she was deep in her dream, the dream from which it seemed there could be no waking.

For the stairs went on and on. Flight after flight, winding up into a darkness that was not quite darkness, bringing her nearer and nearer to a nightmare that was not quite a nightmare; for even in her dream, she knew that this time the nightmare would be real.

The face would be there, its great teeth shown in tears or laughter; it could make no difference which, for the noise would be the same. A hissing noise, so faint, at first, that you might think it was your own weary breath as you plodded round the bends of the stairs. But soon you knew it was not so. It was another breath, and it was coming from above . . . hissing through the bared teeth with a hatred that went beyond human speech. Louder it came, and louder; it was coming in coils now, in spirals, winding, pulling, dragging at your arms, your shoulders, loosening your fingers on the banister and smothering you in the sickly smell that you knew, now, was the smell of death; death, which would be a crashing for ever back down those thunderous stairs . . .

Louise gave a great cry as she woke, and jumped to her feet. But somehow it went wrong; for as she jumped the scullery floor swooped to meet her, and she heard the blow of stone against her skull.

She lay for a moment, wondering that she felt no pain. If you dream of falling, then you must wake before you hit the ground, or you will wake up dead! Which jovial uncle had it been who had stored her infant mind with this particular piece of lore? But he must have been right. That would explain why she felt no pain.

No, but this wasn't a dream. The dream was over, she was back in the scullery, the place of wakening. But if she was awake, then why was there still the hissing and the roaring; why still the sickening, deathly smell . . . ?

'I'm being gassed!'

The suddenness of the realisation seemed to revive her, for she struggled to a sitting position; and in the same moment she knew that Michael was gone.

If only this thundering in her head would stop, then she would know how to find him. She staggered into the kitchen, and began to look for the door. Yes, to look for the door, although the light was on bright and full. All this tangle of chairs was the trouble; this whirl of legged and cornered wooden objects, banging, jabbing, twining round her ankles as she tried to move.

'Mark!' she tried to cry; but her voice seemed hoarse and dream-like. 'Mark!' she cried again, louder; and this time a hand came over her mouth and she was pushed, light as a toy balloon, backwards into a chair.

Vera Brandon's face swayed before her like a face deep down beneath rippling water.

'It's no use calling Mark,' – the words came to Louise's ears with a curious lilting quality, as the ringing in her head rose and fell: 'It's no use calling, I've seen to it that he will sleep soundly tonight – Oh, very soundly. No one will be surprised. You've done some very odd things lately, they all know that.'

'Mark!' screamed Louise again; 'Mark! Mark!' – and her voice seemed to gain strength as she fought with the hands that restrained her: 'MARK!'

And then there came a tapping on the wall. Mrs Philips had been woken up again.

'It will surprise no one,' the relentless voice went on. 'Drugging your husband, doing away with your baby, and then gassing yourself – it's only what they're all expecting!'

'Doing away with my baby – what have you done?' screamed Louise; and the tapping on the wall began again, more peremptorily. Vera Brandon laughed into her face.

'Even while you're being murdered, you're still scared of annoying Mrs Philips!' she mocked; and then: 'He's not your baby. He's mine. You know that now.'

'He isn't! You're crazy! Where have you got him? It'll kill him – all this gas!' Louise tried once more to get to her feet, but again the hard hand pushed her back.

'Stay there, you poor little rat!' hissed the voice above her. 'I shall hold you here till you're dead! It won't take long to kill you, you poor, feeble thing. Gosh, it's like drowning a kitten!' . . .

Afterwards, Louise learned that the explosion had been heard from many streets away. She herself heard no sound. She only saw the sheet of flame that leapt like a radiant blind across the window curtains, and then roared upwards and outwards into the night.

And then she was out in the hall . . . she was up the stairs . . . The other woman was behind her . . . in front of her . . . behind her again, and there was a shouting and a crying, and Mark, half stupefied as he was, was out of bed, bundling the little girls downstairs.

Louise could not remember how she guessed that Michael would be in his cot. But he was there, rather white, and deeply sleeping.

Round and round in a great blanket she rolled him; and it seemed to her that other arms were rolling another blanket, right beside her, helping in some queer way. And the weight was nothing . . . nothing! She could float, she could skim with him through the smoke and down the stairs; so wonderful a thing is fear.

They were all out, all five of them; and the dressing-gowned neighbours were gathering like bees to listen to the crackling, to watch for the little spurts of flame.

'Miss Brandon! Is she out? Has anyone seen her?' cried Louise; and at the same moment they all saw her. Slowly, clumsily in the flickering light she was clambering over the sill of the attic landing window. In seconds, it seemed, a group of neighbours had a blanket outstretched.

'Jump!' they shouted. 'Jump for it!'

But Miss Brandon would not jump. She seemed to be wrestling with some burden . . . something that would not come easily through the window . . .

'Jump!' yelled the crowd again. 'Jump! Jump!'

But again the dark figure paused . . . struggled . . . and by now, by the flaring light from within, everyone could see with what she was struggling.

It was a bundle of bedclothes. Cot blankets – eiderdown – pillow.

'Baby's here! He's safe!' yelled Louise; and the crowd took up the cry:

'He's here!' 'He's safe!' 'It's only blankets!' 'Leave it!' 'Drop it!' 'Jump!'

Had Vera Brandon not heard? Or had she failed to understand the words? Or had she, in this last moment of her life, gone back to a time where speech has as yet no

232

meaning; a time where the smell, the warmth of a baby's sleeping place *is* the baby, for no words, no reason, have yet drawn lines this way and that across the material world?

It was only for one more second that the hunched figure toppled and swayed upon the windowsill. Then it tipped backwards, and fell, like an overbalanced sack, into the blazing space behind.

24

The same set of people, filling the suburban sitting-room with the same air of expectant curiosity, just as they had done that evening forty-eight hours before. Only this time it was Miss Larkins' sitting-room; it was Miss Larkins who presided over the tea-trolley, apportioning milk and sugar; sorting out teaspoons; commiserating with those of her guests who could have been knocked down with a feather when they heard of the disaster; nodding her head sagely with those who had seen it coming all along.

Miss Larkins was in her glory, and she deserved it; for it was she who had taken the Hendersons in on the night of the fire; it was she who had volunteered to accommodate them until they had decided what to do; and it was she, with the somewhat lethargic help of Edna, who had rearranged the house to make room for all five of them. And she was willing – indeed 'willing' hardly describes the extent of her overflowing eagerness – to keep open house for whichever of their friends were brought by concern or curiosity to her door. Edna was a little less enthusiastic about the arrangement, for it involved a lot of walking backwards and forwards; but even she was willing enough, this evening, to sit on the low stool by the window and listen to the whole, the complete story of The Fire.

For the whole story was known now. Mrs Morgan, with a little trifling help from police and other experts, had pieced it all together and passed it over the wall in its entirety. Miss Brandon was a bad lot, of course; everybody had known *that*, except for the people who had thought her such a *respectable* woman, and couldn't get over the shock of it all. But she was clever, too; there was no getting away from it. Her plan for getting possession of the child had been most ingenious. A few days before Easter she had taken a job as housekeeper to a professional couple in an outer suburb; and from the point of view of her employers she had been residing there, with her baby, all the time. True, they had only actually seen the child twice – once on that evening when Louise had left him in charge of Edna (who had since admitted that she had not been to look at him at all, since he had seemed so quiet) – and once on Bank Holiday Friday, when Miss Brandon had boldly abducted him from the fair, confident that the episode would be glossed over by all parties because of Louise's previous humiliating encounter with the police.

But twice was enough for these preoccupied employers; why, indeed, should they expect to see the housekeeper's baby very often when they went out early in the morning and only came back after he might be expected to be asleep? To have seen him occasionally; to find constant signs of his presence in the form of drying nappies on the line, a pram in the kitchen – all the nursery paraphernalia which Miss Brandon had been careful to make noticeable – all this was quite enough to make them certain that a baby was living there. Their only feeling was one of relief that the child seemed to be so little in evidence and made so little noise.

Nor did they concern themselves about what their

housekeeper did in her free time; they neither knew nor cared that in the evenings after her work was done she hurried straightway out of the house and back to her former home, returning to work very early the next morning. Thus, if she had finally succeeded in stealing the child, no possible suspicion could fall on this model housekeeper. If kidnapping was suspected at all, the suspect would be someone who had suddenly appeared in possession of a baby just *after* Michael's disappearance, not someone who was positively known to have owned one before. And meantime the schoolteacher Miss Brandon would have officially left her job and 'gone abroad' (as she had stated earlier, in front of a roomful of witnesses, that she intended to do); and this official departure would, no doubt, have been arranged not to coincide too closely with the disappearance of the baby.

Clever. Oh, undeniably clever. Louise accepted a second cup of tea with a hand that shook a little. She wasn't thinking of the cleverness. She was thinking of a cot in a housekeeper's room; a cot carefully rumpled every morning, and then made tidy. Of clean, dry nappies, endlessly washed and hung upon a line. Of a bottle left ostentatiously about half filled with milk that no baby would ever suck.

But there had been another bottle; just one. On that evening when Edna had been in charge. For one evening Vera Brandon had fed Michael; had bathed him; had settled him with her own hands into that deep, satisfied sleep. For that one evening the vast, heroic fantasy must have come true.

But the story was continuing; the questions from the

company came thick and fast. Had Miss Brandon intended all along to murder Louise? Or had she only been driven to this recourse when she found that Louise had read the diary? Anyway, the plan, however hastily evolved, had almost worked. Michael had been safely extracted from his mother's unconscious arms; the scene was all set for Louise to be found dead in a gas-filled kitchen, apparently by her own doing. It had been outside her calculations that Louise should wake from apparently deep unconsciousness and blunder about the kitchen calling for Mark. It had been outside her calculations, too, that the tiny pilot light over the sink should be on, and should ignite the gas-filled kitchen.

'And we can be thankful, really, that the house *did* catch fire,' observed Humphrey, with an air of profound calculation. 'She would have held you down, Louise, until you really *had* gone right off, and I don't think you could have got away. She was very strong, as she said; she could have stood up to the gas much longer than you could—'

'I don't see that she was strong at all,' interrupted Louise's mother-in-law sharply. 'She just had an obsession about it, that's all.' 'A power complex—' put in Mrs Hooper hopefully, but was silenced as Mrs Henderson ignored her: 'She prided herself on her strength,' went on Mrs Henderson. 'But actually, it's Louise who turned out to be the strong one. Much more gassed than Miss Brandon could have been, and a crack on the head into the bargain, and yet she was the one who kept her head enough to rescue the kid. And, really, it's exactly what I'd expect. These doormat kind of girls – you don't mind me calling you a doormat, do you, dear? – these girls who can't say

Boo to a goose, they're always as tough as rubber really. Well, after all, you only have to ask yourself, which *is* the toughest mat in your house—?'

She looked round in a challenging, argumentative sort of way oddly reminiscent of her youngest granddaughter; and then went on: 'If you want any more proof, it's in front of you. Louise is alive, and she's got the real baby. The other poor woman is dead, and she only got a pile of blankets. In a way, it had to be so. She'd been living in a dream world for months, and that was the logical dream ending—'

'That's right,' interrupted Magda, feeling that this was beginning to savour of poaching on her own special province. 'She was living in a world of fantasy. I knew, as soon as I saw her, that here was a case of inadequate adjustment to the Reality Principle. You see, to some types of neurosis, the symbolic significance of childbearing—'

'Quite,' agreed Miss Larkins anxiously. 'That's what I've always said: it's the faithful attention to one's small daily duties that really *counts*. Isn't that so, Mrs Henderson?'

This technique for silencing Magda left Louise agape with admiration, and she was unable to answer. Besides, what could she say? She would have liked to ask them all why they were so certain, so unanimously, unquestioningly positive, that Michael *was* her child, and that Miss Brandon had been the victim of a delusion. She, Louise, was certain of it, but why were they? On what grounds did society always decide so instantly and irrevocably between fact and fantasy . . . ?

'Of course, it wasn't *real* mother-love,' Beatrice was saying, 'or she'd never have exposed him to the risk of being gassed like that. Really, I suppose, it was just a sort of ex-hibitionism. The fact that she risked keeping a diary seems to me conclusive. No one keeps a diary unless, in their hearts, they want it to be read.'

'No, *I* think it was a kind of pride – a desire to show herself to the world as the mother of a child,' Humphrey contradicted her absent-mindedly; and Louise noticed once again how oddly united the two seemed as they bickered gently over these almost identical opinions.

'And to take him away from such a good home!' Miss Larkins was saying indignantly. 'A kind mother and father – two sweet sisters – why, a *real* mother, one who *really* loved him, would have been thankful to leave him in such a home, so much better than anything she could provide. *Real* mother-love—'

'What most people call mother-love is a sham!' Mrs Hooper had been waiting several minutes for a chance to say this. 'What they really mean is maternal possessive-ness. This is a typical example—'

'And there was jealousy, too,' put in Mrs Henderson senior. 'Watching Louise winning the child's affection—'

'The purely physical pleasure of handling a child – That's what some people call mother-love,' came Magda's voice again. 'It's really only the sublimation of—'

Louise lay back in her chair, listening to them all. Not *real* mother-love. Take away the pride; take away the pos-sessiveness; take away the physical contact; the jealousy; the selfish pleasure; and you are left with Love. Wasn't there a philosophical problem that went something like that? What is a chair? Take away the back, take away the seat and the legs, and you are left with Chairness – the

239

essence of a Chair. But not, one would suppose, with anything that you could actually sit on.

But hadn't she, herself, been falling into exactly the same sort of fallacy when she had tried to store away love and happiness in a drawer 'until she had time'? Thinking she could – or should – keep them separate from the tiredness, the dirty nappies, and the sleepless nights? She felt she could understand Miss Brandon's bitterness as she watched Louise ignoring, neglecting the boundless wealth for which she, Vera Brandon, was starving.

And yet, wasn't it part of the glorious luxury of wealth that you could afford now and then to neglect it – now and then to take it for granted? Only the impoverished soul, surely, need be always counting its blessings?

Outside, in the light of the mistily setting sun, Margery was picking yet again at the paint blisters on the front gate. Through the wall, in their improvised bedroom, Harriet could be heard pitting her shrill desire to move into a windmill against her father's unenterprising hope that their own house might prove possible to repair. And Michael – why, Michael had not cried at all last night; not once! Could it mean that now, at last, he was beginning—?

'Edna, dear, wake up; don't you see that Mrs Henderson is ready for another cup of tea?'

Edna looked up at her aunt, vaguely smiling, as if just roused from sleep; and Miss Larkins nodded to Louise knowingly:

'She's got a young man, you see,' she apologised proudly, in an undertone. 'It – well – it rather takes her mind off things. She has other interests now.' Her tired face beamed with such loving and senseless pride that Louise had not

240

the heart to suggest that Edna's behaviour seemed just the same as usual, and her interests, coiled in blue-grey profusion over the stool and rolling on to the floor, exactly the same as they had always been.

No, not exactly the same. On looking closer, Louise observed that the pattern in Edna's lap was not for the usual Quick Knit cardigan. It was for a man's Fairisle pullover, with a wonderful, intricate pattern, in the finest of fine wool.

Celia Fremlin: A Biographical Sketch

Celia Fremlin was born in Kingsbury, Middlesex, on 20 June 1914, to Heaver and Margaret Fremlin. Her father was a doctor, and she spent her childhood in Hertfordshire before going on to study at Oxford. Between 1958 and 1994 she published sixteen novels of suspense and three collections of stories, highly acclaimed in their day. Sadly, Fremlin's work had largely fallen out of print by the time I discovered her for myself in the mid-1990s. But I was captivated by the elegant, razor-sharp quality of her writing and – as often when one finds an author one is passionate about – keen to learn more about the writer's life. Then, in early 2005, I had the great good fortune of having several conversations with Celia Fremlin's elder daughter Geraldine Goller. Geraldine was a charming woman and I found our discussions enlightening, helping me to understand Celia Fremlin better and to appreciate why she wrote the kind of books she did.

One noteworthy thing I gathered from Geraldine was that her mother (highly academic as a young woman, even before she found her vocation in fiction) was invariably to be found immersed in her latest writing project – to the exclusion, at times, of her family. Geraldine also told me that her mother was notorious within the home for embroidering the truth, and was quite often caught out by her family for telling 'little white lies'. Geraldine, however, read no badness into this trait: she simply put it down to her mother's creative streak, her ability to fabricate new identities for people – even for herself.

Who, then, was the real Celia Fremlin? The short biographies in her books tended to state that she was born in Ryarsh, Kent. Geraldine, however, informed me that her mother was raised in Hertfordshire, where – we know for a fact – she was admitted to Berkhamsted School for Girls in 1923; she studied there until 1933. Ryarsh, then, was perhaps one of those minor fabrications on Fremlin's part. As a fan of hers, was I perturbed by the idea that Fremlin may have practised deceit? Not at all – if anything, it made the author and her works appear even more attractive and labyrinthine. Here was a middle-class woman who seemed to delight in re-inventing herself; and while all writers draw upon their own experiences to some extent, 'reinvention' is the key to any artist's longevity. I can imagine it must have been maddening to live with, but it does suggest Fremlin had a mischievous streak, evident too in her writing. And Fremlin is hardly alone in this habit, even among writers: haven't we all, at one time or another, 'embellished' some part of our lives to make us sound more interesting?

Even as a girl, Celia Fremlin wrote keenly: a talent perhaps inherited from her mother, Margaret, who had herself enjoyed writing plays. By the age of thirteen Celia was publishing poems in the *Chronicle of the Berkhamsted School for Girls*, and in 1930 she was awarded the school's Lady Cooper Prize for 'Best Original Poem', her entry entitled, 'When the World Has Grown Cold' (which could easily have served for one of her later short stories). In her final year at Berkhamsted she became President of the school's inaugural Literary and Debating Society.

She went on to study Classics at Somerville College, Oxford, graduating with a second. Not one to rest on her laurels, she worked concurrently as a charwoman. This youthful experience provided a fascinating lesson for her in studying the class system from different perspectives, and led to her publishing her first non-fiction book, *The Seven Chars of Chelsea*, in 1940. During the war Fremlin served as an air-raid warden and also became involved in the now celebrated Mass Observation project of popular anthropology, founded in 1937 by Tom Harrisson, Charles Madge and Humphrey Jennings, and committed to the study of the everyday lives of ordinary people. Fremlin collaborated with Tom Harrisson on the book *War Factory* (1943), recording the experiences and attitudes of women war workers in a factory outside Malmesbury, Wiltshire, which specialised in making radar equipment.

In 1942, Fremlin married Elia Goller: they would have three children, Nicholas, Geraldine and Sylvia. According to Geraldine, the newlyweds moved to Hampstead, into a 'tall, old house overlooking the Heath itself', and this was where Geraldine and her siblings grew up. Fremlin was by now developing her fiction writing, and she submitted a number of short stories to the likes of *Women's Own, Punch* and the *London Mystery Magazine*. However she had to endure a fair number of rejections before, finally, her debut novel was accepted. In a preface to a later Pandora edition of said novel Fremlin wrote:

The original inspiration for this book was my second

baby. She was one of those babies who, perfectly content and happy all day, simply don't sleep through the night. Soon after midnight she would wake; and again at half past two; and again at four. As the months went by, I found myself quite distracted by lack of sleep; my eyes would fall shut while I peeled the potatoes or ironed shirts. I remember one night sitting on the bottom step of the stairs, my baby awake and lively in my arms, it dawned on me: this is a major human experience, why hasn't someone written about it? It seemed to me that a serious novel should be written with this experience at its centre. Then it occurred to me – why don't I write one?

The baby who bore unknowing witness to Fremlin's epiphany was, of course, Geraldine. It would be some years before Fremlin could actually put pen to paper on this project, but the resulting novel, *The Hours Before Dawn* (1959), went on to win the Edgar Award for Best Crime Novel from the Mystery Writers of America, and remains Fremlin's most famous work.

Thereafter Fremlin wrote at a steady pace, publishing *Uncle Paul* in 1960 and *Seven Lean Years* in 1961. Those first three novels have been classed as 'tales of menace', even 'domestic suspense'. Fremlin took the everyday as her subject and yet, by introducing an atmosphere of unease, she made it extraordinary, fraught with danger. She succeeded in chilling and thrilling her readers without spilling so much as a drop of blood. However, there is a persistent threat of harm that pervades Fremlin's writing and she excels at creating a claustrophobic tension in 'normal' households. This scenario was her métier and one she re-visited in many novels. Fremlin once commented that her favourite pastimes were gossip, 'talking shop' and any kind of argument about anything. We might suppose that it was through these enthusiasms that she gleaned the ideas that grew into her books. Reading them it is clear that the mundane minutiae of domesticity fascinated her. Moreover, *The Hours Before Dawn* and *The Trouble-Makers* have a special concern with the societal/peer-group systems that adjudge whether or not a woman is rated a 'good wife' and 'good mother'.

By 1968 Celia Fremlin had established herself as a pub-lished author. But this was to be a year for the Goller family in which tragedy followed hard upon tragedy. Their youngest daughter Sylvia committed suicide, aged nine-teen. A month later Fremlin's husband Elia killed himself. In the wake of these catastrophes Fremlin relocated to Geneva for a year.

In 1969 she published a novel entitled *Possession*. The manuscript had been delivered to Gollancz before the ter-rible events of 1968, but knowing of those circumstances in approaching *Possession* today makes for chilling reading, since incidents in the novel appear to mirror Fremlin's life at that time. It is one of her most absorbing and terrifying productions. Aside from the short-story collec-tion *Don't Go to Sleep in the Dark* (1970) Fremlin did not publish again until *Appointment With Yesterday* (1972), sub-sequently a popular title amongst her body of work. The novel deals with a woman who has changed her identity: a recurrent theme, and one with which Fremlin may have identified most acutely in the aftermath of her terrible dual bereavements. *The Long Shadow* (1975) makes use of the knowledge of the Classics she acquired at Oxford; its main character, Imogen, is newly widowed. Again, we might suppose this was Fremlin's way of processing, through fictions, the trials she had suffered in her own life.

Fremlin lived on in Hampstead and married her second husband, Leslie Minchin, in 1985. The couple remained together until his death in 1999. She collaborated with Minchin on a book of poetry called *Duet in Verse* which appeared in 1996. Her last published novel was *King of the World* (1994). Geraldine believed that her mother's earlier work was her best, but I feel that this final novel, too, has its merits. Fremlin marvellously describes a woman who has been transformed from a dowdy, put-upon frump to an attractive woman of stature. The reason Fremlin gives for this seems to me revealing: 'Disaster itself, of course. However much a disaster sweeps away, it also inevitably leaves a slate clean.'

Though Geraldine did not admit as much to me, she did allude to having had a somewhat mixed relationship with her mother. This, in a way, explained to me the recurrence of the theme of mother–daughter relations explored in many of Fremlin's novels, from *Uncle Paul*, *Prisoner's Base* and *Possession* right up to her penultimate novel *The Echoing Stones* (1993). One wonders whether Fremlin hoped that the fictional exploration of this theme might help her to attain a better understanding of it in life. Thankfully, as they got older and Celia moved to Bristol to be nearer Geraldine, both women managed finally to find some common ground and discovered a mutual respect for each other.

Celia Fremlin was, in the end, pre-deceased by all three of her children. She died herself in 2009.

To revisit the Celia Fremlin *oeuvre* now is to see authentic snapshots of how people lived at the time of her writing: how they interacted, what values they held. Note how finely Fremlin denotes the relations between child and adult, husband and wife, woman and woman. Every interaction between her characters has a core of truth and should strike a resonant note in any reader. Look carefully for the minute gestures that can have devastating consequences. Watch as the four walls of your comforting home can be turned into walls of a prison. Above all, enjoy feeling unsettled as Fremlin's words push down on you, making you feel just as claustrophobic as her characters as they confront their fates. Fremlin was a superb writer who has always enjoyed a core of diehard fans and yet, despite her Edgar Award success, was not to achieve the readership she deserved. Now is the time to correct that.

Chris Simmons
www.crimesquad.com